#Tweeting the TL

by

Bonnie O'Neill

Irish Cat Media
Hudson, New York
San Francisco, California
www.irishcatmedia.com
info@irishcatmedia.com

ISBN 978-0-9972747-0-7 (paperback)
ISBN 978-0-9972747-1-4 (eBook)

Interior Formatting by Sweet 'N Spicy Designs

Dedication

To my children whom I never dreamed I could love so deeply or feel so loved by. If this novel ever reaches a ten on the embarrassment scale for you, please re-read the first sentence of this dedication. xoxoxoxoxo Mom

To my gem of an Irish father who encouraged me to have a back-up career so that I could write independently in comfort. I've missed you.

To my family of girlfriends who have, decade after decade, been through it all with me. Love you.

And lastly, to Lester Cole who taught me that it's the role of the artist to comment on the politics of the day.

Acknowledgments

To my fabulous beta readers, Ruth Sison, Terri Thompson, thanks you for your time, energy and support. A special thanks to Joellen Ademski who has given me such generous feedback and ridiculous laughing attacks throughout this entire process.

To Deborah McIntyre who has been a guiding light along with the other writers in my SF Writers' Groups.

To my graphic designer Adam Lee who implemented all my scattered visions.

Contents

"It has become appallingly obvious that our technology has exceeded our humanity."

- Albert Einstein

Bitter Asphalt

—#—

DS and his father stopped in for doe-in-estrus piss and bleat calls at the Hunter's Depot in Shawnee on an otherwise sunny morning. When the familiar bout of nausea began, DS took a deep breath as if willing the flow back into the pit of his taut belly as the owner, Buckhorn Bob, rambled on and on about the local forests and how they were home to some of the best bucks in Oklahoma. For DS's father, Richard Strait, Sr., swapping tales with the stiff, grizzly man was an essential part of the adventure. He'd relive the killing escapades from his own childhood when the male bonding simply couldn't have been better as Bob nodded fondly, recalling the sport of the hunt, the love of the kill, that Richard and his father shared. This, however, wouldn't be the same for DS, a scrawny, clumsy kid who suffered the belt of his old man and the youthful belligerence of the students in his fifth grade class in silence.

"Best memories of my life, hunting with my father. You'll see, son. You'll see," his voice roared even during such potentially tender moments.

Worst of mine. Worst of mine. Worst of mine.

DS's father was a cruel and hard-hearted man who had a deep musty odor about him like stale armpits or what one might imagine—if ever there was the need to—boiled ass might smell like. His words only punctuated the guilt that DS had for detesting killing. He cringed when he heard the word "son," tying him to the monster's DNA, acknowledging the potential that the demons might very well be lurking dormant within him.

Days later, in the rickety shack behind their stone home, overgrown with ivy and in desperate need of TLC, DS just couldn't bring himself to scrape away the skin of "the beaut"—not simply a 12-point buck, but an albino deer—that his father had killed in cold blood earlier that morning in the backwoods just miles away. He had rammed DS aside and taken the shot when his son, trembling with a stinging stream of tears running down his camouflaged face, refused to pull the trigger. Instead, the boy stiffened up aside the lovely creature in that instant before death when the eyes of the soul—evil, glorious and everything in between—were in focus. The haunting that sticks forever. The literal sunset of a life. In a blink, it was over.

DS turned away when his father began to remove the hooves at the elbow by working the blade through the buck's ligaments. He cringed at the distinct *snap* after he twisted each joint with a grunt of pleasure and then hung the carcass by its antlers from a meat hook in the center of the splintered ceiling.

"It's your turn, Dickie. You're all set up. Take your knife and start at the base of his neck. Just the skin. Don't go an' spoil the meat." Again, DS recalled the kill moment and froze. His buck knife fell to the ground. His father, that gargantuan man with an easily ignited temper, picked it up and came at DS, the knife's curved edge just inches from his neck.

"I... I..." DS felt the upward flow.

"Don't you get all sissy on me again boy! Take the fucking knife and just cut, damn it!!" DS remained still in the chill of hatred and death. His father shoved the blade closer. A bit of blood trickled down DS's neck. The impossibility of his son ever being able to contribute to venison filets made DS's father furious. The telling vein that cursed his forehead bulged like a worm in heat.

"I... don't..."

"Some son," he dismissed in disgust. "Some pussy son," he taunted, emphasizing "pussy," then lunged his meaty body, shoving the slight, quivering boy aside. DS toppled against a rusty nail, scraping his forehead. His heavy black-framed glasses flew to the ground. DS's father proceeded to cut through the still soft hide, past the membrane that was watery and thin until the red meat was exposed.

Worst of mine. Worst of mine. Worst of mine.

"I... I..." DS vomited next to the hanging buck, which further infuriated the mad man. He looked into his father's eyes, wishing for a sunset.

Not long after, his wish came true.

#

The big truck with a cab the size of a tiny house was in the shop, and just this once, the family had all piled into the front seat of the old Ford pick-up. It was a particularly tight squeeze with his father, mother, DS,

3

his big sister Lulu and the Barney purple volcano she had made for the science fair in Tulsa.

"Can you roll the window up? Pleeeeaaazzze?" Lulu begged her father. Her mother, Juney, a meek little thing, elbowed Lulu the usual warning. DS just sat tight-lipped, not wanting to rock the boat.

"Pleeeeaaazzze? My hair." She begged again and again her mother jabbed her beauty-queen-worthy daughter, this time in the ribs.

"Just shut the fuck up before I belt you!" her father bellowed. Everyone in the car knew exactly what that meant. Too many times Lulu and DS had been stripped down and forced to lean across the toilet seat while their father took out his rage on them until his belt drew blood. The grainy leather sizzled their buttocks and thighs. At fifteen, the strip-downs for Lulu were particularly flagrant. At eleven, DS just took it as part of growing up. "You little bitch. Your hair? I'll shave you good and bald if you don't shut the fuck up." He reached over his wife to grab his daughter's blonde mane and gave it a rough tug.

DS's mother cringed at the words. She tightened the scarf around her head which further muted the words, although at this point, it didn't take much. Her husband had taken to a particular habit with her that had all but knocked out her hearing and left her with a permanent ringing in both ears. Just the night before, he had done it again—held her head in the doorway of their bedroom and slammed it repeatedly until she thought her skull would split.

"Richard!!!!!!!!!!!!!!!!!!!!!!!" His wife let out a blood curdling scream. Richard Strait, Sr., slammed on the brakes.

DS's mother and sister went through the windshield while his father's body toppled across his son's lap, leaving two doe-like eyes staring up. The sound of sirens and the smell of blood stayed somewhere in the recesses of DS's mind.

#

Flodina Strait, Richard, Sr.'s widowed mother, had just finished a Bogart movie and the last Morley in her pack when she switched on the local news, hoping for a report from the fair. The news truck had headed home from the event carrying footage of dozens of Rube Goldberg-like inventions, volcanoes with somewhat believable lava and such. It went live from the accident scene just as the majority of the Strait family perished. A meth head had slammed right into the Ford full speed. Flo thought she recognized scraps of the pick-up, but it was the close-up of the shredded purple papier-mâché on the asphalt, the same one that her granddaughter Lulu had brought by to show off that afternoon, that sent a current through her heart. She rummaged across the cupboard shelf for her carton of Morleys, pulled a pack out and ripped into the cellophane. The smoke swirled around her eyes which were, by now, wide, wet and sick with shock. She stared at the old turquoise phone sitting above her yellow linoleum kitchen counter. She dared it not to ring. But it did.

#

DS slid out of the front windshield of the pick-up when he got his only injury, a small, neat cut on his abdomen that later required stitches. He wouldn't remember stumbling through the smoke and truck rubble calling for his mother, his sister and then, again, for his mother.

"Lulu? Come on... Lu? Momma? Come on you guys. You're scaring me." He called through the thick gray silence. "Lulu? Momma?"

DS wouldn't remember stepping on something squishy in the dark. He wouldn't remember collapsing between the two grayish bodies, face up, strewn on the asphalt, limbs askew, bones poking through tenderized skin. He only vaguely remembered the medics arriving to take their silent, still vitals. Before more police raced onto the scene, DS saw the blankets being pulled over their remarkably calm, intact faces. First they covered his sister's sleek golden hair and then his mother's blue scarf, the same one she always wore when riding with his father who demanded the feel of wind whooshing through the front seat. But the precise moment that had looped through his brain ever since was when their eyes disappeared under that stiff, course blanket leaving him alone with nothing but a raging heartbeat.

The most vivid memory was his father's eyes, the dilated black pupils, the reddish-brown tache noire strip that formed across his left eyeball and the soft feeling of an odd sense of peace as the evil passed. It was a slow motion image in his mind that always froze on that eyeball. Forever.

So, this is how Richard Strait, Jr. came to live with his grandmother in a ramshackle house in Shawnee, Oklahoma. Good Old Grammy Flo. She was always there when the chips were down, but had never ever imagined a scenario like this one. She took DS in and gave him every ounce of love she had, spoiled him with good intentions and watched over him like a feral cat sitting guard over a gopher hole. Nothing, but nothing, would happen to this last member of her family.

Not to anyone's surprise, DS's father had pushed the family into so much debt with his boozing and gambling that there was not a red cent for the burials. Flo spent the last of her savings to make sure the family was tucked properly in the ground so DS wouldn't have to suffer the public humiliation of asking for townsfolk to pitch in.

The funeral came in waves for DS. He stuck by Flo's side for the entire burial as well as the wake thrown later that afternoon in the hall of the Lutheran church. They sat firmly on fold-out chairs, DS's eyes lifting for no one as he clenched a damp paper napkin.

"Let's make some use of these things." Flo hoped he remembered their little game where she'd scribble on whatever paper was available and DS would turn it into an animal—perhaps a snail, upright, dancing with a top hat, or an alligator sitting at a desk. She took a ballpoint pen from her old blue leather handbag then scribbled on a thick white paper napkin and handed it to DS with false enthusiasm. He held it loosely as neighbors and church ladies passed by, patted his shoulder and offered soft, eager condolences.

"Come on, remember how we used to play our drawing game?" The dead air seemed impenetrable. The blue pen was still. "Hey, maybe we can turn my sewing room into a play room." Flo was grasping at straws now. "You can draw there and make things. And we'll fix the backyard up all nice. How would that be?"

DS's silence was of concern to everyone, so hearing even two simple letters would be welcomed. "O.K.," he barely muttered which lifted Flo's hopes, although DS's head remained bowed and still.

"O.K. then! That's the plan. And I'll be doin' lotsa bakin' now that you're livin' with Ol' Gram." Funny thing was that Ol' Gram wasn't actually that old. Somewhere in her sixties but just real old-looking with deep-lined skin and no attempt to youth-up her hair. Just gray and pulled back. But her heart, that heart, it lit up in her eyes. And even through the coarseness of decades of smoking, her voice was still as chipper and cheery as they came, once one got past the gravel baritone.

"You're not old, Grammy. Don't tell me you're old." Finally, more than a mutter. Flo put her paper plate down on the floor and wrapped her thin-skinned hands around her grandson's white knuckles.

"Of course I'm not old, Dickie. I'm your little spring chicken!" She squeezed DS's clenched fist. "Quack, quack," she teased. And then there it was. She finally got a smile from him. "Now, let's get home and watch a little TV. How does that sound? And I'll make us some popcorn with that special caramel you like. Sound good?" He looked up at her and nodded. He handed her the napkin where he had quickly turned her scribble into a chicken with a spring bonnet.

For that moment, the freedom to flee the misery, to leave the mourners and seeking eyes, DS would be grateful forever.

# #

When DS returned to school a week later, he was treated like a hero, or so it seemed to the newly-designated orphan who was normally teased and bullied by the boys and shunned by the budding girls. The lectures from Mrs. Oricello while he was gone tending burials had worked. She was the school's notably macabre science teacher, a fleshy woman with thick rolls under her chin, and she knew the ins and outs of scaring the shit out of anyone.

"Please be kind to Dickie. We all know he's been through a lot. Just think of how you'd feel if your whole family had been crushed, their skin breached and their bones snapped. Just think. I want you to just sit there and think of what that poor boy has gone through. If I catch any one of you giving him even the slightest teasing, you'll have no recess for the rest of the year." The crash had happened in October, so that was a significant threat. To emphasize the loss, the children were led around the room to pieces of organ meat—hearts, brains, kidneys and knuckly bones usually reserved as doggie treats from the Neighborhood Grocery Mart. The organs, once meticulously wrapped in brown butcher paper, had been savagely ripped open by the teacher. In this line of students, you could tell the hunters from the others.

Mrs. Oricello took the first set of fingers she could get her hands on. Jessica Herz was one of the others. She was too positively cute to ever get dirty, let alone bloodied by a kill. She squealed when Mrs. Oricello jabbed her thin index finger into the huge cow heart that sat profoundly atop the piece of brown paper. And then with equal gusto, she shoved the poor girl's curled pinky into a pool of brains. The exercise was under the guise of anatomy, but, really, it was the bosomy woman's morbid way of making her point. "Just think," the evil woman repeated, "how you'd feel."

Jessica had a big heart herself and did exactly what Mrs. Oricello asked her to do. She thought. She thought about the accident. She thought about the guts. She thought about the slippery intestines which had spilled out onto the highway that night on the way home from the Tulsa Science Fair. And she thought about Dickie Strait and how the loneliness must be haunting for him.

While the other students only tolerated DS and basically stayed out of his way from then on through middle school, Jessica always made an effort to include him in class projects and sometimes even lunch.

"Come on, Dickie. Come sit with us." By us, Jessica meant the other blonde, Germanic girls who stuck together like some mini-Reich.

"You sure?" Dickie would scan the table, knowing that Jessica's was the only truly inviting face.

"Yes. Sure." Jessica always waved him over in her own adorable way and pulled him down and offered to share whatever her mother had packed that day. Like DS's grandmother, Jessica's roots were in Munich, which DS was convinced was the only reason that she even paid him the slightest bit of attention.

"Here. Try this." It became a game between the two of them that started with Jessica unveiling her sandwich.

"Liverwurst?"

"With Hellmann's," Jessica would nod as DS pulled out Flo's version of the same. They'd share a laugh and typically that would be DS's only moment of happiness during the wretched school day. By the time they finished dessert, which they both hoped was either a traditional rich chocolate cake or apple strudel, the joy for DS was over. The rest of his time was spent maintaining social space and counting the minutes until he could go home to his comfort zone.

Jessica's friendly attempts continued until high school when the cliques became mandatory and DS soon found himself at the top of the loner/loser list. Not one friend to help him process the stares, bleats and cruelty of the jocks who ruled the hallways. They had all forgotten Mrs. Oricello's butcher shop lesson.

"Hey, faggot." That was the common greeting DS ducked as he shuffled past the classrooms and cliques of goths, cheerleaders, jocks, princesses and native Shawnees who puddled the path to his studies. Sometimes the jocks would crudely cup their cocks with their hands or emulate a terrific ejaculation.

Whenever DS passed Jessica, she would glance at him with those dreamy blue eyes, then quickly spin around. He fantasized that she was simply holding back when, in fact, she had already been fully initiated into the clichéd Bitchy Girls Club and was quickly rising to the top of the ranks.

"Hey Jess," DS braved one day as he passed by her and a group of cheerleaders in tight sweaters and short skirts in the steel-cold high school hallway.

"Who you talkin' to you, you Little Dick?" Wendy wore the uniform and was now Jessica's bestest. She blurted out the cruelty before Jessica even had a chance to spin around from her locker door.

DS wanted to hear a simple, "Oh, hey Dickie." Or even, "What's up?" but Jessica just glanced and rolled her eyes. DS was pummeled.

The days of Jessica Herz rescuing DS like some lost puppy soul were over. There was no heart left in the little golden girl with the starry eyes that DS had crushed on since their first nap together in kindergarten.

There would be no more rescuing in Shawnee.

#

So, the safety net of death that kept the bullies away, as well as nearly everyone else, was null and void by the third month of freshman year. DS was destined to eat lunch alone, study alone. On the bus he sat alone and never went to a single dance in spite of Grammy's encouragement. He skateboarded alone. He did homework alone. Although he found the busy work assigned by ineffective teachers excruciating, he sped through it so he could get on to more important things like video games, films, mastering code or—his favorite—drawing animal characters. Getting it done early also made time for Grammy's movies and TV shows.

"Come on, Dickie. Hurry up. They've got a rerun of the *Streets of San Francisco* comin' on. By God I'd love to see that city someday... the Golden Gate, cable cars, Chinatown."

"Almost done. Be right there." DS loved the comfort of hanging next to his grandmother, munching on her homemade caramel corn as he soaked in all her knowledge, even though the smoke from her Morleys always swirled restlessly in the room.

"Did you know a German designed that bridge? Joseph Strauss." She never had a formal education, only what she picked up on Jeopardy and in the local library, but she clearly had the smart genes. If there was an arrow to the brains in the family, it would be aimed right at that precious little woman stuck in Shawnee who had suffered the loss of her only son in silence. The tough old bird with the big heart. "An' he was a poet, too. Now that's something to have all that talent. An' he used it all, too."

"Seriously, Gram. You know everything." DS meant it. He hoped that all those smarts rubbed off on him instead of the monstrosities that possessed his father, her son.

After the accident, Flo had vowed to make up for the silent cruelty that defined DS's school days. But nothing could make up for what happened in the spring of his senior year. That was the year that Joey Wheeler and the Boys let their testosterone get the best of them.

It was late at night and DS took off on his skateboard. Even before the skate park had been built, Shawnee was the perfect town to master his boarding. Flat and empty. It was on these streets that he tamed his clumsiness. He mastered tricks through perseverance and pain. DS was never a team player and he had always managed to avoid the football players like the plague. But this was his sport. His thrill in life. The wind against his face, the freedom he felt when he zoomed through downtown Shawnee, past the boarded-up shops and the defunct soda fountain that Grammy swore was the magic of her youth. *Krrrrrr, snap, crack. Krrrrrr.* Boarding was his solace, his bliss. His sex.

This night, Friday, the Boys were drinking up behind the old radiator shop. DS didn't hear the belches and crumbling of beer cans and crashing of bottles until his trick failed and he smashed his elbow into the sidewalk. In those moments of cursing the pain, he was oblivious to the wide hard bodies circling him. It was a third of the first-string varsity team, shit-faced and thrilled at the good fortune that had befallen them. Joey Wheeler was the ringleader.

"Well, if it isn't po' little Dickie Strait. Bleedin' like a pussy." "Pussy" got a round of howls from the other players. Joey's brawny body swaggered over to DS.

When he tried to get up, Joey kicked him back to the ground. The circle got tighter. "Piss on this po' little pussy!" Joey tugged on his zipper, the first to jet his urine onto DS. The others followed trance-like under the Oklahoma sky. The beginning of a tribal ritual.

DS scrambled up to his feet, but he was again knocked to the ground, this time by Graham Armstrong who now had his penis aimed right for DS's already drenched head. "Hey Dickhead. Here's another present for you."

He felt the flow and the vomit came fiercely. As quickly as it came up, it was scooped back into his mouth by one of the Boys knocking his glasses to the asphalt. It might have been the blurry streetlight in the distance or an intoxication of the mind, but DS saw an aura. His brain escaped into that light. The streams of hot urine drenched his plaid flannel shirt and flood pants. He tried desperately to stay in that light as his wet jeans were pulled from his body and a craft beer bottle jammed between his spread buttocks. The pain was excruciating. As the aura became more intense, the team scattered. A lone car passed and DS was left in a puddle of piss and blood on a deserted street in Shawnee, Oklahoma. He was pumped full of adrenaline and didn't remember skating home, wet with every bodily fluid. Flo was already in bed. She had left the letter taped to his bathroom mirror.

The timing couldn't have been better. DS was accepted into Pent State University, with a full scholarship, just shy of his seventeenth birthday. The next morning Flo could barely believe her ears. Her little Schnicklefritz off to college with a full scholarship.

DS could barely walk throughout that bittersweet weekend. He returned to school on a gentle Monday morning. Joey Wheeler and Graham Armstrong passed him in the hallway without incident—protected by the range of convenient blackouts. And Jessica Herz's empty eyes could not see beyond the pseudo-power of her cheerleader outfit to give DS the time of day that he so desperately needed.

Sometimes Just Desserts

———#———

DS counted the days until graduation and then the days until he could leave Shawnee and the demons that haunted his childhood. His only regret was leaving Grammy Flo. She had been his savior. That little woman. That little powerhouse. She had sacrificed everything to give DS some sense of normalcy and DS would give back the best he could.

What that came to mean was hanging with the old ladies who gathered for dominoes once a week or accompanying Flo to a church event that called for family. Although not an atheist, DS certainly leaned towards being agnostic, even though both were proclamations of disbelief according to his grandmother's friends.

"It doesn't matter what the word is. The word is Jesus and if you don't accept him into your heart, well... well you know what that rhyme is." Mabel was Grammy's dearest friend, who always wore her Sunday best. Tuesday or Friday, it didn't matter. She was a frequent guest around the red Formica kitchen table, especially in the late afternoon when fresh fried pies were piled atop it.

"You'll well go to hell without Jesus in your heart." It was a Mabel original and DS could recite it in his sleep.

"It just doesn't make scientific sense, Miss Mabel. As much as I'd like to agree." DS had made the argument only once and still cringed at her fierce response about the indisputable powers of the Lord.

Flo gave his shoulder a little swat with a wooden spoon. "Then just do, Dickie. Just do."

Although these encounters seemed like such a pain at the time, they were some of the moments he'd miss the most when he was away. Those times in the kitchen listening to Mabel and Flo argue about this and that, who and what, and why in the world everyone in the world should care.

At the end of the August, after DS had gone through his summer pair of cut-offs, it was time to say goodbye. Flo was down with a bad case of what they called the flu for lack of anything better although it was far from that time of year.

"Don't be ridiculous. I can drive just fine." She hacked out the sentence.

"Please, Grammy. Will you rest? Please? You have a fever. We can say our goodbyes here. I'll be back for Thanksgiving. Promise. And we'll talk. Every night if you want. And write. I promise."

"But it's not the same having Mabel take you. It's not fair. I wanna be the one to say goodbye."

"There will be other goodbyes. The doctor said bed rest. You don't want to end up with pneumonia again. So, rest. And rest assured that I love you."

"Oh shit, now don't go pulling out the big guns. I'll really be a mess."

"I just want you to know that I love you. Seriously, even more than, much more than him." DS started to cry. "You don't know, Gram."

"Of course I know, Dickie. Since he could walk, your father had a mean streak, just like your grandfather. I tried, but I just couldn't make him right." Gram took a tissue from her rolled-up smock sleeve. "Could never make him right."

The discomfort was piercing, but DS just needed to know if she knew. Now, he hated to see her being swallowed by guilt and needed her pain to stop. "But if it wasn't for you and all that caramel corn, I never would have made it. We're good Gram. Real good."

He knelt down, took her frail body in his arms. They both felt their hearts sync into one. It was too much for the old woman's emotions. "Now, get back! Don't be getting all mushy all over me and getting' sick. On your way. Call me when you get there." She gave her nose one last wipe and tucked the tissue back in place.

"Okie dokie."

"Now you cut that from your vocabulary right now! You don't want to give anyone ideas. You ain't no damn Okie!"

"Right, Gram."

"Oh, and Dickie. Turn on the TV. It's *I Love Lucy.*"

"You betcha." DS turned on the TV and adjusted her rabbit ears just as Ricky Ricardo was belting out a badass Babalu conga solo with his band. "Ba-ba-lu!" DS chimed in for one chorus.

"Oh Dickie. I'll miss you." She waited until he was out the door before breaking down. Full on. Not since her son's family had died had she allowed herself that luxury in the quiet. Nobody said it, but everybody knew it. Her fever was just from being heartsick that Dickie was going.

Mabel drove DS to the airport in Tulsa and rushed back to call Flo and give her the blow-by-blow of the traffic, any songs they listened to on the way and what his last words were. "Tell Grammy I love her." By then Flo was out of bed, baking, trying to take her mind off the loneliness.

Later, Mabel headed over to her childhood friend's house and offered the only advice she knew. "You should get a cat, Flo. A fluffy lil' thing to put a smile on your face. They're all over that World Wide Web. Like movie stars, some of these kitties."

"Thanks for the thoughts, Mabe, but I'll be just fine." She had parted ways with too many cherished pets in the past and didn't want to risk any more heartbreak. Flo shuffled through the kitchen in her housecoat and then shoveled a perfectly shaped fried pie stuffed with tender bits of apple onto Mabel's plate and topped it with homemade vanilla ice cream. "Just fine."

#

DS's college days at Pent State weren't significantly different from the rest of his school days. The promise of a new beginning and the end of bullying was just another busted dream although it was subtler now. His freshman year roommate, Bobby "Blotto" Sanders, a jock fond of *Animal House* reruns and *American Pie* re-enactments, found college to be ideal for his frat boy larks. Beer pong to ecstasy—nothing was off limits for this boob. In any other environment, he would be considered a serial rapist and a chronic alcoholic, but in college, he was just one of the guys.

Blotto had no sense of weekend. The week never started and never ended. He would drink himself sick Wednesday through Monday nights, puking on half of them. If there was such a thing as a dry night, it was Tuesday, mostly because he had a late afternoon class topped with a night class which he vowed to make it to at least once a month. And he wasn't alone. It seemed like the whole dorm was on the same schedule.

"Hey dude. What's wrong with your roommate?" Blotto's friend, Dash, couldn't trust a freshman that didn't party. He looked at the picture propped up on DS's desk. It was him with Grammy at high school graduation.

"Dunno. He never goes out. Just to class."

"Pussy." Dash downed his eighth beer, let out an earth-shattering belch and reached for another beer from the mini fridge on Blotto's side of the dinky dorm room.

"Exactly." Blotto echoed, with his own impressive burp.

Even though they were obnoxious as hell, DS was oddly jealous. He had never been just "one of the guys"—only one of the guys that the guys avoided at best, emotionally tortured and beat the shit out of at worst. But DS got through it the same way he did at every other school, by burying himself in a fantasy world of films and video games. He even found a few pseudo buddies in the dorm later on that year who didn't really like to party but loved the thrill of a good cyber kill. Still, mostly, he was alone. And when his roommate procured one of his sloppy drunk blondes for a few hours of annoying moans, DS would just conveniently slip on his headset and slay some demons.

#

"Hey, Mason just got the new Grand Theft. Come on. We're gonna play." Willy was one of the fellow nerds that DS had finally gotten to know his first year at Pent State. There was a whole table of once-loners who merged in the cafeteria over their sheer obsession with playing video games.

"No shit. I've been waiting for it. An hour. I need an hour." DS had gotten good at compartmentalizing his schoolwork in order to play. Willy, a gangly kid from a farm in Lima, knew he was good for his word.

While Blotto was out killing brain cells pledging some fraternity, Willy and Mason, who was a stout and sloppy kid from Fresno, California and Artie, an annoyingly hyper guy from Atlanta, were committed to gaining strength through Olympic-like feats of manual dexterity and speed. It was on nights like these that DS felt normal. Just like one of the guys—at last.

On this such night in their junior year, after DS had had his hour and the game was going fast and furious until an electrical fire at a construction pit caused a campus blackout of monumental proportions. The campus texting alert system indicated the power would be back on in a few hours. Artie still had battery on his laptop and immediately started surfing for something, anything to do besides hanging around the dorm where they could be sitting targets in the night for some of the obnoxious pledges.

"Hey, you guys ever been to a strip club?" Artie turned the laptop around for the guys to see an impossibly huge-breasted woman in nothing but pasties and a G-string.

"Oh, yeah. All the time in Lima." Willy let out a nervous guffaw. "Not." He was the most sheltered of the group, having been homeschooled and rarely free from the family pig farm. He stared at the heavily made-up woman's mammary glands. "Geez, do you think those are real?"

"Doubtful. It's not anatomically possible for a woman to have no hips and balloon breasts." DS was simply deducing.

"Seriously. Never?" Artie was shocked.

"Rarely." Mason didn't seem like the stripper club type or maybe DS was just being judgmental about his friend's enormous waistline that likely would droop and overshadow his penis regardless of its size.

"Well then, gentlemen. Looks like it's time to put Operation Stripper into action. Right? Who's in? I'll drive." Artie was not going to let this opportunity pass by.

"I think I'll hang out. I've got a couple hours of juice left. Johnson's class is killing me." The last thing DS wanted to do was let his friends bear witness to his awkward approach with women, not least at a strip club and especially one called the Pussycat Den in Akron, Ohio.

But before he knew it, he was in the back seat of Artie's Beamer heading down the I-76 to Akron, the default entertainment town for Pent State students with a car.

They arrived at the Den after a stop at a sleazy convenience store ATM where they all loaded up on twenties. It was a seedy joint on the outskirts of the fifth largest city in the State of Ohio. Artie parked down the street and the four piled out like unsuspecting sheep ready for slaughter.

"This is going to be great. Great!" Artie led the herd.

"Do they really give lap dances? Honestly, I've never had a lap dance. Not even close. I'm not even a hundred percent sure I know what they are." DS looked at Mason's girth, his excuse, then at his own slim excuse-less waist. He, admittedly, felt a little excitement at the thought of a girl paying that kind of attention to him, but having to pay for paying attention was not what he thought his first sexual experience should be like. And certainly not in some creepy place where costumed pussycats danced.

"Me either, if we're being honest." He whispered this to Mason, but not low enough to be out of Willy's earshot.

"Me either if ya wanna know." Well then, all was out in the open as the three Virgins followed Artie, who had just recounted his sexual experiences, all two of them, as he pressed the pedal to the metal on the way to Akron. Artie sped ahead to the lit-up neon kitty that adorned the otherwise dark building. It hardly seemed fair to DS that Artie had done it two times as he was always winning the video games as well.

Before flinging open the Pussycat door, Artie gathered his men for some last minute instructions.

"Now, remember. Be a patron not a parasite. Bills in panties, no change on the floor. Break your twenties at the bar first."

The Virgins were near panicked before they even got into the club and Artie's words just made it worse. The smell that hit them as they were sucked into the room was palpable. A mixture of booze, sweat and smoke. The animalistic motif dominated the room, leopard print everywhere and little ears and whiskers on the girls.

Artie, they had also learned for the first time on the ride from Pent State, was a trust fund baby. He paid the hostess off, and after breaking their twenties, they marched behind him to prime front row seats next to a party of old business men and a bachelor with his boys in tow. The girls were hot that night, knowing that pre-wedding parties tipped big, as did anyone who knew how to manipulate a business account.

A couple of the strippers were not just old, but had those kind of hard-life wrinkles that manifest with too many cigarettes and afternoons off in the sun. DS heard The Wrinkled One whisper to Artie who, because he was somewhat of an expert in the pay-for-sexy arena, got the first lap dance. The Virgins observed as Artie ignored the fact that the semi-retired stripper grinding her lumpy ass into his swollen lap was surely old enough to be his mother. Fuck. Maybe even his grandmother. The ancient guys at the next table drooled over the old platinum blonde as she was, after all, closer to their age.

"Over here, doll. Let the big boys take care of you." The guy who spouted this punctuated his command with a huge puff on a fat cigar.

Another option wriggled and crawled her way across the dance floor like a snake with her tongue darting right at DS. She whispered, "Lucy likes to lap dance," to him.

Artie elbowed him. "Show her the money." DS, in a klutzy move, struggled to release a crumpled twenty from his pants pocket and finally flashed it at the girl who barely looked sixteen. If this was her college job, surely she was an early graduate, he thought. Artie motioned for him to stuff the money in her black sequined G-string as she backed into his lap. He secured the bill so quickly it looked like he was afraid of cooties.

"Ah, I didn't hear your name?"

"Lucy. Lucy likes to lap dance." She was on auto-sexy.

Artie and the other two Virgins gave him proud, affirming nods and DS proceeded to try and have one hell of a great sexy time. But as this strange young girl's buttocks were rhythmically attacking his lap, all he could think about doing, obsessively think about in his moment of testosterone pulsing, was smacking her ass like it was a set of congas. And, remarkably, he did just that. "Ba-ba-lu!" Right then and there. "Ba-ba-lu!!" Just like Ricky Ricardo would do. Then DS belted out one huge cheerful guffaw of joy, "I Love Lucy!!!"

The next thing he knew, he, Artie and the Virgins were being roughly escorted from the club by a monstrous square-jawed, testosterone-pumped bouncer. "You never touch the girls."

"Ah, but, excuse me. I just gave Lucy a twenty-dollar bill," DS defended himself.

"I saw it. He snapped it right in." Mason joined in the defense.

"If you four weenies don't get the fuck out of here, I'll snap you all in two. Now, get lost and don't come back unless you plan on followin' the rules." He pointed to a sign that DS desperately wished he had seen on the way in: No Paws on the Pussies.

They got in the car and headed back to Pent State. DS hoped the lights were still off. All he wanted to do was hide in a black hole. Alone.

It was one of those stories that lived on until they got through undergraduate school. By the end of their time at Pent State, if the tall tales were true, both Willy and even tubby Mason had been de-virginated, leaving only DS alone as the sole member of their original Virgin Club.

#

DS's passion for Digital Sciences was insatiable. He took to software engineering like a stud. After the four strip club fanatics graduated, DS was the only one who wanted to stay on to get his MDS. He had to remind Grammy time and time again what the acronym stood for.

"Master of Digital Science, Gram. It's computer stuff." DS, Grammy and Mabel sat in the coffee shop in downtown Pent, slurping colas after his undergraduate graduation ceremony. It had taken the gray haired ladies two days to make the drive and they were still thirsty.

"Computers. They say you can't go wrong with computers." Mabel was, as always, stout and loud. She had talked Grammy's ears off all the way from Shawnee to Pent State for DS's graduation. It was Grammy's only option. Her car wouldn't make it and flying was out.

"You do what you need to do, Dickie. Me an' Mabel got lots of busy-ness going on. Don't we, Mabe?"

"Lots of busy-ness. Church is making new pew cushions and me and your Grandma are leadin' the committee."

"That sounds... busy." Actually, any thought of church now sounded just gross to DS. He had spent a childhood praying for protection—from his father, the bullies, the DNA potential. And it never came. The God he was taught to know didn't give a shit.

"Don't you worry about me," Flo said in her best convincing way. Of course he would worry. But if he kept going straight through, he'd be out with the Masters just as he was turning twenty-three. And then, with some luck, he could jump onto the tech bandwagon and someday give his grandmother a better life.

"It's a great program. Lots of job opportunities with it."

"Like I said, Dickie, no one can ever take that paper away from you."

The three continued slurping their sodas. "Where's that cute girlfriend you keep telling' me about?"

"Yeah... we've been dying to meet her," Mabel chimed in.

"We broke up. A tragic break up. I don't really want to talk about it."

Flo and Mabel eyed each other knowingly. "Well, some things best left unsaid, I always say." Although Mabel said that, it was hard to believe that she would be the one to leave anything unsaid.

Grammy took her napkin and doodled a cat across it. She flashed it to DS who turned it into a fabulous lion wearing a cherry print housecoat, mane up in curlers, baking in Grammy's kitchen. "Oh, Dickie. Look, how clever!" Gram grabbed the napkin. "I'm framing this the very second I get home!"

And she did. It was the fondest memory of her grandson's graduation weekend from Pent State. She perched it right next to her old Montag stove, right where she'd see it first thing.

#

Since his inaugural class at Pent State, his professors had found him a delightful deviation from the crop of hung over students who would only occasionally slip on their pants and make it to class for a midterm or final. But DS had something shared by only a handful of the other Digital Science students. He also loved art. And he was good at it. Ever since he'd been a kid, he would finish his tests early and doodle on the side margins. Animals, all kinds of fantasy animals. Sometimes, he'd use markers to give them extraordinary colors. They weren't just delightful. He created a whimsical fantasy land that no one had ever seen before. They lived in urban areas, walked alongside everyday people as pets. By the time he graduated with his Bachelor's from Pent State, he had a double major in Digital Sciences and Art.

There was one professor in particular who encouraged him to go on and get his Master of Digital Sciences. Professor Gismondi had left Silicon Valley to teach after years in start-ups, the finale being the bursting of the first bubble which he recalled with some degree of agitation. He was a slickish guy, about fifty, who mentored many students, but DS was his real pet. They had long talks over coffee about the possibilities of art and technology—how in the future one would not be able to exist without the other. They talked about the interplay and what it meant on a global scale.

"Tell me Richard. If I asked you if art plus technology equaled art or money, what would you say?" DS was used to Professor's pop quizzes.

"I'd say it depends on the audience."

"Go on."

"If the audience truly respected art, whether merged with technology or not, its commercial value would be secondary to appreciation. If they only appreciated art for its commercial value, then that disrespect would be monetized. The urgency that technology encourages would not allow for the proper development of the art itself." DS's tangents often seemed to be channeled from some neo-sage. He liked to think it was Grammy.

"Exactly. The audience. It all comes down to the audience." Professor Gismondi nodded and made a note on his napkin then buried it in his pocket.

DS would manage to complete his next academic program in less than two years and in that time, expand his interests to Project Management and Team Dynamics. Under the influence of Professor Gismondi, DS had found that, after years of being clammed up, he was not simply an introvert, but an ambivert who, once unleashed, had tremendous leadership potential. So, at the ripe old age of twenty-three, he would graduate with a Master's while some others his age, like Blotto, were still struggling to get out with a BA. His thesis was on everyday applications of holograms and his portfolio of 3D animals was groundbreaking.

#

One afternoon, just weeks before Graduate School graduation, Professor Gismondi asked DS if he'd like to join him along with his wife for dinner at their home in Akron. They had ventured out on occasion for coffee, but this was bigger. This was his future.

"Akron? Hmmm... what part of Akron, sir?" Although the Pussycat Den had been years before, he still avoided the area at all costs. One never knew where that testosterone bouncer just might show up.

"Part? Northwest Akron. About ten minutes from downtown."

"That's nice, sir. Some parts of downtown, I hear, can be a bit racy."

"I wouldn't know, Richard. All I see coming into town is a load of strip joints. And who would want to hang a hat there?"

"Exactly, Professor, sir." DS was just so damned relieved that it was nowhere near Lucy and her decadent den of kittens.

"How's six o'clock on Saturday? I can have Patrick pick you up on campus. We're about twenty minutes away. Public transport never made it our way."

"Patrick, sir? Your son?"

"No. No kids. My handyman. Best hire ever. He does anything. Just email me your address and he'll meet you."

A week later, DS stood in front of his unit at EnviroSuites, a vintage sustainable housing development that he had splurged on for his final year at Pent State. The student loans had piled on, so what was an extra ten thousand? He peered into each passing vehicle, not knowing who or what to look for. A gleaming red 1959 Mercedes-Benz 190SL convertible spun up and parked not two feet from DS. A dapper Irishman, Patrick O'Malley, popped out from behind the wheel. He was not too tall, stocky yet fit for being in his sixties, with a ruddy complexion and gingerish hair.

"Would you be Richard Strait?"

The question was somewhat disorienting for DS as he drooled over the Benz. "Ah, yeah. I would be. Am, that is."

"Grand! I'm Patrick." He spoke with an endearing Irish lilt. "Hop in and we'll make our way back to the house."

"Sure thing." DS did just as instructed. He eased himself into the perfect leather passenger seat and tried not to be too obvious as he ran his fingers past the wood grain of the glove box, thinking all the while that Professor Gismondi must be incredibly generous with the handyman pay.

"Elena has planned a meal fit for the Pope. We don't want you to be late!" DS was fully enamored with the ride and charmed by the witty Irishman who slipped the car into fourth gear as they hit the I-76. All the way, he imagined what the Professor's house and Italian wife would be like. But his vision didn't come close to the reality of the mansion the little red Benz rolled up to.

Westlawne Manor was one of Akron's premiere estates, clearly defined by the magnificent circular driveway lined by enormous hedges. The Benz passed arbors entwined with vines and symmetrical flower beds arranged in patterns. The gardens beyond bloomed with a color wheel of peonies, hyacinths, tulips, lush perennials, chrysanthemums and bulbous hydrangeas. The property oozed decadent wealth and the structures, the brick Italianate mansion, carriage house, apartments and garages for seven cars were all magnificent. No detail was spared in the recent restoration by a crew of specialists who had gone over every inch of the estate with perfection in mind.

The Benz rounded the circular drive with ease. Patrick cut the engine just inches from the impressive front steps. He popped out and raced to open the passenger side door, but DS beat him to it. "I can manage. Awesome wheels, Patrick. Thanks, man."

"Enjoy your dinner. Elena is a master!"

The black lacquered front door opened before DS had a chance to knock. Professor Gismondi and his wife stood perfectly framed by the enormous doorway, side-by-loving-side like those couples atop a wedding cake, but these two had nearly twenty years of marriage under their belts.

"Welcome Richard. So pleased to finally meet you." DS shook the diamond-encrusted hand, careful not to stare, or, worse, drop a dollop of drool on the jewels. "I'm Angela."

"Pleased to meet you, Mrs. Gismondi."

"Angela."

"Of course, Elena."

"It's Angela, Richard. Elena is our chef." The Professor tried to set him straight.

"Of course. Sorry. Patrick mentioned Elena. I just assumed she was your wife. I just sorta got that stuck in my head." *O.K. Just shut up fool. You're stepping in quicksand.*

The Professor's wife was stunning, looked much younger than he and very blonde. Later, when DS would find out that Angela had graduated from Pent State, he would imagine that she could very well have been part of some freshman's late night loot years earlier.

"Come in. Let me show you the house." *House? Come on. Let's be real. It's a mansion. My Professor lives in a fucking mansion.* DS repeated it in his mind as he toured through room after room of exquisite craftsmanship and antiques, delightfully accented by contemporary art. Eclectic but not absurd.

"I chose a Victorian Italianate because it seemed the perfect blend of my past, those years studying in Italy before I was bitten by the tech bug. And who could ever forget those beautiful painted ladies in San Francisco? The essence of each stage is within Westlawne Manor."

"The artists are all from the Bay Area," Angela chimed in as they passed the peculiarly fascinating modern art that lined the approach to the wine cellar. "We've continued to collect their work over the years."

"In fact, I've done a great deal of collecting, as you can see." David Gismondi's arms swept across his body past rows and rows of vintage wines obsessively stacked in the elegant, temperature-controlled cellar. Gismondi ushered DS onto a black leather bar stool at the tasting bar. "Have a seat, Richard. I've got a special bottle I'd like you to see." The Professor gently lifted a bottle of 1985 Henri Jayer Richebourg Grand Cru from an isolated shelf. "Côte de Nuits. The limestone bridge that's at the heart of the Burgundy wine region." He held the label closer, just two inches from DS's now chilly, heavy framed glasses. "You're staring at a twenty-two thousand dollar bottle of wine. Spectacular now. And one that we'll share someday."

DS nearly choked on his words. "Twenty-two thousand, sir? Dollars?"

"That's right Richard. Twenty-two thousand and rising." He slipped the bottle back into its space. "But you're young, and I assume, a wine novice. So we'll start with something fun which I foresee as having tremendous investment potential."

The Professor's California collection wasn't just the typical Napa-Sonoma assemblage. He also purchased from the alternative wine areas and was particularly fond of those from Calaveras County. "I've just started collecting from a promising region. Angels Camp and Murphys in the Gold country. The Sierra Foothills. Nothing like it for wine tasting without the pretentiousness of Napa. Just great wine. Undervalued, and down the line, I'm predicting I've struck a little gold mine there."

"David has such an instinct for wine."

"Palate, love. Palate."

"And that, too." Angela clearly adored her David and stood corrected without flinching as many women who stand behind their men do.

The Professor lifted the bottle of Aspect 16:9 for DS's inspection. "Hmmm, The Ratio."

"That's right, Richard. The Ratio. The Analogue. Why not have fun with wine? But don't underestimate it. This 2011 is a blockbuster. We'll see if you can sense the texture and finish. It's an art, really. And like all fine artwork, it has a story. You know Richard, people buy stories first and then the art."

"Oh, no doubt, sir." And with that, David Gismondi flawlessly opened and decanted the modestly-priced bottle of Grenache and Syrah blend. David and Angela proceeded to teach DS the fine art of wine tasting. DS shoved his nose into the glass as instructed and eventually noticed The Ratio's subtle cherry, leather and pepper aromas in just the right combination.

"I like a little fun in my collection. The elegant stuff gets boring after a while. Fun, Richard. Life should be fun!"

DS continued to nod as he swigged down The Analogue which Gismondi warned was electric. By the time he moved onto the final tasting, a Twisted Oak 2009 *%#&@! Red, DS felt *%#&@!. He desperately searched for those dark dollops of spicy fruit, herb and tobacco. And to his surprise, they were, indeed, right there under his nose. He sensed spectacular.

"Make note, Richard. These wines will develop over the years, and with time, they'll be an investment that pays off. And that's what this evening is about. Richard raised his glass. "Here's to investing. Youth. Potential." By now, DS was starting to spin. The dinner bell could not have rung at a more perfect time.

#

The meal was full of food DS never knew existed. Not just pizza, pasta and prosciutto at this place. Oh no, Elena's mysterious plates and platters were paced to a reach a crescendo from the kitchen: lampredotto, pajata and pork blood cake.

"Nothing in Italy is left to waste." Gismondi pointed to the pile of unrecognizable food before him all served family style. "This is usually street food— cow stomach—but Chef Elena had the good sense to bring it indoors." David, full of anticipation, pointed at a pile of entrails. "And over here we have milk cow intestine. Imagine such beautiful food in Ohio. Elena!" David shouted out for his chef. Elena, a beautiful, voluptuous blue-eyed brunette who looked freshly kissed by the Italian sun, appeared.

"Richard, this is the infamous Elena. I snagged her from a little trattoria in Milan."

"Is all well, Mr. Gismondo?"

"Delicious as always. Bene. Molto bene."

DS nodded, his face distorting slightly. "Delicious. Oh yes. I've never had such... such remarkable Pajata. Ever. Really."

"Grazi, grazi." Elena blushed and backed her way out of the room.

DS felt the familiar upward flow, chugged some water and reached for the warm focaccia, hoping he could somehow soak up the nausea. He thought of Mrs. Oricello and that school day he missed due to services and how it was recounted by students over the years. Surely she would have appreciated this feast. DS got by, pushing the food around his plate and eyeing, with acceptance, the large bowl of Italian Shrimp Caprese Pasta.

As though they were back in the lecture hall, the Professor educated DS on the finer points of pairing wine with food. But more importantly, he let him into his world. The tech world from the ground up. Eventually, DS fully succumbed to the grape and with each glass of wine he became more emboldened. He derailed the Professor's lecture and guided himself to his future.

"So, what was it like? To be there when the bubble burst?" Thanks to Grammy's reruns, DS had a fascination with all things San Francisco. His obsession with Silicon Valley was insatiable and he wanted a rerun from the horse's mouth.

The Professor pointed to the pasta. "The shrimp. The shrimp. Always keep your eye on the shrimp."

DS had a quick internal debate. *Am I blotto? Or is this guy, my mentor, the guy pointing at the Jumbo shrimp, ripped?*

"You see, every start-up launch party in the late Nineties had a mound of shrimp. The bigger the mound, the faster they'd fall. It's my no-fail mound of shrimp theory."

DS nodded. *Mound of shrimp theory.*

"When I was an angel investor, it got so bad that I'd spin down 680 in my Mercedes, and shit, there it would be, right there on drive time news. Another one of my start-ups gone belly up. By the time I got to work, there'd be the fatal pink phone message. Huh, imagine that? Getting a pink phone message today. You probably don't even know what I'm talking about. Shit, I'm getting old." He reached for another pour as DS thought, *shit. My professor just said shit. Twice.* "You get enough of those and you cut your losses and end up here in Ohio teaching code." He made a toast. "Here's to code and to your future Richard. May you never be the victim of a mound of shit." *Shit. Did he really just say shit again?* The Professor let out a hugely uncharacteristic guffaw. "Shrimp. Shrimp. Not shit. Shit, not shit." His wife let out a girly giggle and simultaneously spilled the red Juice of Gods on the stiff white tablecloth. No one cared.

DS toasted and took another warming gulp of wine. It would be the last he'd remember that night. No amount of espresso or tiramisu could sober him up. Had he not blacked out, he would have known that the Professor had some big plans for his pet. He also might have remembered the slobbering ride home in the Benz with Patrick and how he insisted they spin past the Pussycat Den. DS most definitely should have remembered the familiar square-jawed bouncer that he flipped off as they sped passed the Pussycat. But, thankfully, he didn't. The embarrassment would have been devastating.

#

The decision to walk in the graduation ceremony was huge for DS. He had no family coming to cheer him on. There were no dinner reservations in town or special meet-up places for his parents during pre-grad events. There was no one, but DS walked to shake that hand. The hand that thrust that symbolic paper into his hand. And it would be his forever.

"You stay in college, Dickie." DS could hear Flo's words as he marched across the stage, shook hands with the college President and gripped the paper. "It's the one thing that can never be taken away from you. Your house, your job, your family—well, I don't need to tell you," she would always say. "But no one can ever take your degree away from you." Of course, she had no real interest in what the degree was. In her book, a degree was a degree and the fact that her Dickie would now have two college degrees was just the icing on the cake. "Just get the damn thing, Dickie. Just get it."

He took the placeholder paper back to his seat and fingered the edges knowing that the real deal would come in the mail at a later date, just as his undergraduate one had. All the memories of the late night phone calls home during freshman year, warning Gram that he was miserable, that he'd have to leave school, that he couldn't handle his roommate another day. But all of those memories dissolved as he realized that he had stuck to his goal. And in the process, DS had paved his way to escape from Shawnee even though it might only be temporary.

Grammy hadn't made the trip because her best friend Mabel had died suddenly of a pulmonary embolism and she was torn between the funeral and stepping onto a plane for the first time, especially since she read somewhere that those deadly clots often started on planes. She had a list of reasons she never flew besides money and paranoia, so the choice was easy. And DS didn't encourage her either. In fact, her absence relieved his anxiety over what would surely be her nagging request: "Come on Dickie. Let me meet your friends. Where are your friends?" For nearly six years he had sent her letters, life fabrications, downright fantasies about all his college friends, the roomies/best friends that never were. This was his gift to Grammy who was so addicted to worry.

"And your girlfriend? What about your girlfriend? You said you had someone special." That was the biggest perpetual lie. The one that caused DS an onslaught of gut-wrenching guilt. He had packed on the college girlfriend myth for years, during every holiday and escape trip back home to Shawnee. But there was no girlfriend. Never. Not in undergrad or grad school. Not even close. Never. In fact, at twenty-three, DS was still a virgin. He had never even come close. Or rather, the closest he ever came was a wicked voyeuristic night freshman year when his roommate, Blotto, was passed out and a dizzy blond stumbled onto his side of their dorm room. She was sloshed and DS could have done the deed right then and there. She'd never have known the difference, but then he'd be one of them. One of the serial guys that he so detested. Instead, he let her gently fall asleep on top of him and made sure that she continued to breathe. She pinned him down like a kitten in the night. And he was excited to have her near. That comfort was reassuring for a boy from a place like Shawnee. *I wasn't a faggot like they shouted all those years. I just never had the chance. Someday, though, when it was right...*

#

DS moved back to Shawnee the day after graduation. There was really no reason to stay on after Professor Gismondi had wished him well and told him he'd be in touch.

DS returned to his hometown with little fanfare but for the triple chocolate graduation cake Grammy baked from scratch. There was a comfort in being back home, being tended to as only she could.

"It's good to have you home. My little Dickie, a college graduate. I missed having someone to bake for. And now that Mabel's gone... well, it's just good." She sliced another piece of cake and slid it onto his plate.

"DS Gram. I go by DS now."

"DS. Don't be silly."

He would just have to let it go for now. It wasn't like she might embarrass him in front of friends, after all. He had no friends in Shawnee.

"So, what now? I talked with Tommy Freitas at the repair shop downtown and he said they might be looking for someone. Seems all the newfangled appliances got them computer chips in 'em. No one 'round here has the trainin' to fix 'em. I told him you just got a degree in fixin' things." Grammy popped out of her chair and headed to the fridge.

"That's not exactly," DS searched for a judicious choice of words, "not exactly what the degree is. But thanks, I'll figure something out."

"Well, you should at least be polite and go have a talk with him. Seems none of the college grads come back 'less they're gettin' married. I told him you weren't quite there yet."

"No Gram. Not quite." *Wow. Not nearly quite.*

Gram held a can of whipped cream over the last few bites of his second piece of cake. "How 'bout some whipped cream? Bought it just cuz you were comin'. 'Member how much you loved to empty near the whole damn can in your mouth when you were a kid?"

"Not today. I'm stuffed."

"Oh, come on. Have some fun. Open up!" Grammy let loose with the whipped cream and its ribbons of white fluff immediately laced the table. She thought it was hysterical.

"Gram! You crazy? Knock it off! Stuff's all over."

"Oh, don't be such a spoilsport. That's your problem. Always been, Dickie. You just don't know how to have fun. This summer, we're gonna have fun!!"

"Fine." DS took the can of whipped cream and sprayed it right into his mouth. His mouth was so full, there was barely room for words. "We'll have fun!" She couldn't resist one more dose. "Thata boy!"

"Hey Gram, did I ever tell you thanks? For everything?" He dabbed at the thick white liquid still oozing from his mouth.

She turned her back so DS wouldn't see the tears. "Say, when you're done maybe you could pick up some cleaner at the $1.29 Store for me. I plum ran out tryin' to spiff everythin' up for you."

"Hey, if I didn't say it before, thanks." He snuck up from behind and tickled her until she laughed like a schoolgirl.

#

DS agreed to head into town even though he knew the pain lived on in his cells, eagerly waiting re-ignition. Venturing through those streets, there would be a pulling down memory lane, only now those sidewalks were littered with ex-cheerleaders and football players whose bodies were withered, their mouths sporting brown teeth, their skin full of pits and scabs. Although Tulsa had been known for a time as the meth capital of the world, it was Shawnee that had the customers.

"Sure Gram. I'll skate on down, just like old times." Old times. Those good old times. DS spooned in the last bite of decadence and took off. The $1.29 Store was just far enough to dump DS into the meth zone. The deals took place right in front of him in the parking lot. As luck would have it, he ran into, literally, the skeletal villains of his past. Joey Wheeler and Graham Armstrong had spent all their high school years in football fantasy—girls, plays, sodomy by craft beer. By the time graduation came around, their hormone rushed little brains had trumped their big one and they were left with nothing but generic recruitment letters from the college football scouts. They used meth to try to raise their grades in senior year, but it was too late for that miracle. What had started as a laser study aid ended up deflating their bodies. One-time hunks became dehydrated willowy figures with mere patches of hair.

DS did a double take as he left the store. If it wasn't for Joey's beat-up truck with the fake testicles hanging under the license plate, DS would have just hopped on his board and been free.

"Hey Dude. Dickie? Man, is that you?" It was Joey, hushed, his once baritone voice now weak from years of inadequate saliva. "Hey, how ya doin', man?"

DS was tempted to just skate on into the sunset, but there was a desperation in Joey, like a hungry dog too weak to beg. "I'm good. Really good. Just graduated from college. Again."

Graham came alive on cue. "College. Dude, really?" Yellow teeth, what were left of them, emerged from dry, cracked lips, the dips filled with old brown blood.

"Really." Pride pulled a brief smile from DS, exposing his mostly perfect teeth.

"Well, hey. Me an' Graham want you to have a little present." Joey dug into his ratty pocket and pulled out a plastic packet. "And there's more."

DS flipped his board. "Piss off." The words flowed freely shocking even DS. "Piss off." He repeated the ironic words in rhythm through the streets of Shawnee vowing to escape the street scum as soon as he could.

One day in Shawnee was all it took to send his self-esteem plummeting. It wasn't just the meth heads, ex-cheerleader mamas, camouflaged everything and boarded up buildings. It was simply the dead of it all. The dead eyes of those kids from Mrs. Oricello's class. The remains of carcasses hauled through town in the beds of gas hog trucks. The dead legs of heroin.

Even Jessica, who had once squealed at the touch of a muscular warm heart as a means of aversion therapy, had succumbed to the needle. The day that DS recognized her slumped against the brick siding of the old train depot downtown, he felt the familiar sinking in his stomach. He saw both legs bandaged with scab-infused gauze tinted green and could only imagine what was underneath. Uncooperative veins putting up their wall of dried pus and blood. The thought of Jessica Herz, the squeamish, once vibrant girl who DS had secretly crushed on, pushing a needle into one of those scabs, turned his stomach. He wasn't sure that she recognized him, but Jess did, and in fact, as he skated past something awakened inside her and a rare tear fell.

The pathetic truth was that the only life in his world in Shawnee was Grammy, her movies, TV and his video games. So obviously true. There was nothing else there for him now but for doodling away any extra boredom. For a time, he thought of staying, building a career as an independent consultant to repay Grammy for her years of kindness and commitment. Buy her a big screen TV with surround sound, a new stove and maybe even a safer car. But he was smart enough to know that staying up 'til four every morning, fueled by Mountain Rain, killing characters to gain strength, wasn't much better than living for the little baggie of meth or heroin or shooting bucks. He would become one of them, just a different version, if he didn't escape.

He would contact Professor Gismondi as soon as he got home.

#

DS opened his email the next morning, which now meant the crack of noon, and was pleased to see that The Professor had gotten right back to him. The heading on the email simply read: LOOKING FOR A JOB?

Was he looking for a job? *Hell yeah!* They had an engaging phone call that afternoon.

"I just can't help but thinking about your thesis and that one discussion we had. Or your 3D animals. At first I thought they were too common. And I was partly right. Dozens of companies are working on hologram animals. But I've done my sleuthing and none of them have your flair for really fantasizing them."

DS didn't know where this was going, but had a feeling it was leading to something big. "Like I said in my paper, it's the future. The world is ready for custom pets, 360 degree moving objects that float in space. Just think of it! Owners can view the objects from any angle and soon be able to interact with them. Far superior to the average hologram, sir."

"Exactly. I think you're absolutely right. So much so, Richard, that I'm willing to bet on it. Tell me, what would make yours different from the pets that are already in development? Surely you've been keeping track of the market."

"Well, actually, yes, sir. I spent all my free time researching it last semester. And I still say we need to look at 3D pets like fine art. Anyone can create a barking dog, but it takes a vision and an artist to birth a purple and pink zebra that wears a saddle and sings show tunes. Or, commissioning well-known artists to create their own name brand 3D pets."

"And that's the brilliance, Richard. You knew years ago that we weren't far away from everyone on the street having the ability to see a 3D prancing zebra.

And you were right. Now the time has come for the designer pet to become a status symbol, not unlike the Tesla, a Patek Philippe watch or a fine bottle of wine. And we will, I assure you Richard, respect this art. And make a fortune charting its course."

Just hours later, Professor Gismondi called back with the excellent news. DS was scheduled for a Skype interview with the head of a start-up that Gismondi had invested in. NuMilieu was a company that did hologram entertainment. DS would spearhead the new 3D pet arm. "This is the chance of a lifetime, Richard. I've spoken quite highly of you to Justin Hardy and it's yours if you want it."

It's yours if you want it. The words were dizzying. "Do I want it? Do I want. It?"

"I took the liberty of negotiating your salary and options. I cut quite a good deal, even if I do say so myself, despite the fact that it's a dent in my own pocket. But you're worth the investment. You'll be dead center in the brain of the tech world. San Francisco. With Silicon Valley just down the road."

Down the road. DS was pumped! He had a fantasy flash of himself behind the wheel of a silver Mercedes CL65 Coupe which he quickly environmentally upgraded to a Tesla. "Oh my God, Professor Gismondi. You're a life-saver. Literally. A life-saver. I can't tell you what this means to me."

"You're the best man for the job, Richard. In all my years, I've never met anyone as focused and talented. You're all set. Get yourself a little place, roll up your sleeves and dig in. Let's face it, with you there on the team, I know my investment will be protected."

A little place? The way The Professor was talking, I'd be able to get a mansion. Maybe even one of those Painted Ladies!! "Thanks again, Professor. I won't disappoint you."

So, there it was. Apparently DS was part of the deal that Gismondi had been working on all along. Had he not blacked out during their dinner back in Akron, he would have known all of this had been in the works.

Word Nybbles

———#———

The day of their Skype meeting, DS went through his limited wardrobe and settled on a white shirt and slim tie, the same that he wore for dinner with the Professor and his wife. But suddenly he wasn't comfortable in a tie with jeans, not that it mattered from the Skype angle, so he stripped those off and was going to opt for a pair of gray graduation slacks when the warning echoed throughout the house. He chased to the dining room table where the Internet had its best chance and plopped down in his tighty-whiteys just in time to answer the Skype call. A sort of goofy looking man-kid loomed before him, larger than life.

"Hey Richard. I'm Justin. Nice to meet you. David Gismondi says you're the man."

DS first felt a blush and then the chill on his naked legs as he became incredibly self-conscious.

"Right. Well, that I am." *Well, that was stupid. Now that we've confirmed I'm a man, what's next?*

"David says you're a genius with code, and you have the artistic side as well." *David. He calls the Professor David. Oh God. Genius.* "He said you're focused, dedicated. A real laser brain." *So, basically, he already knew I didn't have a life.* "Let me tell you a little bit about our start-up and where I see you fitting in."

So that was it. That's how the conversation started and it continued until Grammy wandered towards the dining room in her cherry-print housecoat and pink curlers. DS tried desperately to shift the screen to keep her out of his interview.

"Why on earth are you sitting in your undies and a tie?" She was making a beeline for the dining room table and DS signaled madly behind the screen for her to stop. The poor little thing looked offended but he had no choice. He had warned her of the call, but witnessing her first Skype conversation was obviously too much of a temptation. He sliced his arm through the air once again. An emphatic "go away" motion that Grammy heeded.

"Richard? Still with me?"

"Yes. Yes, sir."

"Sir? No sirs on this end, Richard. Just Justin."

"Well then, DS on this end."

Crisis averted. Grammy turned about and headed back into the kitchen with her plate of Jell-O. Minutes later DS chased in, slid across her slick linoleum floor, screaming from head to toe.

"Gram!! Oh my God... Gram! I got it! A job. Gram... a big job! A really big job! Ninety-thousand a year big! With stock options. Fifty-thousand shares!!"

"Well, who in Shawnee has that kind of money? Don't tell me you're thinking of going to Tulsa?" And there it was. The reality hit. How could he break this woman's heart and take off again?

"No, not Tulsa."

"Well, thank God for that."

DS knew he had to cut her off before she spilled her sentimental beans.

"No Gram. San Francisco."

Flo slopped a wobbly block of crimson Jell-O onto a vintage cowboy-themed plastic plate. "Coagulated blood" his sister had called it when the red gel appeared for dessert on the eve of her first frog dissection at Shawnee High. Like many survivors, DS had PTSD and the flashbacks came without warning. Teasing DS had been his big sis Lulu's favorite hobby, right behind humping thick thighs in the cab of any football player's truck. DS wiped his memory of her clean by focusing on the mysterious cottage cheese mixture that had set beneath the Blood-O. He watched it spread in slow motion like asbestos across a bad Seventies ceiling. Cowboys on little ponies circled the "food"—perhaps a subtle acknowledgement between the two sole survivors of the Strait family that DS was headed West.

He took a good firm look at his grandmother, the hunched over little thing that menopause had not treated favorably, and wrestled with the familiar ghost of guilt that circled the room.

"It's not the end of the world, Gram." He crouched beside her.

"Never said it was. Don't be spoonin' words in this old gal's mouth."

Grammy Flo slipped the syrupy dome of a canned peach onto one of his ponies.

"I didn't raise you since you were a little stink to poop out at the end. Besides you got that NDS... DMS..."

"MDS Gram. Master—"

"That's right. Mr. Dickie Strait MDS!"

"DS Gram. Remember?" *Oh my God. How many times did I have to say it?* "I'm not your Little Dickie Strait any more!"

"That's right, Mr. Biggie Shot."

"DS or Richard. Please."

"My Dickie—" Grammy Flo could never accept it. Those.

"DS."

"—off to the big city."

DS scooped up some pink-tinted asbestos, vowing to enjoy every bite as if it might be his last, now that he had gotten The Job.

"It's not forever. It's a start-up and they end-up as quick as they start. Plus, lots of people clawing for jobs out there. Who knows if I'll even last."

"Well, bet none of them have the letters like you. Your mother and father are surely cheering from their graves seein' that their son graduated with half the alphabet behind his name." Flo unrolled her duster sleeve which enveloped a ratty piece of tissue. She dabbed a filmy eye. "Biggest relief of my life was when Big Dickie walked across that High School stage. I never thought he'd make it with that temper and all. I can't tell you the times I got called up by the Principal." She blew her nose as if to punctuate the memory. "And now you, the first Strait to graduate from college. Twice!" The reference was muted by the subsequent tragedy. And of course, the fact that this poor, proud woman had only the slightest idea of the monster of a son she had spawned. No one else really knew his father's full capabilities for abuse except his mother and sister and they were gone. DS always figured that Flo didn't need to be bothered with the depth of his secrets at her stage of the game and he settled on just keeping the dirty little details to himself.

Regardless, not a day went by that DS didn't flash on the past that was robbed from him so unfairly that night. The image of his mother haunted him, she who would calmly hold his hand through the after-school bully tales while his sister ushered him through his prepubescent nerdom. That night. That night taught DS to be careful for what he wished for. The sunset of a life could never rise again.

Flo chattered on. "And now you—with an S and an M."

"MDS. Master of Digital Sciences, Gram. Remember?" DS was a genuine nerd, a good boy, and now an arty software engineer with a grand idea who wore his denim too short, his shirts too buttoned and his black-framed glasses too thick. His charcoal hair was short with an uncontrollable cowlick at the crown. He was certainly not one to respond, nor even really get, a silly S and M reference. Surely a couple of months in SF would seed the acronyms in his brain. And now that he had a job at a start-up in San Francisco, SMS would have to become his way of life.

"All these letters spinning around the world today. I don't even care what they mean. IM, LOL, LMAO. Just got one of those in a letter. A regular paper letter, Dickie! What happened to words?"

"DS," he muttered with defeat. "You worry too much, Gram." OMG he loved this little bitty, chain-smoking-pain-in-the-prat old woman. "Words will never disappear."

"Hope not. One word can tell the future."

"How so?"

"Plastics." Of course, there it was. *The Graduate.* Grammy the closeted movie buff had struck again. She was obsessed, really. DS was raised on three things with her—love, comfort food and film. At times like this, the obsession served them both well.

"Fact is, ever since you graduated, I've been scratchin' my head for one for your future. Then, there it was, right in front of me, plain as that sweet little nose on your face. That's it."

"What's it?"

"Word."

"Hmmm?"

"Word is your word. The word is the future. Not initials!"

"Acronyms Gram. I think you mean acronyms."

"Fuck the acronym. That's what I mean!"

Oh dear. And there it was. The little slip of dementia that scared DS to death. Guilt dripped into consciousness. Could he really leave her? What if she had the Big A and started roaming the neighborhood naked or stopped eating? Or became a head banger or lit the house on fire?

"I want words again. Dialogue. Full sentences."

"I suppose 'word' is—"

"This initial, acronym crap is just one big fake in my book. Fuck. Fuck it. Fake, fake, fake."

Now she was really worrying him. He had read that cursing, a loss of impulse control, was a sign of Alzheimer's. "Even fuck is fake, Dickie. There was no such thing as Fornication Under the King."

O.K., then. She said it. She came full circle. DS rolled his eyes up to the bumpy ceiling. *Thank God.* It was clearly intentional, called for. Profanity would be ruled out in diagnosing dementia for the moment. DS could go to California semi-guilt-free.

It took a few minutes of witty repartee for the news to really settle in. Grammy steadied herself by the chair then firmly collapsed into it.

"Leave this dump Dickie. Take your heart to San Francisco."

#

That night, DS felt a comfort settled on the couch next to Flo, watching a San Francisco film marathon that she had carefully selected. He snuggled next to her, shared a blanket and alternated turns scooping popcorn drizzled with homemade caramel. Just like old times.

Of course, they started off with Hitchcock. They had watched *Vertigo* at least a dozen times and knew all the locations: Fort Point, Mission Dolores, the Palace of the Legion of Honor, the Palace of Fine Arts, and of course, Ernie's Restaurant. They had a no-talking rule for first runs, but from then on it was allowed.

"There, right there, Dickie. The Bridge. There! Just think. You'll be seeing that bridge soon. In real life!! Walk across it!!! With all those big bucks, you can pick up a new phone with a camera. Send me a shelfie."

"Selfie."

"Selfie, schmelfie. You just promise to send me everything. Pictures, videos. And get yourself a cat. I love cat videos. Mabel used to show me all kinds. They'd be takin' baths, singin', playing the piano. One even swingin' around on a fancy chandelier! Poor Mabel."

"I'll get you all set up. Promise. Smart phone. A new computer with a Thunderbolt screen. We'll even get you set up with the highest speed Internet. It'll be just like we're in the same room. I promise. And then, as soon as I get settled, I'll bring you to San Francisco. Double promise. For good, if that's what you want."

They plowed through movie after movie.

"O.K. Ready? *The Birds.*" Grammy called from the kitchen where she was heating up more butter, corn syrup and sugar for the popcorn. "Name 'em."

"Easy. Union Square. Bodega Bay."

"O.K. Smarty. *Family Plot?*"

"The Fairmont. Grace Cathedral!"

"Bingo! You win another bowl." Grammy set a huge bowl of warm, shiny popcorn down and they cued up *The Birds.* "All set. Let's start."

They sat tucked together, munching through scene after scene of perfect blondes. It was during this marathon that DS wondered to himself if this was what established his blonde obsession. Or maybe it just started with Jessica. Regardless, a blonde was certainly on his wish list.

After a night of Hitch babes, Grammy insisted that the next night they celebrate with *The Graduate.* She was quick to point out the biggie film mistake about the Bay Bridge and how she had read that Benjamin was actually driving on the wrong level of the bridge when he was supposedly heading to Berkeley.

"They say he should have been on the lower level. Doesn't matter now. It's a different bridge. Just think! You'll get to see that new Bay Bridge, Dickie. They say it's spectacular. Even though it's got those stupid-looking palm trees. Seems like those are for the beaches in Los Angeles. Don't matter. You'll get to see it all. You can say if they look stupid." Her voice trailed off. "I'll miss you. Again."

Grammy slowly leaned over onto DS's lap. His hand cradled her head. He had never once known her to cry. The wetness on his hand was odd. He lifted her head slightly and looked into her old, moist eyes, unsure of how to define the downpour.

Booking It

———#———

DS was to be in San Francisco by Monday of the following week. What at first was excitement in booking his flight soon turned to panic as he sorted through Craigslist and the various rental websites. He saw his $90,000 quickly dissolving into thin air as he scavenged through listings. And after a couple of phone calls with agents, he sank further. If the $3,200 rent for a 350 sq. ft. studio wasn't bad enough, parking was going for an additional $550. Surely he'd need that for when he got his Tesla. He found that without being able to show three months in paystubs or get a co-signer, he'd be out on the streets. For just the briefest flash, he thought of calling the Professor and Justin and backing out.

"Now watcha doin'?" Flo took a big drag from her first Morley of the morning.

DS shut his laptop on the dining room table. "Maybe it's not the best idea after all."

"Whatcha talking' all silly about?"

"Gram, the rents. The rents are crazy. By the time I get a decent place, half my money's eaten up. Maybe I should just stay."

"Stay? Stay and what? End up with all the crazy, spinnin' eyed idiots you graduated high school with? Or stay and work at the repair shop? Dickie, I was just sayin' about that job when you got home to be kind. I had no idea you had this biggie chance come your way."

"I know. It's just so, so big. I mean, I don't know anybody there, really. And, it's really expensive. And—"

"Hey, hey, hey. You're not takin' away my one chance to get out of this dump, are you?" She stared him down. "Now, you get out of here." She placed her wrinkled hand over his chest. "You take this pumping machine to San Francisco, now. You hear?" She took another fat drag from her cigarette and opened the laptop. "You just get back on that computer and find yourself somewhere to hang your hat. You can switch later. Anything'll do. Just make your way there. And remember, don't ever let anyone call you an Okie. We ain't got no dustbowl at the moment."

Within minutes, Plan B went into effect.

Grammy sat chain smoking all that afternoon next to DS as they sorted through hotel after hotel.

"Try that low price one. You know, with Captain Kirk. I sure liked that Captain Kirk. He wouldn't steer you wrong! He'll take you where no man has gone before, right?" DS was quiet. "Come on, now! You're a man looking to go where's you ain't never been before. So, why not?" They'd exhausted all the other hotel websites and everything was becoming a blur. They clicked on the Express Deals and gambled on a three star in the target mid-Market area and up it popped.

So, with Grammy's encouragement, DS settled on booking a quaint little European hotel on Market St. between 6th and 7th, just a couple of blocks from the start-up's office and down the street from the biggest tech and social media companies in the world. Heck, if the neighborhood was good enough for them, it was surely good enough for DS. It was $225 a night with a shared bath, so it just had to be nice. He imagined the high-tech cafes and restaurants that were certainly up to Professor Gismondi's standards. DS visualized Market St. full of boutiques, maybe even like the Rodeo Drive he and Grammy saw in *Beverly Hills Cop* and *Down and Out in Beverly Hills*.

In fact, that's just how DS pictured all of California—sunshine and Armani in Southern California and fog and Armani in Northern California. Another wave of panic set in. Armani. DS was never one for paying attention to clothes. He had a few decent plaid flannel shirts, a hoodie and some silkscreened tees with ironic sayings. Every year he bought two pairs of skinny jeans, one dark, one light. Grammy would routinely cut the light pair off right at the top of his knees when summer rolled around. But he knew all that would change because San Francisco didn't have summer. "The coldest winter I ever spent was a summer in San Francisco," were words of warning incorrectly attributed to Mark Twain, but a fair warning nonetheless. Regardless, DS would have to dress fancier. He just knew that even though these new start-up offices looked like high-tech playgrounds, he would have to spiff it up a bit for his first day.

"I wouldn't be worried about clothes right away. You can see what people are wearin' in the area and pick somethin' up soon as you get there." Grammy pointed to the calendar on the screen. "See, you'll have Sunday to shop, clean up and then head to your first day all fresh."

"You think all the stores are open on Sunday?"

"It's California. Of course the stores are open on Sunday. Beautiful as it is, they got heathens out there, Dickie. Don't let them drag you into hell."

"I won't. Don't you worry about me. I'm gonna miss you, Gram. But, it won't be long. Soon as I get settled, we'll get you a ticket. First Class."

"Ahhhh, First Class."

"Sure. Why not? You deserve it. Heck, I'd charter a plane if I could."

Grammy blushed. "Maybe we should just settle on the train. I'm still a little shaky on bein' up so high."

"Gram. It's nothing. Nothing will go wrong. Flying's fun. And the flight attendants are always super nice. They'll help you with anything you need."

"Well, we'll see."

"Exactly. You'll see. No smoking, though."

Grammy's face soured. "Ain't no one taking away my cancer sticks. They're my best friends 'sides you, Dickie."

"Well, I'd like to think I'm in better company. You'll just have to do without when the day comes. Wouldn't hurt to practice every now and then, though." It was a constant struggle between the genes. One that DS would lose every time.

Wanderbust

—#—

DS had scheduled his arrival in San Francisco to the precise minute, but cut it close to departure because Flo had wanted to cook him one last meal. Surely getting to the airport closer to boarding time wouldn't make a bit of difference in the long run. He just needed to get to SF in time to pick up a presentable outfit and get a decent night's sleep before his first day at NuMilieu. Anything would be better than the skinny jeans, plaid flannel shirt and hoodie uniform he would wear in flight.

Flo insisted on driving him which is never a good thing when one suffers from Restless Legs Syndrome like she did. Violent RLS. They lurched into the Tulsa airport parking and after prying herself from her treasured 1959 Nash Mechanic that could only top 45 mph, Flo steadied herself with her gnarly fingers pinching the elbow of DS's hoodie. Her free hand grasped a silly little lunch bag with liver sausage and mayo sandwiches, homemade Rice Krispie bars (most desserts in Oklahoma were a bar of some sort) and a couple of juice boxes. The comforts of home for DS's first flight to San Francisco.

Grammy was a total mess and fingered the unlit Morley she held between her fingers as they shuffled through the airport.

"I'm sending you nicotine patches, Gram. You've got to cut those things out. You want to be nice and healthy for California, don't you?"

"Now don't start nagging me again about my smoking. It's all I got left now."

"Still, I'm sending patches." He was adamant and she finally stopped arguing.

"Over there. US Flightways check-in." Grammy followed DS as best she could, elbowing her way through the crowd of travelers.

By the time they made it through check-in, the good-bye was down to the wire. This was it.

"We have to say goodbye here. They won't let you through security. Remember where you parked?"

"Of course I remember." Of course she really didn't, but she had nothing but time to get lost once DS departed.

"O.K. then. This is it." DS reached out, wanting to give his little heroine a hug she would never forget. Flo leaned back and tucked the crinkled sac of goodies under his arm. "Goodbye my little Schnicklefritz." The phrase drew a few questionable stares from potential seatmates.

"Shhhh Gram. Shhhhhhh." DS hoped no one knew the exact etymology—little boy penis or little rascal. Grammy grinned, knowing full well that she had made a lasting impression and shuffled off before it got mushy. DS waited for her to turn around one last time. She did, with a huge smile and waved like a little school girl.

"Have a great flight Schnicklefritz!" For a wee thing, she sure could bellow. Her call from down the terminal drew looks from the same crowd that DS imagined were already googling Schnicklefritz as they waited forever in the horrific line. One stoner glanced up upon hearing the urban word for weed.

It was forty-five minutes and three Morleys before Grammy found the ol' Nash Mechanic. She cried halfway home knowing the emptiness she would walk into, now that both Dickie and Mabel were gone.

And it took those same forty-five minutes for DS to make it through security. He ran to the gate, hoping there would still be room for his overstuffed duffel.

#

DS was late and skimped on baggage fees. He finally got through security with his duffel but getting past Old Iron Balls was a different thing. The flight attendant was about Grammy's age, so at first she won DS's endearing glance. The overheads were nearly full, so he began to do a bit of assertive rearranging. He apologized profusely when the tip of his bag brushed by the shoulder of a lovely Indian woman who was settled into the seat next to his with a sack, perhaps of fruit, on her lap.

The voice took him back. Literally. "What do you think you're doing?" Had it been a bit deeper, he would have thought it was his father, risen from the grave, intent on haunting him.

"The overheads are full. You'll need to check that." He turned to see one crazy looking pair of eyeballs spinning with hate.

"But, my laptop. I need my laptop." Before he knew it, he was being herded back to the plane's doorway and that's when things quickly went south as the gnarly crew member accused DS of hitting her with his duffel when he turned in the aisle of the cabin.

"He hit me!" The sagging flight attendant immediately scanned the cabin for witnesses. There were no takers, so she piped up again, this time a near-howl. "He hit me!" By now the other attendants were circling their elder.

"Evelyn? Wha—?" One of her mentees, a pleasant woman with perfectly manicured lips comforted her.

"He shoved me just like this." And with that, Old Iron Balls motioned with her arms thrusting through the air.

DS gasped. "I never! No way. I was just turning the corner. It was my bag. Really. See?" And with that, DS motioned to the bag and repeated the fateful movement.

"I know when I've been hit!" Old Iron Balls reached for the phone and the next thing DS knew, he was under interrogation by the Captain who then called security.

"Oh geez, really. I'm so sorry. I would never hit anyone, especially an old..." *Oh dear, did I really just call the bag old?* Apparently yes, because the attendant's face contorted.

"I know when I've been struck, Captain. He went just like this." Again, she motioned the air shove.

The next moment was borderline surreal as the little Indian woman stood up from her seat in mid-cabin, dumping her lapful of oranges. "He hit me, too!"

"Wha?" *This can't be happening. Surely this can't be.*

A humongous man stood up. *Oh, please don't let him bear witness too!* "I saw the whole thing." *Shit.* The man approached the Captain and discreetly flashed his badge. In that moment, DS learned that an Air Marshall trumps a crazy, stressed-out, disability-seeking flight attendant and equally whacko Indian woman. Nevertheless, for another twenty-five minutes, DS stood feebly at the front of the plane in full sight of every pissed-off passenger who just wanted the air turned on and to take off. And not in that order. He offered heartfelt, desperate apologies for the misunderstanding(s), then made his most sincere eye contact while simultaneously trying to keep Grammy's final luncheon meal of meatloaf and mashed potatoes down. The last thing DS needed was to puke in the aisle of hell, for surely he would not be able to survive that mutiny.

Finally, he was escorted back to his seat, sans duffel, by Miss Manicured Lips and eased into his seat next to the angry, once-lovely woman who had taken great pains to collect her oranges. *Thank God that Air Marshall is right across the aisle.*

It would have seemed that from that point on the flight would be unremarkable, but truth be told, his interrogation had caused the Rube Goldberg of all delays which would get DS and the ever-growing cast of haters on the flight to land not in SF late that afternoon, not even late that night. In fact, Flight 147 didn't arrive in San Francisco until 6:05 a.m. the next morning. And it was fifty-five minutes after that landing, while DS watched the last of the demon passengers pick up their luggage, that he was informed his duffel had been lost. With his laptop. *Could it get any worse?*

DS had no choice but to climb onto BART and pray there would be some shop, any shop, open in time where he could pick up some clean clothes (he would settle for just a nice white shirt at this point) and head to the hotel for a shower. If all lined up, he could still make it to his first day freshly showered and clothed.

So much for wishful thinking.

#

BART, Bay Area's Rapid Transit, wasn't the problem this Monday morning. There were no suicides on the track, no protesters to contend with and no strikes by station agents. In fact, there were no police activity delays at all. DS was safely delivered to the Civic Center Station by 7:55 a.m. and he just knew the moment he popped up above ground, he would find a store open. And a warm shower waiting.

DS emerged from the stench of the underground into a swarm of San Francisco's best and worst. The best, the well-tailored attorneys and civic leaders heading to the gloriously crowned City Hall and Courthouse, were few and far between. The worst looked like apocalypse survivors. He vaguely recalled a reference to "The Homeless" in The City, but had ignored any mention. Surely that wouldn't be where NuMilieu would be officed, nor anywhere near where he would be living. Not his San Francisco. But within minutes of emerging from the station, he saw them everywhere. They were the walking dead, their skin tough and dark from the elements, their hair clumped, their smell palpable. The fountain at the top of the BART station sprayed high streams of water. DS looked up to take in a moment of glory, but when his eyes landed back down at the foot of the fountain he saw rows of them, zombie-like and one with the seagulls. Needles were littered about.

"Hey, what the fuck you lookin' at? You lookin' at me?" DS refocused his attention to a heavily dust-encrusted, bent-over fellow struggling to balance with his pants down to his ankles and a crinkled newspaper propped in his hands as he took his morning constitution in the fountain. Next thing DS knew, the guy was shimmying over, ankles still bound by his dropped pants. He was pointing wildly. "You! You! You! You! You!" The man, DS wasn't sure if he was twenty or fifty, sounded like a broken record. He glanced around to see if anyone had noticed the encounter, and soon found himself surrounded by a dozen or so other homeless stumbling up to debate the event. In the distance, unbelievably, another man was stuck crouching with his pants around his ankles. DS had learned long ago the value of an early exit and took off in a speed walk with the dome of SF's glorious City Hall against his back. When he turned around for the briefest, curious glance, the crowd had somewhat dispersed, all but for the two men crouching by the fountain.

His senses kicked in and his eyes burned as he passed the spray and the heavy stench of urine mixed with chlorine from leathered people of all ages using the fountain as a urinal throughout the night, all just blocks from the SF Symphony and Opera. Who would have dreamed that *La Boheme* would ever have anything in common with the streets of San Francisco? It was the $1.29 Store parking lot morphed.

With his eyes still stinging, DS had one hour until kick-off and started his mad search for a place to pick up some fresh clothes but stores along Market St. were still caged up. Siri said nothing would be open until 9 a.m. He'd just have to explain to Justin what happened with his luggage and do his best to clean up. He checked the hotel address on his phone. One block down on the right was his hotel. *Well, finally something's gone right!* The marquee looked promising. DS made a beeline through the swarm.

#

The Hotel Baida was something of a legend around town these days. Its interior was a decrepit Art Deco throwback begging for restoration. The lobby featured an old-time record player with swirly, gold-embossed detail. A sign by the elevator, handwritten in struggled letters, instructed all guests to sign in at the front desk. DS arrived in time for the breakfast that should have warmly welcomed him had he not fucked up Flight 147. Instead, only stale doughnuts greeted him under a cloudy plastic dome. The reservation desk was behind more protective plastic where a moldy Asian woman held guard. DS dinged the bell. She barely looked up. For a moment, DS thought she might be slumped over. Dead. He dinged again. This time the woman stirred from her online Mahjong game.

"You have reservation?"

"Last night. Strait, Richard. I'm here for the week. My flight was delayed."

The little woman tapped the metal tray of her cage. She didn't care about his personal matters. Above it a sloppy sign read: I.D. and credit card. No checks. DS slid the required under the window. The woman examined it with a magnifying glass then looked up at DS. Several times.

"O.K. We still have room. Sign." The woman slid the forms through the tray.

"Great because I need to take a shower and—"

The woman grabbed the signed docs and slid a key with his room number, 315, under the glass. She pointed to the elevator. "Breakfast at 6:30. Bathroom down hall. And no bring in hotplate. People try to make kitchen in room. No kitchen in room." And with that, she turned her back and re-entered her world of Mahjong.

The hotel appeared empty. Odd, DS thought, for a bustling San Francisco morning. In fact,

the hotel in general had a creepy vibe. Sort of a cross between doom and death. Later that afternoon DS would get the full scoop.

There's an App for That

―――#―――

DS arrived after a frigid shower at his new job in the heart of mid-Market. The exterior was underwhelming, but once he set foot inside, he was blown away. It rivaled the best in cool, arty playfulness and casual wear. Everyone looked like they fucked up US Flightways Flight 147. And this receptionist was worlds away from Mahjong Woman.

"Hi there." Her teeth sparkled. In fact, everyone's teeth sparkled and were shades lighter than the average yellow-tinged ones in Shawnee and what seemed dozens of shades lighter than the meth heads. "You're DS, right? Justin's out for the morning." Mindy's hair was glossy California blonde. Just what a guy from the Midwest would imagine. Her eyes were get-lost-in-blue. DS was in love.

"Yeah. Me... DS." *Yeah, me DS. Me caveman, you cavewoman. Fuck. Did I really just say that?* "I mean, yes. I'm Richard Strait. DS."

She popped up out of her ergonomic chair and for a minute DS thought she was going to high five him but instead this babe wrapped her arms around him and gave him a bounteous hug that, literally, touched his heart. "Welcome to NuMilieu. I'm Mindy. I'm the

Vibe Manager. So, like if you need any special pillows or stuff like that, I'm your girl." *Vibe Manager?* "I'll show you around. You can get comfy before Justin gets back. The dentist. I told him he's too young for root canals. Poor guy. He's a starch addict, just as bad as sugar. At least that's what our Wellness Guru says." *Wellness Guru?*

And so the tour of the nearly empty space began. Mindy pointed out where the play room, the workout room and amphitheater would be once they got more rounds of funding. There was already a yoga studio and fully functional organic dining room, though. It was staffed by Chef Louis whose only job was to pamper employees with anything from sushi to tandoori with organic produce at the core of each meal. DS noted the lavender lemonade on tap. And then there was the rooftop deck with loads of potential. DS took in the view of the Ferry Building. The word "TRUTH" was spelled out in large black letters on the brick siding of a neighboring structure.

"Dave and Justin picked this space because of that. Truth. It was a message to a former mayor painted by his arch enemy so he'd have to stare at it everyday from his office in City Hall. Cool, huh?" *Dave... did she say Dave? His Professor Gismondi?*

"Yes. Cool. Very cool."

"They want everyone to be truthful in mind, body and spirit. But DS, you look like a hipster and you guys are usually straight shooters." *Hipster. Did she just call me a hipster?*

"I... no one's ever called me that before."

"A straight shooter?"

"No. A hipster."

Mindy twinkled as she giggled. "Listen to your Vibe Manager here. It's all about the truth. And the truth is, oversized black frames, plaid flannel and skinny jeans equals hipster. We're all about hipsters here. I'm all about hipsters."

So, Flight 147's debacle served its purpose. Only an idiot would show up in a fresh shirt and tie at this place. And Mindy was into hipsters. Life was starting to look up for Little Dickie Strait.

#

By the time Justin returned with a half-paralyzed face, DS had seen it all, as well as having his first sushi roll which he tried desperately not to spit out. Mindy, Frances and Marika were his lunch companions and for a moment DS didn't mind death because he thought he had died and gone to heaven as he sat around the kidney-shaped dining table in the NuMilieu Cafe. Frances, a flaming redhead, was the web designer and Marika, with her silky black hair, was an award-winning graphic designer. Together they completed the neo-Charlie's Angels trio. Yes, indeed, DS was in heaven. Except for the dragon roll. Eel would definitely not be one of his acquired tastes.

"So DS, where are you from?" Frances had one of those ethereal, angelic voices that made a guy sing in his head.

"Shawnee. Oklahoma."

"Sounds small." Marika led The Girls in a private laugh that pierced DS's initial security. The really shitty bully memories had formed connections in DS's brain and certain things, like private laughs, sent an electrical current straight from his head to his heart. "I'm jealous. I was born and raised here. Always wanted to live in a small town, though. Anonymous gets old."

"Put it this way, if hunting and fried pie is your thing, then so is Shawnee."

"Who fries pies?" Another private laugh, this one led by Mindy but this time DS joined in. There was the slightest spark that he was one with them. One of them.

"My Grammy and every other real baker in Oklahoma."

"How cute, Grammy. He has a Grammy." Marika wanted more.

"Yeah, she raised me. Grammy Flo."

"Oh My God! A Grammy Flo!" Mindy was clearly impressed.

"My…" DS couldn't go there. Not today. "My parents weren't around much."

"Were any of ours?" blurted Frances. The three cackled, though Mindy's was a bit subdued. They were all from the Bay Area. Rich little suburbanites whose parents were both either workaholics or they had stay-at-home moms who spent their days at the gym and on the tennis court and their nights slugging back weekend Napa wine purchases, usually Chardonnay, a.k.a. Peninsula Crack. Or, as in Mindy's case, raised by a single parent. It was obvious they knew each other inside and out.

"So DS, where are you staying?"

"I got lucky. Found a little hotel until I could scope out a place to rent."

"Good luck with that. It's a jungle out there." Frances had spearheaded a rental hunt years earlier.

"But the strong do survive and sometimes even get a studio for under $3,900." DS gagged. The rents must have gone up as he was in transit. "We got in just before the greed. And under rent control. What hotel?"

"The Hotel Baida." The three nearly spat out their sushi and raised their eyes like does in the path of death. The details quickly emerged—Marika gladly led the reveal. "There was a really, really gross murder there. Two weeks ago. The Tenderloin Butcher."

"Seriously? You didn't hear about it? It's all over the news." Marika was stunned.

"The guy chopped the fingers off a guest and sprinkled them out a third story window." Frances recounted the gory details.

"Third story?" DS gulped and suddenly felt the outline of his room number 315 key pressing through his pocket, next to his skin.

"And then he tossed out the arms for good measure." Marika found a weird pleasure in the gory details.

Marika elbowed Frances. "No *Criminal Minds* recount needed."

"You can't stay there. It's not safe. You'll have to stay with us until you find a place," Mindy pleaded. *Us. Stay with us? I mean, poor guy, arms and all but... well, just but, that's all.*

"It's the second TL murder in four weeks," Frances squinted.

"TL?"

"Tenderloin, silly. They think it's drug-related, but who knows? You can't count on the SF police.

Severed body parts are the biggie clue, though." *Yup, Frances loved the details.*

Marika piped in. "They say if you want to commit a murder, do it in San Francisco. No one's ever caught here, let alone prosecuted."

Mindy checked a text on her cell and read it out loud. "He's back. Puffy but back. Come on DS, time to get to work." Mindy's correct left and right air quotes were just another endearing gesture from DS's dream girl.

#

Justin's office had been off the initial tour. DS entered the world of tech fantasy in wide-eyed awe. Two huge monitors framed his sleek desk. The requisite office diversion games were scattered about. A collection of neo-pop culture artwork blurred the lines between high art and low culture.

"Well, I'll leave you two brains alone." With that, Mindy swirled an about face, accented by a cute little toodles wave.

Justin, his face wrapped in gauze holding an ice pack, emerged from beside a Warhol-ish life-sized image of Steve Jobs wearing his standard black turtleneck and jeans. Justin wore a designer hoodie that had set him back seven hundred bucks. His speech was slurry. The ice pack digging into his cheek caused the occasional *sh* to get buried in his words.

"DS, good to finally meet face to distorted face." Justin repositioned the cubes. "Here we're dead center in the tech world, but ice packs are still the only revenge for a yanked tooth. And that's after two fucking root canals. Nothing worsh. Ever had one DS? A root canal?"

DS struggled to understand the words. "No, knock on wood." DS looked around—wood, real wood was a rarity in the tech world where antiques were often looked on as rubbish unless they were reclaimed. Simply too brown. He gave up the awkward search and unrealistically vowed in his head to avoid starch and sugar.

"They stick a fucking rubber shling in your mouth to catch any tooth dust you don't shnort. And, you shnort a lot of tooth dust DS. Feels like a gram. And then, after that torture fails, they go in for the kill and pull the fucking thing out. The crunching sound alone is enough to drive anyone insane." Justin pulled a snotty rag from his pocket and blew with a ferocity that DS had never witnessed before. "And just as you're leaving, they give you the instructions. Don't blow your nose." Justin then spit a wad of blood into the rag. "And no spitting. It's all impossible. Now I can look forward to an implant. That's code for 'I'm getting screwed.'"

"Sounds intense." Really, what else could he say?

"But, that's yesterday's tweet. Today we need to focus on you and NuMilieu."

As Justin then slurred on about the company and the destiny they would create together, DS felt an odd ever-presence, like someone else had lingered in the office long after Mindy made her adorable exit. The thought haunted DS to the point he couldn't concentrate on a single one of Justin's words. And then he saw it. High in the corner of the office was an eyeball the size of a medium cantaloupe mounted on a thin strip of metal. It blinked to the beat of the dub step in the background. For a guy like DS, a genetic nerd who could even potentially be on the spectrum of Asperger's, this environment was an assault on his brain.

"I'm sorry. I missed that." DS snapped his way out of the diversion.

"I was just saying that our goal is to make our investors proud. Line their pockets. Then line ours!" With that, Justin escorted DS from the office. "Now get to work. We have a team meeting at 4:30."

"Great. Sure. 4:30. See you then." Justin shut the door and DS stood in the hallway, certain that his career was short-lived, killed in the blink of an eye. But Mindy came to the rescue.

"So, not a clue, right?" She swept her arm around Justin. "Not to worry, no one ever has a clue what Justin wants. That's what I'm here for. I suggest you prep some bits of brilliance for the 4:30. You know, how code can transform the new industry. Anything code. Justin just loves code. And any images for those pets we've heard so much about."

"Code. Right. Code. And images."

"And don't forget that you're with us tonight. We'll pick your things up from The Baida after the meeting."

"Things? Oh, things. US Flightways has my things."

"Ha! US Flightways!! Figures. From now on only Virgin for you."

"Virgin?" *How could she possibly know? Do I have a scarlet V carved into my forehead?*

"Airline, silly. They're the best. Lots of goodies."

O.K. then. Virgin it is.

#

After DS spilled his bits of brilliance, both impressing and intimidating Justin, the trio dragged him from the office to The Baida to check out and then to Urban Outfitters to pick up some temp clothes. They must have all loved to play paper dolls growing up, because they had the dress-up thing down. They basically parked him in the dressing room and turned him into their private model. They started from scratch, first insisting on new boxer briefs even though he had been a longtime tighty-whiteys guy. In the end, DS left with three bags of shirts, sweaters, pants, print boxer briefs, including, but not limited to, Homer's Donuts and dinosaurs, and a $1,759 bill. But, according to Mindy, Marika and Frances, he was looking good. And that was worth every red cent to DS.

#

As DS would soon learn, The Mission was an ironic, vibrant and influential neighborhood in SF. Its Latino history was deep and its gentrification was a slap in the face to many of the families who owned the alleys, ethnic shops and aromatic eateries. Its street art wasn't merely graffiti but explosions of elaborate colors and themes that would have made Diego and Frida proud. Clarion Alley, one endless mural, was just one such example.

The Mission had a smell, an energy, and a tradition that it struggled to preserve. The influx of rich techies who demanded high-end, chichi food along with their burritos sometimes put the neighborhood on edge. And when the Mission was on the edge, the whole city was on the edge. It never took much—a Giants win, a police shooting anywhere in the U.S. or another building getting knocked down for an upscale apartment, a bookstore or cafe relinquishing its lease because of a rent hike—any such event could get the fever raging. And when it raged, it poured passion. People would flood the streets, jump on cars and ride up and down Mission Street on the roofs throwing M-80s like condoms from a Gay Pride parade float.

DS's first night in the Mission was this kind of night. Yet another white-on-black shooting in a Blue state had left tensions running high. The Girls ushered him through the streets. When a stack of firecrackers was tossed at his feet, DS danced like a dragon on Chinese New Years to avoid the singe. People with bats were breaking windows everywhere and messages were spray painted on corporate targets by bandana-covered protestors. By the time they arrived at the three-bedroom flat, DS was a hot mess. The Girls led him through the retro funk living room to the under-used kitchen.

Mindy and Frances headed for their rooms. "Be right back." Mindy gave the trademark adorable wave.

"It's not always like this. You just hit a weird night." Marika threw her purse on the kitchen table. "We'll get something to calm you down. After all, you're in San Francisco now!" Marika shouted through the flat. "Hey, who's got herb? DS is a little scrambled."

"I'm out. Thought you guys had some." Frances' voice floated through the rooms.

"I'm out, too."

Marika yanked out her cell. "Shit, who's going to deliver through this street rage?"

Frances entered. "Try Green Cross. They deliver rain or shine, riot or rave."

Marika brought up her weed delivery app and read the Green Cross reviews. "Forget the rain or shine. Pit bulls. These guys even deliver through pit bulls!"

"Hey, no hating on pitties. Some just have bully owners," Frances defended the breed.

DS's eyes bugged open when he glimpsed the app. "Is that for marijuana?" Shock began its descent into the room. "Uh, you probably won't believe this but I... I never—"

Mindy entered the kitchen as if on cue. "Oh My God! A virgin!! We love virgins!!!" *If only they knew the extent.*

Frances chimed in. "Too much fun!!" An M-80 went off outside their window. No one budged but DS who braced himself firmly against the built-in China cabinet.

"Let's see. How about some Blue Cheese?" The Girls gathered around the app like they were sharing a dinner menu.

"Sunset Sherbet's supposed to be amazing. See? Battles ADD, depression, arthritis and relaxes the muscles. Perfect for him."

"Ugh, I don't have arthritis," DS piped up.

"Yeah, but you were on that plane forever. Your muscles gotta be sore."

Within ten minutes, as the app promised, The Green Cross delivered. Within seven minutes of that, DS was flat on his back on an impossibly comfy couch with flowing giggles as Marika jacked the widescreen with a *Criminal Minds* marathon that lasted 'til 3 a.m. Had he been coherent, he would have heard their detailed praise of how adorable he looked as he slept.

While The Girls let him chill, his mind had flashes of panic about the next morning, sort of like when he was gassed at the dentist's office once, mind racing, body like a tree trunk grounded by an entanglement of roots. But when the sun broke through the fog early that morning, he woke up as refreshed as ever, dug through his Urban Outfitter bags and headed for the bathroom.

DS opened the door on Marika, who was entirely naked, stepping into the shower. "It's O.K. Come on in. Water conservation. We still all need to do our part." Before he knew it, Frances peered out from the curtain, her head crowned with white foam.

"Oh God."

"Get in here silly." Marika stepped outside the shower and pulled him into the stream. It was a tight squeeze. They teased him to off the Homer's Donut boxers, but DS clung to them with his life. Thank God he was blind without his glasses otherwise his stares would be awkward. *Look up. Look up. Look up.* DS wasn't sure if he could handle the pace—new job, protest, weed, showering with two hot chicks before work all in 24 hours. A bit much for this Shawnee transplant. But, when in SF...

#

DS and his Girls, all freshly showered, took the 49 Muni towards Market St. Some day, if all went well, the company would have their own luxury work bus to shuffle them to and from work which, when complete, as told by Justin, would come with a signature coffee bar in the morning and open bar in the afternoon.

"Toast. I want toast," Mindy obsessed.

"Mmmmm, me too." Marika moaned, equally emphatic. Mindy was laser-focused on her cell phone.

"I could have made some if I knew. I saw the toaster and bread." DS wanted to give back to these girls who had given him sooooo much. Suddenly, an evocation from the evening before swept through his mind, or maybe it was just a vague recollection of his early morning dream. All DS knew was he couldn't get the image of himself eating a huge bowl of spaghetti with some kind of improvised pistachio ice cream sauce. *No, I didn't. Did I?* And then he remembered the empty container sitting on the kitchen counter as he entered the kitchen that morning. The Pistachio Gelato container. It was slopped between the toaster and a crusty bowl of dried red sauce and noodle remnants. DS questioned his sanity.

"Ahhh, how cute. Making toast." Frances pinched his cheek.

"But we're talking toast. Toast toast. Real toast." Mindy checked her phone. "Wrong direction. Get off! Now. There's our Uber. Perfect timing." The streetcar stopped and like a miracle, a black Uber was waiting next to it. "Right there!"

The Girls herded DS from the packed vintage streetcar and into a spotless Black Expedition. "The Staff has the best toast in The City." DS couldn't imagine there being such an emphatic distinction but on that ride to The Staff on Divisidero, DS soon learned that San Francisco had long fetishized bread and this purveyor had brought it to a new level. Sourdough had no hold on this craze.

"Oh My God, I'm salivating already!" DS glanced and Mindy was dry but her pupils were a bit dilated in anticipation of—toast.

"You're gonna love it! Chef Louis is amazing but his toast sucks. These guys are the real deal. And only four dollars a slice."

DS stared down Mindy in disbelief. "Four dollars? For a piece of toast?"

"Yeah, can you believe it? Bargain." *No, actually, I can't.*

They arrived to a line of tech hipster hybrids at The Staff in designer shades, eight-hundred-dollar jeans and nine-hundred-dollar shoes, sans socks. DS imagined they could surely afford a toaster and some grocery delivery service plus their own chef to do the honors. And certainly they had the means to buy a pair of socks. Here DS had his first slice of bargain four-dollar toast—a hunk of seed studded bread with a spread of clumpy cream cheese and sour strawberry jam. It was not much different from the fixings he'd get at the local diner back home for free with an order of eggs but, surrounded by The Girls, it just tasted better, plus he didn't have to attend church first. Still, he couldn't help but wonder what an eight-dollar piece could offer. Just as he finished the last bite and avoided the temptation to lick the last bit of strawberry from his finger, he felt his phone vibrate.

"Do you mind?" The Girls were deep into their second order and could have cared less. At first. "Grammy! Hi!! Sorry I didn't call. It's just been really crazy." Her smoker's voice graveled from the phone. She had been worried sick. DS covered the phone and motioned to The Girls, "It's my Grammy Flo." He lowered his voice. "I know Gram, I just seemed to have lost a day." By now Mindy, Marika and Frances were hanging on every word. "I'll tell you all about it tonight. Yes, yes. I promise. Yes. Yes." He lowered his voice but it was not lost on his colleagues. "I love you, too."

Marika gasped. "Ahhhhhhh, did you hear that?"

Mindy chimed in. "Grammy Flo."

Frances wouldn't be left out of the Grammy grab. "I want!"

They talked as though she was some sort of pet that could be bought on Overstock. He addressed no one in particular. "What about yours?"

"Dead."

"Dead."

"Dead."

O.K. then, apparently there was a shortage of grandmas in the Bay Area. Surely his would be a hit if she ever made it to SF.

#

The four Ubered to the office in style and no one blinked twice at the fact it was 10:30 and they were just getting in. Justin was still home nursing an investor hangover from too many mixologist specialties off the Million-Dollar Cocktail list at The Moonlight Room. His last indulgence, a two-hundred-dollar drink, appropriately called the Devil's Share, was a concoction of pricey Cognac, Walnut Liqueur and 20-year Tawny Port served in a snifter that was washed and then skillfully flamed. He didn't remember finishing the drink, his parting words with his angels or the crackhead that punched him in the face when he stupidly decided to walk home through the Tenderloin just so he could get a little fresh air. Justin turned up at the office at about 1:30 in the afternoon, his face still swollen from what was developing into a raging gum infection but now with an added black eye.

Meanwhile Mindy and the Wellness Guru were helping DS organize his office when his duffel arrived, sans computer. Several calls to US Flightways only elevated his anxiety which would prompt a call from Mindy to The Green Cross before lunchtime.

"That's right. The duffel came, but no computer." DS grimaced at the response. Mindy grabbed his cell.

"I'm just about to send out a social media blast if we don't get the computer back now," she grimaced. "Manager. Get your manager. I don't have time for this shit."

DS looked on half-impressed, half-embarrassed as his Vibe Manager bitched herself up the chain of command, simultaneously pulling up US Flightway's executives' email addresses then warning the poor customer service agent, who no doubt regretted revealing her name was Sandy Jenson, that she'd be out of a job if the computer wasn't delivered by 5 p.m.

It was a motley crew that afternoon, but somehow, during and after lunch, they seemed to have mapped out a flow chart for success that would impress the investors at their subsequent dinner, the same dinner that Justin would literally "blow" through that evening. This time at lunch, DS finished his sushi, aptly named the Monkey Roll, which best described his playmates in this zoo of an office. DS was not just adapting to his new environment, but quickly becoming intoxicated by the whole scene.

And, luckily for Sandy Jenson, DS's laptop miraculously appeared at 4:59 that afternoon.

#

Mindy's eyes pierced through the candlelight that flooded the flat. Frances and Marika were out. Mindy plopped on the couch. "So, what was it really like growing up in Shawnee?" *Oh God, did we have to do this now?*

DS drank from a huge goblet of red wine that would make Professor Gismondi proud. "My family, parents and big sister were killed in a car crash. I was in fifth grade. I was the only survivor."

Mindy expected tears, but there were none from DS. Hers compensated plenty, though. "I..." she tried to herd some words. Any words. "Shit, DS. Why didn't you say something?"

"I am saying something."

"That's the worst thing I've ever heard from a real person. I mean, you always see it in movies and stuff, but for real? For real is awful. Trust me. I know real, too."

Yes. For real is awful.

He confessed more of the details when he felt the vibration. Mindy saw that it was Grammy again.

"Answer it. Answer it. Oh my God! Answer it!!"

"Hey Gram. I was just settling in to call you." Mindy cuddled next to him like a kitten in the night, much like the one who snored those hours away in his dorm room. But this one purred and listened as DS recounted to his grandmother everything from the moment he set foot on Flight 147 to this very moment on the velvety soft couch that enveloped his body. She wanted to know every detail and he gave it all to her with the exception of The Green Cross, The Tenderloin Butcher and The Shower. This time, when he spoke of his new friends, he conjured up the painting on the side of the building across from his. Truth. This was the Truth. When he hung up, Mindy gave him one of her heart massage hugs. He felt a convergence of pain and love, a cellular change within his body. This Vibe Manager really knew her stuff, even after her fourth goblet.

"Well, I think it's bedtime for me." DS knew he had to distance himself just as any good employee would do.

"Ahhh."

"Big day tomorrow. I'll see you in the morning." Mindy wanted to grab him by the arm and pull him into her room, but showed a rare moment of restraint instead.

#

Great as his temp living situation with The Girls was, DS decided to take an afternoon to apartment hunt. He wanted to settle in before work stepped up, as Justin warned him that it would soon, especially with their launch party on the horizon. Although DS's 3D designs were new to the company, NuMilieu had every intention of showcasing them.

"I don't want to put you guys out another night." Chef Louis had fixed them a Mediterranean feast for lunch and DS picked his way through a lumpy, foreign-looking substance.

"No way. You're staying. We love having you. Right?" Frances angled her question towards Mindy and Marika.

"You're not leaving," Marika echoed.

"I have to get my own place. But I'll be over. Lots."

"Promise?" Mindy had grown fond of his slender, boxer-clad body parading around the flat, but she understood his motivation. He wanted a place Grammy could come and visit, hang her hat.

"Promise."

"Okay then, here are the best sites." Frances provided a list of websites beyond Craigslist. "Padhopper is awesome."

"If you like frogs," Marika grinned. "Just kidding. That's how we found the flat."

"Stay away from the Tenderloin. Especially with that psycho killer on the loose. TenderNob's O.K. though if you get desperate." Frances knew the rental market inside and out.

"But only if you're really desperate," Mindy chimed in.

"Tender Nob?"

"Nob Hill on the border of the grunge." Frances explained.

"Got it. The grunge."

"And don't commit to one agent. Use 'em all. They'll lie through their teeth to get you to sign an agreement. Check the crime stats. Turn on the faucets. Make sure the oven works. And no building built after June 13th, 1979 or you won't get rent control. Ask for a certificate of occupancy. And listen. They only have open houses at quiet times. Expect some of the alleys to be twice as noisy at night. At least. Bum fights don't have boundaries in San Francisco. And don't take any apartment next to the elevator. It will drive you nuts after a while." Frances was full of sound advice.

"Or a garbage chute. Been there, done that." Marika chimed in.

So, with a little digital frog in his hand, DS embarked on an apartment hunt that would test every ounce of his patience as he shuffled between grimy, potential residences.

The last stingy studio was packed. It was his seventh open house that afternoon. This one was in the TenderNob but more Nob than Tender.

"I'll do the tour once. Follow me. Anyone interested should fill out an application online. You can scan stubs, references, attach credit." The rental agent was a fast-talking guy with muscles that stuck out through his Armani suit. He would never have fit in at NuMilieu.

DS followed the sheeple. They were a well-dressed herd, mostly twenty-something techies, each wanting to make the best impression. Like DS, they were desperate. The housing costs were rising daily. This was a "large" pre-'79 studio tucked into a fabulous flat, not too gross and everyone wanted it—"vintage" yellow linoleum, crooked blinds and all.

It was hard to have a private conversation in the 325 square feet crawling with a couple of dozen apartment hunters. DS cornered the agent. "Uh, I don't have any stubs, yet. I just got to SF last week." The sheeple collectively turned and sighed a mixed sense of compassion and relief as one more competitor was about to hit the pavement.

"But, I have a job. A good job." DS couldn't contain himself. "I make $90,000 a year!" No one was impressed. After all, it wasn't even six figures.

"No stubs, no apartment." His attitude was cavalier at first, barely glancing at the prospective tenant he was chastising.

"Nothing? There's nothing in this city? I don't even need a kitchen."

The agent must have felt DS's pain. He pulled him aside from the group just as the herd was beginning to turn on each other like cannibals in heat. They pushed and shoved, checked the gas stove, faucet flow, felt compelled to pull the chain attached to the light bulb on and off in the teensy, mothball-y closet.

"I've only got one option for guys like you, but it's down the hill. Not quite a micro. An aPodment."

"aPodment?"

"Listen—" His eyes gave the name cue.

"Richard. Richard Strait."

"Listen, Richard. It's in San Francisco and it's bigger than a jail cell. And the rent starts with a one. One thousand nine-hundred ninety-nine. Furnished."

The guy gave him a condescending pat on the shoulder. "Temp until you get those stubs. Right?"

DS took the card offered from the agent's well-manicured hand. He rolled his index finger over the raised gold letters: Jason Taliaferro, Owner, Broker. Jason noticed that DS noticed. "I only did this open house as a favor to my pal. He owns the block now and someday, when he cashes in on the raging gentrification, I'll make that commish." Jason wrote the address on the back. It was on Hyde St., down, way down from the cable cars. "I'll be there in two hours."

#

If ever there was a walk from heaven to hell this was it. The descent from the lovely Victorians, most refurbished and pristine, was striking. People walked their pedigree pooches with pride. It was nearing sunset and the dogs were dressed appropriately in little designer frocks for the fog that was beginning its journey from the Bay. In this moment, DS thought of Flo, wishing that she could be there as the heavenly moisture coated the sky. This was the magic that was San Francisco. The jazzy ring of a passing cable car accented the moment.

DS checked the address again. He was on track. He continued down the hill, block after block, and noted the cultural shift. He was definitely heading back into the zombie apocalypse, in parts near ankle-deep in rubbish. Empty plastic bags, now outlawed in San Francisco, took flight in the mysterious, whirling air. He was close enough to the aPodment and had time to kill. He googled the nearest Meet's which The Girls vowed was the best bet chain coffee. Takeaway caffeine was a newly-acquired addiction and this would give him the jolt he needed. A damn good fix.

The line was made tolerable by an entertaining barista who announced his drinks with a deep, refined golden voice. "One large extra-hot extra shot soy sea salt caramel macchiato, ten pumps sugar-free vanilla, two pumps sugar-free mocha with a pretty leaf on top." A skinny woman with two toddlers on leashes grabbed the drink. "Half-caf cappuccino extra shot cream two pumps hazelnut no pretty leaf on top." This went to the man with quarter-sized spacers in his ears. The barista turned his eyes to DS. "And. One. Tall. Hot. Blonde." DS blushed as he reached for his simple large latte and suffered the attention the impromptu drink name brought from the eclectic line behind him.

He still had a few minutes, grabbed the rare Meet's seat and took it all in. Every last character, and there were many. A woman, perhaps old, perhaps not, shuffled through the doors all hunched over. DS noted the vertical tattoo of a marijuana leaf on her chin. From the hips up she was spineless, walking horizontal to the ground. DS inspected her as she inspected the brown floor tiles with laser-like curiosity and zeroed in on what DS thought had to be a coin. Instead she picked up a crumb on her index finger and examined it against the recessed light. She added it to the invisible pile in her leathered hand and continued her search below the next table. No one seemed to notice her obsession, the urine stain on the legs of her torn khaki pants, the pills on her grubby wool coat larger than the crumbs in her palm. Not even the lower Hayes Valley crowd, some also dressed in khakis sans stains, who had ducked out of their cool buildings away from their raw food cafeterias and playground-like offices, noticed the slouched-over body. Crumb Woman was not an anomaly. DS wanted to point, call the Manager, write Grammy Flo, but instead he stared into his phone as though that would absorb his shock. *So, this is what tweeting is for?*

The Girls had encouraged DS to set up a twitter account, but until now, he had never really been convinced of the purpose. Sirens roared in the distance, one after another until their sound was one. Had he been social media savvy like they insisted, he would have known, even before it hit SFSlate, that the Tenderloin Butcher had struck again. But since DS hadn't followed their emphatic advice, he headed back to the Hyde St. address on the back of Jason's gold-embossed card.

Jason was pacing inside the iron clad entrance. DS felt dirty when he arrived. Not that the street filth had actually rubbed off on him, there was just sooooo much of it. Piles of garbage, human shit, the potent odor of concentrated urine and the random expired bird amongst the needles. A half-dead crackhead napped mid-sidewalk, his matted hair cushioned with an old spare boot. No one so much as blinked as they stepped around the mound. If it was an animal passed out, surely someone would come to the rescue but apparently in San Francisco humans didn't quite carry the same clout.

"The neighborhood is a little iffy. But remember, it's temp, right?"

Jason ignored the sirens roaring in the background and let DS through the initial entrance. The marble steps were encouraging but it was downhill after that. He recognized the odor that wafted through the dark maroon hallway. Whether it was either Blue Cheese or Sunset Sherbet, he couldn't tell.

"So, it's got an elevator but don't expect it to work. Ever. Just being honest here, Richard. I'm always honest with my temps."

"O.K. Thanks for that."

"You're up on three." As they climbed the stairs, DS convinced himself it was Blue Cheese.

Jason opened the door and DS slid through before him. He looked for a corner to turn, but there was none. A small refrigerator with a hotplate atop it, stood in a pseudo nook. The room was furnished in chipped Swedish furniture. A twin bed lined one wall and the smallest desk and chair were centered on another. That was it. The bathroom was nearly big enough to turn around in without grazing the sharp handle of the stall shower.

"A hundred seventy-five square feet. And no street view or alley which is good. That means no traffic or 3 a.m. bum fights." Jason opened the dusty window shades. "Decent light and you do get a little depth." DS looked out the filthy window. The neighbors were directly across the light well and DS could see into all four aPodments. "It's sort of like *Rear Window*."

"*Rear Window*," DS mumbled under his breath, "my Grammy's favorite."

"Mine too!" And with that Jason had sealed the deal. "All utilities but Internet. PT&T cell service sucks here. Z-Mobile is great in SF if you need to switch. Cheaper too. The aPodment's wired for high-speed. Terms are two months minimum. By then you'll have the stubs."

DS was cornered. Literally. "Fine. I'll take it. Two months." *How bad could it be for two months, really?*

#

DS took the nondescript elevator off of Mission St. as instructed by The Girls. The walls were lined in poster board and every night guests used marker pens to create graffiti that rivaled the best in town. The new temporary, interactive installation was added to a collection that was auctioned off to benefit local charities at month's end. An artist throwback to the Beat Generation, Jack Frizz, complete with black beret and a very goat-y goatee rode up and down until all walls were filled with visions of culture. DS exited into heaven. The outdoor rooftop restaurant had one of the most heavenly views in The City and his angels were flagging him down from a prime table.

Mindy spotted DS from across the floor and chased up to give him her fabulous hug. "Thank God you're here." She dragged him over to their table.

Frances gave him alternate cheek kisses. "We were sooooo worried you got tied up in it."

"It?"

"It. You know. It. The Butcher. This time arms and legs." Here was Marika again with the morbid details. Surely she and Mrs. Oricello would have hit it off. She backed her narrative up with a map. "The open house was here, right? We had you tagged." She shoved her phone with a plotted app in his face. Sure enough, the crime scene was just a block from the aPodment.

"Marika's obsessed with *Criminal Minds*. This is her amateur hour," Mindy explained.

"And thank God for that." Marika defended herself while poking the phone under DS's nose once again.

"Fuck. Double fuck." DS immediately excused his language, it was just that East Coast, West Coast thing. "Fuck" was not only becoming his new "um" but he was using it as a noun, verb and an adjective, much like the hipsters spread out over The City and so many New Yorkers. The Girls set down their ultra-aged margaritas. "I just signed a lease there." They leaned into the little dot that DS pointed to. "One block away."

For a team that hated football, particularly since the Niners made their hideous move to Santa Clara, this trio sure knew how to Monday morning quarterback. "You did what?" Frances was the first to scold.

Then came Mindy who was most concerned, even tearful. "I knew it. We should have gone with him."

"Well the good news is, The Butcher has never struck within a block of a prior murder." Marika, being a graphic designer, had mapped a visual of each murder. And she was right. DS was, according to her theory, potentially safe for now.

The three took to social media and within minutes had access to all of the gory details. A video of one woman covered in blood was a trending tweet link.

"I was just walking, minding my own business and plop, a fucking leg drops out of the sky. A leg. From the sky!" The link was hard to watch. She held up her red-streaked glasses. "These got caught on the tendons." The tech worker had just recently rented a temp apartment in the TL and was walking home. The video showed her surrounded by the other three limbs before the police put up the crime scene tape.

As if on cue, the news report came onto the one television above the El Sketcho bar in the distance. The newscaster, himself a bit rattled, reported from behind the yellow tape. "Once again, the Tenderloin Butcher has struck in this neighborhood. Police say they expect to step up patrols and are actively asking any witnesses who saw anything, to please contact them. They'll be reviewing all camera footage from the area as well. The department is working under the assumption that the string of homicides are gang related. They encourage all residents to be on guard and keep all doors and windows secured. Again, anyone with any suspicions should call the police immediately or send a tip by text to TIP411." If one strained, they could see that poor, bloodied woman in the background shivering in the fog, surrounded by investigators. Surely she hadn't seen anything or she would have dodged that leg.

"It's only for two months until I get the stubs," DS reasoned. By then I'll know the neighborhoods better, and who knows, maybe rents will come down."

Frances charged in. "Who knows? We know. Rents won't come down until the next bubble bursts or The Big One hits."

"But it's only temp." DS flagged down the waiter with the distinct Dali knock-off mustache. "I'll have what they have. And this is all on me. I don't know what I would have done without you three."

"Woo-hoo... hey, big spender!" The Girls toasted DS. Little did he know until the bill came that ultra-aged tequila equaled one-hundred-dollar margaritas. Even in The Mission.

#

DS held on to Marika's observation that no murder had taken place within a block of another. He had paid the two months' rent plus security deposit and wasn't in any position at the moment to make a change, especially with those ultra-aged margarita bills.

Moving day was not at all an elaborate ordeal. Basically, DS packed up his duffel with his Urban Outfitters loot and shuffled to his new home. Crime tape still webbed the neighborhood and the police presence was, indeed, high. The spree had now attracted national news which caused the mayor to attempt to quickly clean up the streets, to preserve the tourist dollars coming from people who wanted to maintain the Golden Gate bridge/cable car fantasy.

DS found out that there was a good amount of truth in that fantasy, though. Anytime he got outside of the TL zone, he saw the magic just like all the movies promised. The Victorians, the views and the little cable cars really did reach halfway to the stars. DS was star-struck. In those first few days, a couple of times, after his first cable car ride, he jumped onto a random Muni and just rode the distinct streets of San Francisco. Other times he'd pick a random destination and Uber up and down the hills. Sometimes he'd even get lucky and have a driver who really knew the hidden gems of the The City. Soon he came to know the neighborhoods outside of the TL and Pill Hill: North Beach, Deco Ghetto on the edge of the Mission, the Haight, Dogpatch, Chinatown. There were so many that he thought it would be impossible to really taste them all.

His first few weeks in the apartment weren't so bad. Just a place to hang his hoodie in between work and explorations. He was even starting to appreciate the cheap Vietnamese food in what some had ironically called the Splenderloin in its pre-Butcher days. And then there were The Girls. This band of babes were now his best buds. They adopted him like a new pet. They fed him, groomed him and gave him lots of hugs and kisses and a little—emphasize little—housewarming he'd never forget, or realistically, found himself hard-pressed to remember.

That particular night, just a few days after he officially moved in, the three girls had stood outside his iron cage front entrance with arms full of essentials. Leave it to Mindy, an official people pleaser and partier extraordinaire, to think of everything: a rubber ducky, a French Press with a pound of Meet's coffee, a toaster oven, hotplate, luxury bath items, coconut candles, wine and champagne glasses, collapsible "kitchen" goods, Thai food, chopsticks and disposable bamboo plates. DS led them up through the layers of hallway scents, the weed, curry and vanilla that trailed into his hallway. He paused at his front door as though working up his nerve to reveal his little pod.

"Come on, come on. We're dying here." Mindy was carrying both the Thai food and a Magnum that she could no longer conceal.

"K, but remember, it's—" Frances cut him off.

"Temporary," the three panted out in unison.

With that, DS sprung open the door. There was a brief, awkward pause as they adjusted to his reality.

Marika snooped around, an action that took a matter of seconds, not minutes. "Hey, it's not so bad. Clean at least."

"Yeah, and you've got a view. Sort of." Frances peered through the two windows that opened to the light well. Across the way, two Latino men were arguing. They drew down the shades which blocked any potential voyeuristic view.

DS squeezed the rubber ducky. "If only I had a tub. These were my favorites growing up."

"Soon enough. Two months. But a bathtub is essential." Mindy put the ducky on the shower floor. "We'll let him rest here until he gets a real home."

Mindy popped the massive bottle of Dom Perignon, filled four flutes and toasted to the aPodment. "Here's to a Tenderloin Butcher-free tenancy." Well, not the most encouraging, but it was the thought that counted. DS lifted his glass.

Within an hour, the four were ridiculously loud. A neighbor, sort of surfer boy type, knocked on the door. He pushed it open. "Hey, just wanted to say hi. I'm Tracy. I saw you when I was pulling down my shades. Across the light well." Tracy pointed to his apartment and then immediately brought out a fat blunt housewarming gift.

It was one of those remarkable nights that one should remember, but when DS woke up, the details were fuzzy. In fact, weaving together the night's narrative was impossible.

#

DS vowed this would be the last wild night for a while. At least he was pretty sure it was wild, although not one hundred percent. He was new to blackouts and didn't want to make them a regular thing. It never seemed to phase Marika or Frances. And Mindy was particularly immune to the shame. While DS slumped into his office, he could hear them chirping down the hall all rise-and-shiny. He had the blank stares when Mindy knocked.

"That Tracy's something else, huh?" Mindy searched for some kind of content in DS's red-veined eyes.

"Huh?" He had never used a French press and this morning-after wasn't the one to figure it out. "Sorry. Sorry. No coffee yet."

"Ahhh... I told you last night, all you had to do was nuke some water, put in an inch and a half of Meet's, stir, wait four minutes, press and then heavenly happens." She gave him a cute pinch on the cheek and did a swishy about face.

"Wait. Huh? What did you mean something else, huh?"

"Nothing. Nothing else. He seems really... sweet. That's all."

It wasn't until DS was done with an espresso and onto a latte that he pulled his attention back to the "something else." For a brief fantasy moment, DS actually thought that she was jealous that he might have a new friend, but then all the ugly insecurities came flooding through. *Idiot. Why would Mindy ever be jealous? She's perfect.*

#

The Girls were DS's comrades at work while the male contingent at NuMilieu were an odd lot. Some were predictably hipsterish, a few fatty nerds, but mostly neurotic workaholics. The free food and all was great and did the trick to keep employees in the office and out of any fog or intermittent sunshine. With Mindy's insistence, it wasn't long before DS had signed up and fleshed out all the typical personal and public connections via social media that a guy in his twenties needed in order to brand himself as a SF hipster. On the Internet, his life was starting to look amazing. Shit, sometimes DS was even jealous of himself. He had an instant presence on every possible social media site. And that was just the beginning. Before he knew it, in a matter of days, DS had become one of "them" and would now fit right in when a generation of Dowager Humps began to devolve into a downward height trend. Perhaps the cave wasn't far away.

In just a short time, DS had synthesized the bones of the company, and although he wouldn't boast this yet, he knew intuitively how to take this company from A to Z on a bullet train. But the morning after the housewarming, the train was slow. He did his best to stay under the radar until the new yoga class that was set up just for his group started.

The company was broken into teams that worked on specific tasks. His, like most, was a bunch of young guys, sort of the industry standard. Perry, Hayden, Khalil and Ted. They were all hand-picked by Professor Gismondi who had contacts from across the country and in India to hire the best. Frances and Marika, who had family money invested, were in Creative. It didn't take an eco-sociological study to know that it was a sexist industry. But the truth was, The Girls were magical at what they did and they were the energy behind the growth. It was O.K. for employees to cross-pollinate and float between groups if the idea moved Justin, who then had to move Professor Gismondi and the investors.

So, now that DS had added social media to his skillset, the sky was the limit. Not only did he know how to work it, he had ideas for new sites that could help drive their product. But most importantly, he knew how to create the software to create the most amazing interactive 3D pets the world had ever seen. DS was originally hired for his specific pet designs, but as he got more integrated into the marketing side of things, the strategies that he shared in staff meetings became legendary. He did, indeed, have it all. And he wanted to share it all with NuMilieu.

#

DS didn't mind the Downward Dog. What he did mind were the farting noises coming from Ted who was stretched out in front of him. The little *ratta-tat-tats* squeezed out like soldiers going into battle. He was a flabbish guy who had clearly spent the majority of his youth playing computer games without the benefit of caffeine fueled sodas. No, not Ted. His play fuel was just pure crap food—bags of chips, rows of rich cookies, vats of chocolate milk. And now that he had moved to The City from San Jose, regardless of the delicious, organic foods served up by Chef Louis, Ted came to work fully stocked with his supply of doughnuts, cookies and milk. The only difference now was that he only frequented the best—Dynamic Doughnuts, Finkie's Bakery and any other four or five-star sugar house his smartphone could dig up. And when he ran out, there were always a slew of delivery services at his fingertips. Ted had successfully fooled himself that maple bacon doughnuts and chocolate brownies with pistachios and sea salt were somehow healthy, but his ever-expanding belly knew better.

Yogi Bhar, the ironically large and hairy Wellness Guru—surely a lumberjack hipster complete with red flannel shirt and suspenders on the weekends—had encouraged the late afternoon yoga class for DS's department to bond and get the Qi moving but apparently all that was moving were Ted's bowels. Yogi circled the mint green yoga room and made sure that each of them were properly stretched, especially Ted, who was having a hell of a time supporting his weight in any pose, especially a Downward Dog. Before long, his arms were convulsing and the drips of sweat falling from his crimson face onto his mat were audible, until a full puddle formed, which diminished the liquid *plink* sound only slightly.

"This is a time to really free up your mind. Let your brain rest. Enjoy your Downward Dog." Yogi's Bhar's voice was invading the peace.

DS had a hard time emptying his mind. By default, his thoughts inevitably wandered to his childhood. He flashed to the pooch he had had growing up before the accident. Bailey, a chocolate lab, was his best buddy and his only comfort when his father would launch into a drunken tirade about this and that and anything and nothing. He loved that dog dearly—all but his smelly dog explosions. In fact, ever since the craft beer incident, DS had had an overly sensitive olfactory nerve that was activated at the subtlest out-of-the-ordinary odor.

"Feel that stretch. Really let your body settle into the pose." Yogi Bhar's voice was soothing, very Wellness Guru-ish. "Breathe deep. In through the nose s-l-o-w-l-y and out through the mouth—" Yogi didn't even get to the "s-l-o-w-l-y" before the most hideously sounding, bubbly fart DS had ever born witness to shattered the silence. He could not believe or stand the putrid smell that wafted his way. It was clearly beyond any of Bailey's capabilities. He tried desperately to ignore it. Perry, Kahlil and Hayden didn't possess any such willpower. At all. It started with a snicker from Perry, a snort from Kahlil and then a chuckle from Hayden that quickly developed into a guffaw that drew Ted into the act. Hardly maintaining his Downward Dog, Ted started to chortle rhythmically until his farts were in sync, a full-blown war in his bowels that was killing his co-workers one by one.

Although DS was nauseous from the invisible plumes, he succumbed to the silliness, himself now dropping tears onto his mat. The full blown attack was soon acknowledged by Yogi Bhar. "Excellent. Excellent. Yoga not only clears the mind, but the body." His tone was overly tender which got the department of temporary jesters going, on yet another round of cackles and further plumes until Yogi was thoroughly disgusted by the group.

The Wellness Guru had no choice but to bring out his Tibetan bells early. Their sing-y charm did nothing to soothe this bunch. In fact, if anything they were ammunition for more hysterics. "Please, respect your bodies and this moment." No dice. By now his entire class of five was Jello-armed, their strawberry-red faces contorting with increasing snorts. "Well then, let's gently move from our Downward Facing Dog back into our Child's Pose." He again spoke s-l-o-w-l-y, monitoring any progress. "Go into a high push-up position, lower your knees onto the mat, press your hips back towards your heals coming into Balasana. Press your forehead into the mat, arms next to the body, palms facing up. Allow your chest to rest upon the thighs."

The five tried hard not to make eye contact as they shifted clumsily into the balled-up pose. They almost made it until the contraction of their bodies forced what could only best be described as one gross case of mass human synchronicity. As if on cue, each of their bodies expelled one loud body note which didn't stop there. The symphony had just begun. Ted, of course, led the melody with the others poofing out the harmony. Thank God they were already collapsed on the floor because there was really no where else to go. With each snort, the sequence elongated until the five were little more than cackling, drooling idiots in their appropriately-named Child's Pose.

The NuMilieu Guru was getting pissy and brought out his big gun, a large Tibetan singing bowl. He straightened his spine, leveled his shoulders and held the brass bowl, big enough to serve eight, at solar plexus level and then circled the rim with the mallet which he held specifically in his hand to allow for an evident peace sign. The sound was meant to soothe, move the energy through the chakras but instead it turned the group into one messy crescendo.

Yogi Bhar was at the end of his mallet. "All right, what's really going on here?"

Kahlil, who had been born in India but educated in England, was the only one to answer. He spoke in perfect High English with his face still smashed against the mat. "I believe we are fahr-ting."

Well, that was it. Yogi threw the mallet across the room, hitting the back wall leaving a large pistachio dent. "I'm out. This place is fucked up!" And with that proclamation, the job opening for a new Wellness Guru opened up at NuMilieu.

DS wasn't sure if he was about to pass out from the fumes or the contagious laughter, all he knew was something felt good. Laughter, whether a giggle or a full on uncultured belly laugh, was the medicine his life had been missing. And although Yogi Bhar would never know this, his yoga class did indeed achieve its goal. The group had bonded.

In fact, that yoga class became legendary among the team. DS's group would never be the same. What had been a tentative series of planned social interactions outside of work, grabbing a beer or a bite, soon turned into a hybrid of a daily consciousness raising group and a full on bromance, and for some, much more. Weeks later, Perry and Hayden came out of the proverbial closet to the rest which happened to be no surprise to anyone.

The Plunge

———#———

After only a month on the job, DS seemed to be the go-to guy in the small start-up for everything. He could navigate marketing as easily as tech and everyone saw him as the shooting star of the company. He had the allusive "it" that so many of his co-workers were lacking. He was on the fast track. Justin, NuMilieu's anointed leader, noticed the team's spirit and credited it to Mindy and the Wellness Guru replacement, Yogi Smith, who managed to handle the rowdy Broga sessions with a balance of camaraderie and authority. But soon Justin, who often had a superior air about him, felt alienated in their meetings and was, simply, being left out. He didn't get the innuendoes, the private jokes or a single invite after work. What he did get was high. Extremely high.

The office deliveries never seemed suspicious until Mindy entered Justin's office unannounced late one afternoon. Justin looked up from his desk with a dusting of powder under his nose. She carried on like it was nothing although it explained his constantly running nose and over-the-top self confidence. If anyone knew drugs, it was Mindy. She was no stranger to experimentation. It was an industry staple for some and dealers had passes to most of the tech giants downtown. The Eighties thing was back with a vengeance, catering to execs who had relied on shrink sanctioned amphetamine hook-ups in college and now had endless money to blow on blow. Mindy was no drug virgin but unlike other areas of her life, she drew a sloppy line at heroin.

"What if he doesn't stop with coke? Or it's cut with meth? I've seen it. And heroin? What if—" Mindy was beginning to panic. She loved the company. Her father had invested nearly everything in it and she was his remote overseer.

"I've seen it, too. Shawnee had it all." DS had become the best ear to bend. Sensitive. Never one to jump the gun, but he'd had his suspicions as well.

"This is my future. If it goes south, I... I don't know what I'd do."

"I'd imagine you'd do just as your dad. Build your own empire. You've got that in you. You don't know how lucky you are to have it."

"It?"

"It. The connections, the background, the know-how. Know-how to travel, know-how to pick up the right fucking fork, know-how to use that intelligence and vision." This coming from the guy that she knew truly had it.

But boy, if any words could swoon a mid-twenty-year-old neo-feminist, these were the ones. Mindy held his eyes for longer than a glance required, maybe in the back of her head thinking of the article on her Facebook feed that morning that guaranteed love. She had practically memorized it—four minutes of staring into a potential partner's eyes on top of a deep conversation was all it took for love to blossom. DS had passed on the article in his feed and if he ever did read it, he certainly wouldn't buy into such a crazy idea. It didn't matter for Mindy, though. She had become smitten with her hipster from Shawnee.

Mindy kept the iris memories of DS to herself. She kept it from everyone—Marika, Frances, even DS. She simply buried it. No one needed to know. She was good at keeping secrets, especially the big ones like why her mother had died; not from an aneurism which was the party line she was sworn to, but from a drug overdose. Mindy had lived with her mother's depression forever, and now that her mom was gone, the Vibe Manager realized she had lost the one person she could have told her secret to. So her DS infatuation and Justin's drug indulgences would remain secrets unless they were, in her humble opinion, getting out of control.

#

David Gismondi made a surprise visit to the new offices. DS did a double take when he passed Justin's window.

"Professor?" Gismondi bolted from Justin's office to greet his former student who had just mouthed the question. "I had no idea."

"Exactly. No one did. That's the key here. Keeps everyone on their toes." The Professor guided DS into an empty room. "Tell me Richard, or, DS. I understand from everyone that, after all our years together, you prefer to go by DS."

"That's right, sir."

"No 'sir.' We've been through all that. David. Plain old David."

"Yes, sir. David."

"Let's hope with a little work, you can get that down." David softened up with a laugh. "So, DS, how's the place running? I hear you've got some great ideas that Justin wants to implement. Anyone can learn code, but what I saw from you at Pent State was someone who was an innovator, and so far, you haven't disappointed. I'm thinking you might work well with the Marketing and Communications team as well, strategizing the growth of the company. Think you can handle all that? We tend to bounce between departments at this start-up."

"Wow. Really? That would be amazing." Amazing because he'd be on the team with Frances and Marika, even though it would be tough now to fit it all in.

Justin came searching for the two. "In here, Justin."

"Hey, the investors are on their way up."

"Come on DS. Meet the others."

DS was beside himself. Gismondi was opening the door to the club even further. "Sure. Great."

A conference room was meticulously set up for the meeting. A computer with a projector and about a dozen white leather chairs surrounded a hammered steel table. In front of each seat was an assortment of designer bottled water (yes, there is such a thing, thanks to France). A barista set up a station in the corner and quietly took orders from around the table. The four Old Guys had Americano diner coffee, a stunning Asian couple ordered green tea, the leftover hipster types ordered Gibraltars and flat whites. DS really needed an espresso. Justin and Gismondi passed.

"So, everyone, this is Richard Strait, who, by the way, prefers DS." Gismondi beamed like a new father. "He's the newbie here at NuMilieu. He was brought on board to create a new brand of designer 3D pets, but now, it looks like he might also be taking on, with the help of your daughters, the branding of the company through social media." DS could pick out the parents by the silent beams that they exuded—the two Old Guys and the Asian couple. "DS, I'd like you to meet Marika's parents, Sally and Edward Fong. Frances' father, Franklin McSweeney and Mindy's dad, John Montgomery."

So, there they were. The investor parents of his angels. What could he possible say? *My God your daughters can party!!*

"Hi. Pleasure to meet you. You—you all have amazing daughters. Bright, awesome. Lifesavers, really."

"We heard it was a rough start for you." Edward spoke for his wife. She was slim and elegant, held her little pinky away from her tea just so.

"But now, you're all settled in and up to speed I understand." Gismondi guided his shining star.

"Oh yes. Absolutely. Settled." *Into a smaller than micro apartment with a local Butcher on the loose.* "Settled for sure."

"Then I say, let's get to work. Tell us, DS, how are things going?" It was the first time that he noticed Justin's nervous twitch. A little bout that caused his left shoulder to dart up to his ear.

DS launched into a dissertation on not only the state of the brand he had been developing since undergrad school, but the economy in general and how their start-up would end up given his projections. He didn't know where the words came from. Grammy had flashed across his brain screen as though encouraging the flow and he just started channeling. "With the help of your daughters"—DS scanned the row of parents—"and Justin, of course, I can see NuMilieu creating an entire market that, for the most part, is nonexistent. All within twelve months. Let me access some files to give you a better picture." His espresso had obviously kicked in.

"And this is the young man I've been telling you about for years. Always at the ready. No prep time needed. And he's always got the right stuff." He looked directly at his protégé. "The right stuff is rare."

DS proceeded to dazzle the group with images and projections, graphs, analogies and stories. More impressively, he brought one of the NuMilieu Pets into the room. The purple and white zebra pranced about, sat in one of the chairs and mimicked sipping tea. And then, the zebra told his story. If there was one thing DS had learned from Professor Gismondi it was that stories sell. And Zebbie had one tall tale of his escape from Africa, sleeping on a hammock in steerage and working as a police zebra until he retired to San Francisco to be closer to his sister at the zoo. DS's story wasn't half bad either as he had a unique ability to turn the numbers and bland facts into the story of a start-up that was irresistible.

When he was done, the group literally bounced up out of their chairs and gave him a standing ovation.

DS forgot every word that had just come out of his mouth, raised his eyes above and gave a nod to Flo. Later that night he would check in with her from his little nest and share it all.

#

That night, the Professor arranged dinner at Aromatic in Hayes Valley, a quaint yet lively neighborhood place. A sumptuous table was set in the private dining room. The seating looked like a 50s family dinner with the kids, Marika, France, Mindy and DS on one end of the table and the parents, The Fongs, Mr. McSweeney, Mr. Montgomery and the Professor at the other. Justin sat like an awkward orphan in the middle. The Professor handed DS the wine list. "Your choice, DS. A red and a white."

This is a test. "Sure thing." DS hadn't had a chance to do the wine tasting thing yet, but it was certainly on his list. He opened the heavy menu, trying to remember the Gismondi's wine tasting lesson and scanned the selection. His jaw nearly hit the table. *$21,000? For a bottle of wine?* He divided it by 4 in his head. *$5,250 for a Mindy size glass of wine?* He wanted to throw up.

Justin looked nervous. At least that's what his twitching shoulder seemed to indicate. "They have some fabulous Romanee-Conti here." There was little response from half the table, and a nearly palpable shiver from those that knew it to be a five figure brand.

Concentrate. Just concentrate. DS scoured the list again. The words popped out at him to stitch the story together. "Hmmm, great suggestion, but I don't want our company to fall victim to the famous Mound of Shrimp Theory, so I suggest a moderate Old World Red from Italy to honor The Professor's love of all things Italian and a New World from Napa to signify a peaceful, solid beginning for NuMilieu." The elders cheered internally. DS told the waiter, "We'll go with two bottles of the Montevista Chianti and two of the Blue Rock Chardonnay for the table." *Settled. Four sentimental bottles for under $200.* At this rate, it wouldn't be long before DS took over Justin's number one spot. If, of course, that's what he wanted.

Mindy, being the excellent Vibe Manager that she was, comforted DS throughout the dinner. In the middle of her third glass of Red, DS could have sworn that the hand she had slipped so innocently onto his leg to rest during one of her father's endless stories, that very hand, he thought, but couldn't be one hundred percent sure, had now shifted slightly towards his inner thigh.

"So, DS, have you ever been to Europe? Any travel stories to share?" John Montgomery's burly brows knitted together. This was either the sign of welcoming encouragement or a blunt fuck-you-get-my-daughter's-hand-off-your-cock warning. DS couldn't imagine it was the later, but, nonetheless, he shifted in a way that surely would cause Mindy to reposition her hand. And that she did, directly atop the undoubtedly throbbing bulge that needed no more attention at this moment, thank you.

"I actually haven't done much travel yet, but look forward to doing so as we expand. Speaking of expanding," DS shot up so fast that Mindy's good vibe hand fell numb-like aside her chair, "I'd like to propose a toast to expansion." He raised his glass as the Professor tapped his to get everyone's attention. "As we expand our wings, never let us forget to enjoy the view." Right after he took his sip, he realized that it was a near rip-off of (yes, of all things) *The View*. As in Barbara Walters. Oh God, he hoped no one else pieced that together. Surely Grammy would have. Afterall, it was with her that he watched the show for years and years of summers.

Suddenly, Mrs. Fong, who apparently was nowhere near a teetotaler, slammed her glass down on the table. "Didn't ya just love that Babs? Why'd she have to go?" Fortunately, her bad form trumped the toast and DS was off the plagiaristic hook.

DS stumbled through the weed-laced halls into his aPodment at 9:45. He owed Flo a call and knew she would have finished *The Tonight Show* and was probably onto *Late Night*.

"Hey Gram. Bad time?"

"No, course not dear. What time ya got there?" She spit a big wad of cough-up into a tissue, stuffed it up her sleeve.

"About a quarter 'til 10. Who was on tonight?"

"They had one of 'em new comedians. I don't know anyone any more. All downhill without Johnny far as I'm concerned." Grammy chain lit a Morley and stubbed the finished one out in the ashtray. It was down to the butt.

DS looked through a bag of snacks on the floor and pulled out a rope of black licorice and began to chew. "It's somethin' else here, Gram. Nothing like they show on the TV. More, way more."

"Tell me about that little Vibe person. What's her name? Mork?"

"Mindy, Gram. Mindy."

"Right. Mindy. We need more alphabets in this world. No sense reusing the same ones over and over again. It's boring."

"She's fine. I think she might even be interested in me."

"Everyone should be interested in you, Dickie. You're the most interesting person I know, more than anyone on TV."

"Interested. Like. Like interested."

"Oh, that kind of—"

"Yeah, but I don't want to mix work and you know. That."

Even with all those new connections that DS had in cyberspace, he still relied on this little woman to listen. Really listen.

"Well, they say that's a risky thing. 'Specially if you want to go up. The ladder, DS. You are going up, right?"

"Well, yeah. Sure hope so. They have me doing stuff that the boss was doing before. I think he may be up to no good."

"No good. What's no good?"

"Not a hundred percent, but I think drug no good."

"Well, I'd imagine if it's here in Shawnee, it's even more there in Frisco."

"No one says Frisco, Gram. If you come here, you can't call it Frisco. I mean, people here are violently opposed to it. San Fran, maybe. But Frisco can get your head bashed in."

"Sounds like you're hanging around with a buncha anal retentive commies out there. Hope not, Dickie. I sure don't want to see you turn into one of those protesting this, protesting that nuts. I see the news; it looks like that's all they're doin' out there. Do people actually work out there, Dickie?"

Well, that certainly was the million-dollar question. "Word, Gram. Word. The word is work."

DS heard the faintest knock on the door. "Ahhh hold on a sec. I think—" DS opened the door a slit. Tracy was standing there dangling a blunt between his fingers. "Uh Gram, I'll have to call you back. A neighbor is at the door."

"A neighbor! Well you don't know how wonderful that makes me feel, that you're friendly with the neighbors."

"K Gram. Call you tomorrow. Promise."

"Not so fast, Mister! You'll be getting a package from me. A big one. Got your skateboard in it and some of those ratty tees you love and few other tidbits."

"My skateboard! You're awesome Gram!! Thanks so much!!! You get a good night's sleep. We'll talk tomorrow. K?"

"Always in such a hurry out there. What do they have in that water? Some kinda speed drug or somethin'? I hear they take little doses of LSD just to come up with fancy ideas. Takin' it just like I take my mornin' baby aspirin."

"It's definitely somethin'," DS conferred. "Listen Gram. Tomorrow. We'll talk tomorrow. Promise. Love you." DS tucked the phone into his back pocket.

Before he knew it, Tracy was through the door and lighting up. DS went into a frenzy. "Hey, wait now. I... ah... we've got an early day tomorrow." Like the one and only time he had met Tracy before, he had a long lock of sandy blonde hair covering one eye.

"Well, it's not like this will keep you from getting a great night's sleep. I mean, sure you won't have any dreams, but who needs 'em? Besides, the best dreams are in the day."

DS had to really think that one over. "I... I get it."

"And that's the techie dilemma. No real isolation. Sitting in front of a computer doesn't count. You need that blank stare time. And that, DS, is what weed is for."

"Hey, you know, I don't think I know... ahhh, honestly, don't remember what it is you said you do. A magnum is a lot of champagne." Tracy teased him with the king-sized joint.

"I didn't. No one asked. You were all too busy talking about your stock options and rich daddies."

"Well, hey, take me out of that category. Mine's dead and even if he was alive and rich, I wouldn't take a cent." On that note, DS took the blunt and a huge hit. He exhaled dramatically followed by a hideous coughing fit.

"I'm an animator."

"No kidding! We're working on—" DS bit his tongue, sworn to silence by the non-disclosure agreement.

"The next big thing?"

"Exactly."

"Everyone in this city is working on that same big thing. Come on. Give me a hint."

"Well." DS was speechless and really high in one of those orders. He wasn't sure. "It's got to do with animals."

"Come on. Don't be shy or I'll start guessing." DS shook his head and Tracy pushed, "Let me see. You've got a sheep that can entertain someone's little peep." Tracy came closer. "Don't be afraid. I won't tell anyone your secret."

"Well, that's random." All DS could think of was that he hoped his phone call from Flo was truly disconnected. In fact, that very thought harnessed him from saying another thing. He tinkered with his phone, just to make sure, but was never internally satisfied.

DS's senses were heightened and when Tracy got up close and personal he looked slightly like Mindy. It was uncanny. The same color eyes. Same starry look. *Whoa, back up.* For a guy whose only sexual experience was a passed-out co-ed snoring on his bedspread, this was a pretty big, sexy day. Mindy's under-the-table challenge and now Tracy, at least in DS's really high head, making moves.

And then, in the midst of awkward silence, he heard her words, "Dickie? Dickie? Are you still there?"

#

DS bounced into work the next morning after a remarkably deep sleep. The Girls were all comparing notes on their phones with what was streaming on Mindy's desktop.

"Did you hear?" Marika wanted to be the first to break the news. "He's struck again. This time on Eddy St. They're interviewing a witness now."

The four zeroed in on Mindy's computer screen where a crackhead was being interviewed and streamed live by KZO. The newscaster was clearly out of his element in a sports coat and slacks. He was being swarmed by street zombies. Sirens blared up Market Street. Juan Chavez just happened to be at City Hall when the call came in and he raced over with his crew. This was his big chance to break the story live. Maybe even a national feed.

"Man, next thing I know dis head come flyin' out dat winda and look... just look here." The crackhead stepped back waving his arms in every which direction. "Who gonna pay da dry cleanin' bill? Huh? Da City gonna pay da dry cleanin' bill? I gots blood all over me." His clothes were little more than stiff rags although he had somehow scored a pretty nice pair of red running shoes. Thank God those didn't have to be dry cleaned.

"Can you point to the window it fell from?" The newscaster was trying to get the facts before the police arrived in full force and he was asked to back up from the crime scene.

"Dat window. Right up der. Dis head just came flyin' out. Looked like a ball but den der was no bounce. No damn bounce. First I thought it was a flyin' saucer or sumptin' but den, da blood came rainin' too. Who gonna pay my dry cleanin' bill? God damn flyin' saucers. Fuck The City."

The interview was going downhill or uphill fast depending on one's crackhead tolerance scale. This morning the entire city was highly tolerant; some might even say morbidly entertained. Next, the crackhead addressed the newscaster directly. "Do you make movies?" The news team just kept rolling. "Cuz I make movies. Got me a big company down der in Los Angeleeeezzzz. Gots to think big in this business. Flyin' saucers is big." Slowly but surely the interviewee's cred was going downhill as the officers streamed onto Eddy St. like blue ants on a pile of trash.

"This is Juan Chavez live from the Tenderloin in San Francisco for KZO News. We'll continue to report on this story throughout the day as details emerge. But, for now, what we know is that it appears that the Tenderloin Butcher has struck again."

The station cut back to *The View*. DS felt the flow of disgust. "Shit. A head."

"From a window." Frances gagged a bit.

"Raining blood." Mindy finished the sequence of disbelief.

"Oh my God, the internet is exploding!" Leave it to Marika to follow the pulse of the story. "The police are looking for a guy in a black hoodie."

"Good luck with that. Half of The City wears a black hoodie." Frances was not really exaggerating.

"Are you sure you're O.K. staying in the TL? You can always stay with us." Marika and Frances seconded Mindy's motion.

Marika brought up her Butcher map. "According to my calculations, you're still in that sweet spot one block perimeter. But, you never know."

DS's phone vibrated. He checked the I.D. and answered. "Hey Grammy!" The Girls simultaneously ahhhhh-ed.

"I was just watching *The View* and they done broke in." There was no avoiding having The Girls hear her. Poor thing was in hysterics and erupted into a most fervent pitch. "What's this about some Butcher tossing heads from windows? And isn't that your neighborhood? The Tenderthigh? Or is it hip—"

"Loin, Gram. Tenderloin."

"Loin. Fine. What's goin' on out there, Dickie? They say there's a butcher on the loose. Is it true? Why didn't you tell me?"

"Dickie?" Marika questioned softly.

"Dickie." Frances affirmed with a nod.

"Dickie." Mindy just hovered in the moment.

"Because I knew you'd freak. I'm fine, Gram. My place is in the zone."

"Zone? What zone? The news didn't say anything 'bout no damn zone. Just that your neighborhood is rainin' pieces of people."

"Now listen Gram. Really listen. The killer never strikes within a block of his previous killings. That's my zone."

"Don't give me no zone shit, Dickie. What happens when he runs out of blocks, huh? Then what? You still in the zone then?"

"Well—" Dickie tried to get a word in edgewise but it was no use.

"No. The answer is no. Now you listen to me. Really listen. I didn't bring you up since you were that darlin' little cutie pie only to have some whacko play basketball with your sweet little head. Promise me you'll find a new place. Promise me Dickie or I'll just die from sleeplessness before I get a chance to walk that Golden Gate."

"Kk. Promise, Gram. I'll start looking soon as..." DS caught himself. "Right away. I'll start looking right away."

By now The Girls were huddled together hanging on every word.

"And one more thing."

"What's that Gram?"

"The cat. You promised you'd get a cat and send me some videos. Hell, that's all anyone ever talks about today. Cat videos. Maybe a Siamese."

"Sure. Maybe."

"They're supposed to be real good protectors. Sounds like you might need some protectin' out there, Dickie. Sounds like that Wild West never died. And what was all that soft talk about last night?"

"Ooops Gram. Gotta run. Meeting." DS looked up to see Justin's bloodshot eyes zeroed in on him. The Girls scattered like kittens from a sheet of tin foil.

"O.K. then. We'll talk later." DS hung up before Justin could get a sound bite from Flo.

"Soft talk?" Mindy mumbled to herself, not sure if jealousy was in order.

#

From Justin's office, the sound of helicopters could be heard whirring just blocks away. They whipped up more than just distant street debris from the collection of night trash that littered the sidewalks and alleys from the homeless dumpster diving in the dark. Those blades that chopped away were the trigger of fear—the lock your doors, close your shades, buy an alarm, get a dog with a decent bark and maybe even buy a gun or at least a tazer kind of paranoia—that was quickly becoming the new norm, not just in the TL but throughout The City.

"I think it's time." Justin was staring out his office at the Truth mural on the opposite building. DS sat before the designer steel desk, waiting. And waiting. The thought came slowly in sync as Justin turned to face him. It was that moment, in that crystal light which broke through the fog, as if on cue, that DS saw the familiar. The pallid skin, the thinning hair and sickly teeth that comes with addiction. Justin could have been just one of the guys outside the $1.29 Store in Shawnee or even one of the TL street people stretched over a manhole for any kind of warmth at midnight. But for the clothes and the bank account, he was no different. In the end he was an angry, desperate man-kid who only cared about his next fix.

"Time? Justin? You were saying?" *Is he stepping down? Doing one of those chichi thirty-day rehab stints?* DS suspected his assumption was on the nose. This guy was talking a big fat time out.

Justin's words were disjointed and the delivery painful to observe. "I think it's time you know that I don't appreciate all the fucking backstabbing you've been doing. Last night was the final straw. Where do you get the balls trying to show me up in front of David Gismondi and the other investors?"

DS started his defense with a nervous laugh which didn't go over big with Justin. "I never... I don't..."

"What's so fucking funny, DS? The fact that I hired you and now have to fire you or that you have to go back to bumfuck Shawnee because no one from here to Silicon Valley will ever hire you by the time I'm done strategically demolishing your reputation in cyberspace?"

"Fire. Fire is a strong word. You shouldn't shout it unless you mean it."

"Yeah, that's just the kind stuff I'm talking about. Mr. Downhome Folksie. Who the fuck do you think you're fooling? Gismondi is a pushover, but not me, Mr. Dickie Strait. That's right, I've been doing some investigating. I've got your number—the poor boy playing on the sympathies of the investors. Mr. Wannabe-Rags-to-Riches. You've had your eyes on my seat all along, haven't you?"

"I... honestly, Justin. I think this is about something else. I think we all had a lot of wine last night and the news this morning didn't help. Everyone's on edge."

"Well, let me help you away from the edge. You're fired. No scrawny-ass punk who screwed his professor is going to take me down. Got that? You're not taking me down!"

Screwed his professor? Seriously? Did I just hear that one right?

"Before you take me down so I don't take you down, could you just go over that one more time? Are you talking about Professor Gismondi?"

"Don't play stupid, back home boy. You know fucking well."

"Actually, I don't."

The crystal light in the room had shifted and was now glowing around DS. It cast an undeniable aura of innocence.

"Oh, come on." Now Justin had a smirk of disbelief stretched across his face. It melted in the innocence. "You don't know, do you?" After the most awkward moment of silence, Justin broke down. Simply broke down. Slumped into his ergonomic chair and cried.

"David... David and I... were lovers. Until this trip and now all he can talk about is you."

Oh God. TMI.

DS's gulp was audible. "I... uh... uh... all I can say is... I'm in love with Mindy. Yes, I'm in love with Mindy. So, if David thought anything, well I certainly... I mean, just watch us together. I know you don't have x-ray vision, but her hand was right here last night." DS cupped his hand over his crotch. "Right under the table. That's how close we are."

Mindy couldn't believe what she heard through that slight crack in Justin's door, the one that he thought he had slammed so tightly shut. She had passed by just in time to affirm her heart and stayed only long enough to imagine him with his hand on his crotch.

Justin raised his head, wiped his eyes. "Oh God. Please, please don't tell anyone. I just assumed you were—you and David—were close. You know, close–close. I feel like such an idiot. You can't tell anyone. It'll cost him a fortune if he has to get a divorce."

#

Mindy slid away from the door, down the hall and dissolved in her office. She only vaguely remembered her strategic hand placement from the night before, but DS had now confirmed it. Now what? Isn't that always the question in a young woman's mind? It's never easy living for the moment when the past and the future offer up so much potential drama.

Mindy picked up her phone and texted:

Lunch Runi at one. Not an option. Just us. Us three.

Marika and Frances were deep into a creative session when the simultaneous vibrations came through.

"Uh-oh. Not an option." Marika looked up to Frances. "Us three? Something's got to be up. Justin? DS? Maybe it's the new Wellness Guru?"

"DS was on a roll last night," Frances insisted.

"Yeah, but did you see the daggers Justin was shooting him?"

"I think he's doing the powder. A lot of powder."

Marika showed Frances a picture on her cell. "Exactly. Or something. Have you seen this whacko he's taking meetings with? Guy's a total tweeker."

They huddled by Marika's cell phone screen and stared at the particularly gnarly looking man who had been "meeting" with Justin, just long enough to drop off his dose.

#

They got the perfect table at Runi. Close enough to see the Market St. bustle but nestled enough to share without fear. It was one of their favorite haunts and they always got the usual. A round of Death in the

Afternoon champagne cocktails, the highly touted $54 roast chicken (tax, health tax and tip included) and a round of kale salads. Given that the chickie takes an hour, this would give them plenty of time to get to Mindy's news.

Mindy bounced in after Marika and Frances were settled in, waiting to toast. Mindy held off until a drink was firmly in hand. "O.K. Big announcement here." She lifted her flute. "I'm about to be in a relationship. Like, I think, I might even be posting it on Facebook soon." Marika and Frances stared with flat affect, waiting, waiting, waiting for the name. "He just confirmed today that he feels the same way. I'm sooooo freakin' happy!"

"We're waiting Mindy. The only hint is that it's a guy." Marika knew Mindy through her college L.U.G. years, so a girlfriend wouldn't have been a shocker.

"You must be lurking around. Who knew you were even seeing anyone?" Frances was, frankly, flabbergasted.

"O.K. I'm going to tell you but if you let on for one second, I'll... I'll... I'll not invite you to the wedding."

"Wedding? Now you're getting married?" Marika couldn't stand it any more. She took the flute away from Mindy. "Tell us now or you'll never have another sip of Death again. I swear!"

"O.K., O.K. I know you guys will keep it under wraps, just don't breathe a word. Promise?"

"Promise. Promise." Marika and Frances were in unison on this one.

"It's DS. I'm in... going to be in a relationship with DS." She waited for the big reaction and boy did she get it.

"DS!!!!!!!!!!" Both Marika and Frances shouted it at the top of their lungs. It was pure impulse.

Mindy, the sweet Vibe Manager got up and pushed her little button nose right into their faces. "Shut the fuck up! You promised!!"

Mindy waited and waited for a less public reaction. It came in a slow motion wave as her seemingly best friends processed the unthinkable. It took well over an awkward minute until Marika could come up with some kind of response. "Well, who knew? Congratulations on the coup."

That would be the end of Marika's private scheming. Her hipster from Shawnee was taken.

#

The email from David Gismondi came with a red flag. DS, who now had his own red flag for the married man who was crushing on him, opened it with trepidation. It was succinct:

We need to talk. I'll be in at 10:30.

DS had been up all night worrying about Justin's blurb of information about Gismondi. He felt a familiar grief, not unlike the night his family perished. It was the death of his mentor, the kind man who had given him so much. It was the end of the closest thing he'd ever had to a decent father and now to find out his patriarch was into incest—well, that was what was on DS's mind when the email came in. He role-played the meeting in his head—of David confessing his infatuation, of David denying the infatuation, of David professing his undying love for his wife, of David telling DS that he had hired a new genius to take his place and giving him the boot with no severance. But, in reality, this was litigious San Francisco and DS knew that there were firing protocols in place so the latter would be unlikely. He would just have to wait out the next two hours and get in gear for the talk that would dictate his future.

That morning, a couple of Blue Bulls and an espresso got him up to speed. In what was the industry standard, he was an adrenaline-driven junkie who, unlike Justin, relied on legal stimulants. But he could see how one could fall into the trap. The day-into-night-into-day work was the norm and that was something that couldn't be taught in school. That training came from video game play.

DS recalled his weekend marathon sessions over the years with *Halo*, *Splinter Cell* and *Grand Theft Auto* when Grammy would rise and wander into the living room only to find DS in yesterday's hoodie and jeans which, effectively, were the same as the day before and the day before that. She never questioned the increasing liters of caffeine charged sodas in the overnight trash. As long as he kept his grades up and made time for their movies, life was a green light. And for DS, that was a cinch. He aced every test without studying and did any essential homework in lightning speed just to get to the reward—a video game. A new game was all he ever wanted for his birthday or Christmas. Like most of his tech worker team, video games helped nourish the brains behind the brawn.

That morning before David arrived, DS's head simply raced. He tried to avert the worst scenarios, even tried to get some work done, but soon he found himself pacing.

"Hey! What's up?" Mindy looked amazing this morning in her short, poofy skirt and $550 ankle boots she picked up on Valencia St. Her eyes even looked more—more something—thanks to the real mink eyelashes from the Lash Lab that cost her nearly as much as the boots. "You're putting out a pretty stressful vibe there, Mr. DS." Her tone was jokey, but DS was in no mood to disclose the source of his anxiety.

"Just getting ready for a meeting with David. You know."

"Oh, right. He ordered lunch for your office at noon."

"Really. Lunch?" This freaked DS out. What he thought might be a quick, intense meeting had already involved into an ordeal. DS sat down at his desk, hoping to signal to Mindy that he was busy, but she unabashedly batted the minks.

"Yeah. Hey, speaking of lunch and meals—"

"Were we?"

Mindy, like always, saw the adorable side of DS. "Well, yeah... sort of. Anyway, come for dinner tonight. Frances and Marika are out hunting down a neo-revival at the Fillmore. St. Paul and the Broken Bones."

"St. Who and the What?" DS was proof that life passion came in basic categories and hybrids. His was video games, film and TV while Marika and Frances (outside of *Criminal Minds*) were obviously obsessed with music.

"Some soul band from Alabama that they swear affects them on a nostalgic cellular level. I thought we could watch a film."

"A film. Hmmmm." O.K. then, there it was. That was her category, too, or so it would seem to DS on that particular morning. But, really, Mindy had put the Grammy two and two together with film and knew that would be a way to reel DS back into the apartment.

"Uh, can we hold off on that until later this afternoon? Not sure what David has in mind." Well, actually Justin had filled him in pretty well what David had in mind, but still, he would just have to wait and see. He might not be the best of company. Mindy's minks battled a tear. Here she thought DS would jump at the chance. Now it was her turn to wait it out.

"Kk... just lemme know." With that, Mindy did her classic, adorable about face and headed to her desk to let out her vibe. "Fuck," she fumed under her sweet breath. It wasn't just the $350 she spent on two Kobe beef steaks, guaranteed to come from Wagyu cows who were routinely massaged and given a beer a day before being slaughtered for their marbled flesh. It wasn't even the fabulous little $275 cheesecake she had driven up the Pacific Coast Highway from Recherché Cheesecakes in Half Moon Bay. It was the lack of the "Fuck Yeah" because in Mindy's book, that lack was just a "Fuck No.'"

"By the way, have you seen Justin this morning? He was supposed to be in on a conference call at nine."

DS just shook his head. "Nope. Haven't seen him." If only Mindy knew the details.

#

Justin was lucky enough to live in a great flat right on Noe St. which had been under rent control since his days as a graduate student at USF. It was one of the sweetest tree-lined streets in San Francisco with the rare cozy, neighborhood feel.

After his self-confession to DS, the only way he could deal was by escaping. He wanted to run, jump, fly. After much internal debate, he decided it was time. That afternoon Mindy had walked in on him while he was snorting coke, he made a point of nixing the office deliveries and, instead, arranged for pick-ups on a side street by the office or, sometimes, in the Tenderloin. It was the seedy side of Justin that few suspected until lately.

Now that Justin was beside himself with grief over David's shifted attention and the fact that he bared his soul to DS, it was time to increase his bag of tricks. He met his dealer, Marcus, the same one who had been snapped on Marika's phone, deep in the Tenderloin. It would be a fast deal. This time he brought an empty leather satchel where he had assembled his kit. By the time he left the TL, it was filled with fifty baggies of heroin and a three grams of pure cocaine. He kicked his way through the trash back down to Market St. and took the F Castro streetcar home.

According to the sign above the seat across from him, the charming vintage streetcar was built in Milan in 1928. Justin sat down with his satchel securely on his lap and searched his cell for something Italian. He pulled up Pavarotti, the only Italian singer he knew by name, and listened to the one song he would likely ever recognize by the Master: Ave Maria. The sun burst in slivers through the afternoon fog as the song filtered through his brain. The white-haired woman tucked next to him saw the water puddled in Justin's eyes and gently cupped her hand over his, which was flat atop the satchel. They spoke no words but the slight warmth of her thin, veined hand was more comfort than he had felt in years.

As he walked home, he said his faint hellos to some familiar neighbors. He even grabbed a latte for good measure at the soon-to-be-defunct Java Jive, making himself doubt whether he was really ready to take the next step. He'd done all his druggie research online and if ever there was a time to mask the pain, today was the day.

Justin sat in his favorite chair, a well-broken-in burgundy leather number, for a long while before he took a packet of heroin and an 1/8th of coke and cooked it up with some distilled water. He ran his nose past the spoon much like his mother did when she made him chicken noodle soup when he had the sniffles. He took a fresh little insulin needle from his satchel, ripped off the plastic wrap and filled it up. He knew the hit took, after he jabbed it into his arm and saw the kickback of blood. And then, literally, he took the plunge. Immediately every nerve from head to toe was hyper stimulated. Lightning struck. Heaven. Nirvana. The potential arc of life and death.

Justin loved the feel of water over his body and floated into the bathroom with his bag of tricks, ran some hot water and stripped down, imagining the warmth of a womb.

#

David entered the office and immediately shut the door behind him. His gaze swept the room, the limited view of the Truth building and the vibe musings hand-picked by Mindy: blinking Japanese eyeballs, a mini swearing punching ball, requisite stress balls and some wind-up chattering teeth. "Quite a set-up you've got here." David picked up the teeth and gave them a wind. As they clattered away across his high-tech steel desk, David just stared at DS.

"Well, hey, great dinner the other night. You and the Mrs. having a good time in town?" *Could I have been more awkward? Why not? Are you and the Mrs. really not fucking in that suite you've got for the week?*

"Angela's been shopping every day. You know how women are." Well then, if that wasn't subtext, DS didn't know what was.

"Oh, I absolutely know how women are. Why, I don't know anybody who knows how women are better than I now how women are." *Overkill. Pure overkill.* "They just love those new, crisp shopping bags. Especially when they've got boxes inside the bags. Shoes, right? They love the shoes." DS watched David watching him.

"May I?" David pulled out the cushy chair in front of DS's desk and positioned another side chair, too close by for DS's comfort. "Sit."

DS sat down and slyly scooched his chair back a tad, wanting desperately to break through that 18-inch intimate boundary into the personal space zone. If it was his way, he'd be in the social space zone, but today David would have it his way.

"DS, you've been like a son to me. Someone I've always tried to nurture and give some amazing opportunities to. And now, I've come to trust you. Trust. It's important in work and in any relationship to be able to trust. What I'm about to tell you isn't easy for me." David looked pointedly out the window.

"Right. Trust. Important."

"I've been carrying a big secret around most of my adult life."

DS twisted in his chair. *Oh God, please push the blurt off button before this guy spills his beans.*

"When I was younger, in the Valley, I was having some kind of identity crisis. I... I wasn't quite sure where I fit in."

"Are you sure this is something you want to share with me? Maybe your wife should be in on—"

"Oh, Angela knows. She's known since the day we met."

"Wow. Really?"

David didn't acknowledge DS's comment, he had a story to tell. "I was experimenting a lot and—"

DS couldn't take it any more. He leapt up from his chair and just started chattering. "Alright then, sir. Ahhhhh, can we just please talk about something else? Hunting, let's talk about hunting."

"DS, what in the world is wrong with you? Here I'm about to pour my heart out—"

"X-actly."

"—about my addiction and you're talking about hunting."

David was getting a bit pissy. DS had never seen this side of him and would rather keep it that way.

"I really don't want to hear about your addiction, sir."

"Well, you're going to hear about it because I don't want the same thing to happen to you."

"Oh, it won't, sir. I'm a one-woman man."

"There you go again. What are you talking about?"

"I'm talking about what you're talking about."

"Well, I'm talking about my drug addiction and you're babbling on about some woman."

DS might as well have been bashed for saying Frisco. It was a hard hit and he had no immediate comeback. "Are you saying—?"

"I'm saying that I'm an addict. A drug addict. That's why I had to leave Silicon Valley all those years ago."

DS let out a huge sigh of relief. "Well, you don't know how relieved I am." David could barely believe his ears. "I mean sorry but relieved that you're in... in a good space now."

"Well, I was until last night."

"Last night?"

"Last night brought it all back home. At my worst, I was speedballing, heroin and cocaine. It's what Sherlock Holmes did for hyper-productivity. It's also what brought Belushi down. I ended up in a psychotic break which was lucky because I could have had heart failure instead. I was really whacked out, screaming, hallucinating. I wanted to die but my business partner saw the signs and gave me an out if I went to the obscure rehab he recommended. I got an over-the-top buyout and started over. It saved my life. It took me years to taper off with methadone, but I did it. My only weakness now is liquid resveratrol.

"So, what happened last night?"

"I got a call from Justin. He only had one. He was arrested yelling at some hooker on Broadway. I went to bail him out."

"A hooker? Like a hooker, hooker?"

"Well, I guess. Short skirts, slinky halters. You know the type. After all, you said you know women, right?" It was a bit of a tiptoe into the taboo. "I think Justin was figuring out things. You know. Those things. Who he was, all that. Trying to prove he was something that he wasn't. Justin was very confused. He built up a whole fantasy world that included me, but unprofessional as his overtures were, that's not why he's gone. He's gone because this is an industry full of addicts. I pride myself on choosing my team carefully. Obviously, with Justin, I was wrong. The temptation was too much."

"So, you two were never—? He mentioned you were his—" DS just couldn't finish that question, and really, what did it matter now? David was staying at a nice personal distance and as long as he kept it at that, well, what the hell. DS looked out the window and took in that word Truth. "Professor Gismondi."

"David. David, damn it."

"David. I really appreciate your honesty. What can I do to help?"

David broke down. A spastic stream of tears and through them, the words hit DS like a waterfall. "Help me with a story. About Justin's death."

"Death?"

"His landlord got a complaint about running water. They found him in the bathtub with a needle hanging out of his arm."

DS felt ill. "Oh shit." He struggled to suppress the inevitable flow. "I should have seen that one coming. He had some creep drifting in and out of his office. Looked like a tweeker."

"I can't let this out to the investors. I've got to keep it quiet, but I just had to let someone know. I had to let you know because—" Gismondi took a soggy handkerchief from his pocket, "I couldn't bear the thought of something like that happening to you. You're like a son to me."

"Professor. David. I would never, ever get involved in anything like that. Blue Bulls and a little Blue Cheese is my limit in that department."

The joke was unintentional, but it did lighten the mood, if only for a moment. "I'll need you to run my ship, DS. Ange and I leave for home tomorrow— shopping bags and all—and I need to know you'll keep this boat afloat."

"Really, sir? David. Sir David."

"I thought we'd just say it was his heart. After all, isn't that what drives one to such nonsense? The heart?"

"I guess you could say that."

"Well then, that's it. It was the heart and the funeral is private. No one needs to know anything different."

"Exactly. Got it."

Professor Gismondi switched back into business mode. "You'll move into Justin's office, of course. And I want to know everything that's going on. Who, what, when, where and why. The why is the important W. If you can't establish why this company is taking any action, then we shouldn't take it."

And so the rest of the meeting went. So much for sentimentality.

Wag Time

—#—

DS was devastated. When Mindy came into his office within minutes of his mentor's departure, DS was staring out the window, wondering about David's truth. "I heard the news. Horrible."

"Horrible. Guess he never even knew he had a bad heart. And no funeral. The family is very private." DS towed the party line well.

They sat for a bit in awkward silence.

"Marika and Frances can't believe it either." The lull was brief. "You think it was drugs?"

"Drugs? No way. Justin just had a bad heart."

"Right. A bad heart." They both nodded equally in silence. Finally, Mindy broke it. "Well, I understand that you're about to man this ship." Mindy's eyes were propped wide, waiting, longing for some reference to her earlier offer. There was none.

"For the moment."

"Right. David said he's bringing in support. Fair warning, it may take a few weeks. David is super picky."

"So I've heard."

"K then." Mindy felt some moisture on the minks and turned away, resigned to spending a night alone with her Wagyu. Suddenly, she spun around and lurched towards DS with a burst of bravery. "Any thoughts on dinner tonight? I think we could use some cheering up."

"That's for sure."

"Home-cooked," Mindy tempted.

"Yeah. Sure. Sounds perfect. I'd love that."

Love. Mindy loved that word. She wanted more of that word. "Great. 7:30. See you then!"

While DS efficiently worked his way down the list that David had left for him and packed up his office, Mindy took the afternoon off to perk up the love nest. She started with a painful Brazilian wax, just in case.

# #

DS's cell began vibrating off the edge of his desk at 8:35. It took him well into the evening to pack up Justin's things and move his own in. He spaced on the time and Mindy had now propelled herself into the "Fuck No" zone. She was three quarters of the way through a bottle of pricey Old World Red and starting to strategically pick at the fondant dome of the heart shaped pecan praline cheesecake when she called.

"Oh my God. Mindy! I'm sooooo sorry. On my way." DS collected his coat and backpack frantically.

"No. Never mind. You don't have to."

"Don't have to? But I was planning on it." He looked over at his skateboard that Gram had just sent. "I'll be there in ten minutes!"

Mindy went back to "Fuck Yeah" mode, capped the bottle of wine and stored it. Next, she put a fresh bottle on the counter and brushed her teeth. Game on.

DS flew past the late night traffic by using the bike lanes down Market St. His right foot propelled off the green painted asphalt swiftly again and again while his left foot remained firmly planted on his deck. When the bike lanes ran out, he zoomed his way up and down the sidewalks, flipping a few masterful tricks along the way.

By the time DS rang the doorbell, Mindy was ready. Really ready. "Well, that was quick."

"Oh my God, if only you knew the list that David left me with. Again, so sorry." Mindy went in for the classic heart massage hug, only to be slightly repelled by DS who had the sudden concern of mixing business with pleasure. "Something smells de-lish. Stew?"

"Wagyu filets."

"Wag what?"

"Yu."

"I? What? I'm confused."

"Wagyu beef, silly. The best in the world. You'll love it. Trust me."

Trust. There was that word again. DS needed to trust that he wouldn't take any action with Mindy that he'd later regret or that David might consider an unprofessional overture. "I'm game."

Mindy opened the bottle of red and didn't give it a second to breathe. She wanted DS to catch up fast.

"Here. Here's to Justin." Mindy lifted her goblet. "Poor Justin. He was so starch dependent. But you know what? Tonight, in honor of Justin, it's starch and sugar all the way!" She took a huge swig and landed her eyes on DS. "And here's another toast to you manning the good ship NuMilieu!" Her next swig emptied the goblet.

Mindy managed, barely, to get the food to the table without slopping anything on the floor. She was that tanked after one additional glass of wine. Nonetheless, DS devoured the Wagyu, wolfed down the scalloped potatoes, picked at the kale and passed on the asparagus for no other reason than he hated that queer smell of his urine afterwards. And by the end of the meal, he had eaten nearly a loaf of black pepper parmesan bread from The Staff. By the time the cheesecake appeared, it didn't matter that one half of the bottom edge, the side facing Mindy, had been picked off. She served that first with a faux "Ooopsie! Musta gotten wrecked in shipping."

DS dug into the cheesecake. "My God, this is decadent!"

"Decadent is good, right? A little low morality never hurt anyone, I always say."

DS was slightly appalled. "Well, I prefer high morals, myself."

Mindy moved in closer. "Oh come on. Don't be such a prude." DS pulled back to wipe a bit of sweat on his brow.

"Well, you know what they say, you can't unboil an egg."

Mindy laughed hysterically. "Oh DS, you and those cute little sayings!"

DS pushed back from the table. "This was over the top. Thanks Mindy. I loved it. Every bite."

"But you skipped the asparagus. Come on. Next time we have to beef up your veggie list."

"It's the—" *Oh God. She doesn't need to know about the pee smell thing.* "It's a texture thing." He rubbed his stomach, not for emphasis but for some kind of relief. "But really, Min. This was amazing. That meat. Fantastic. Really fantastic. Thanks for a great evening."

Those sounded like retiring words to Mindy and she wasn't about to let DS go. She crept closer, trying not to slosh her red. "It's the Wagyu. They do this special massage on the cows that gets the marbling just right." She clonked her wine next to DS, stood up behind his chair and started to massage his neck. "They just rub and rub."

The more she talked obsessively about the marbling, the more grossed out DS got. In between deep tissue digs, he started to overthink the cut of the flesh that he had just devoured. Mindy literally spun around and straddled DS, staring at him with her albino doe eyes. The next thing DS knew, he was back home, next to that poor hanging deer. It wasn't two seconds after that when he felt the pending flow of vomit. It was probably the stress, the three glasses of red wine, eating too fast, the fabulously rich cheesecake, or just the flashback to that buck that got him. Or maybe it was just the pressure of the lap-dance-in-the-making. All he knew was that he had to bolt that very minute.

"I hate to run Mindy, but it's been a long day. And that list. That list is waiting." DS eased himself out from under Mindy. She barely got a hug out of him at the front door as he left. The harder she pressed him, the further up the flow flowed. He had no choice but to grab his board and scramble from the flat, leaving Mindy alone with her mink eyelashes and fresh

Brazilian. But as long as there was still cheesecake, she'd be fine.

#

Frances and Marika strolled home from the Broken Bones not long after. About three doors down from their flat, Marika stepped in a wide puddle of vomit, a creamy mess with at least $100 worth of Wagyu chunks, cursing the anonymous asshole that had the nerve to heave on their street. After all, their neighborhood was not the TL.

Inside, they found Mindy face down in the cheesecake, fork in left hand, little bits of pecans and praline covering every digit of her right. Marika checked her freshly manicured ring finger. Empty. Obviously the night had not gone as she had fantasized.

They woke Mindy up, held her hair back as she expelled her share of Wagyu and pecans, then put her in bed next to a vintage bottle of Trader Jack's Blue Italy. She woke up in the middle of the night and crawled into Frances' room, desperate for clarity.

"I blacked out. Everything. I don't even remember DS leaving."

Frances grunted and pulled open the covers for passage. "Get in. But I'm sleeping."

Mindy crawled in with her blue bottle. "I know we ate. I just saw the dirty dishes."

"You puked your brains out and we put you to bed. No sign of DS."

"Oh God. What if we did it and I don't even remember?"

"Doubtful. You were dressed. Face planted in cheesecake, but dressed."

"Oh shit. What an idiot. I blew it." Mindy smashed her pillow over her face like a child in the midst of a tantrum.

#

The fresh air and emptier stomach revitalized DS. By the time he got home, he had his second wind. He ran into Tracy in the hallway, dumping some trash down the chute. The door to Tracy's aPodment was wide open. Music from within played through surround sound speakers.

"*Requiem for a Dream*? Loved that movie. God, I haven't had time to watch one since I got here."

"Come on in. I've got it streaming. It's a totally addicting score."

"Right?" DS looked around the aPodment with its wall full of DVD's categorized by director. "Dude, this is fucking kick-ass."

"You know it." Tracy signaled to the wall. DS inspected obsessively.

"I grew up with a film buff, my grandmother, but her tastes were old school."

"Hey, nothing wrong with that. I grew up on classics, too. Check these out." He pointed out sections of classics from Hitchcock to Billy Wilder and foreign directors from Italian Neo-Realism to French New Wave to British Kitchen Sink. DS was in awe.

"My Gram would love this!!"

Tracy's place was the identical floor plan to DS's. The only difference was the sleek leather chair. "I brought my own chair. I couldn't stand all the cheap stuff, even if it is for just a couple of months."

"Ha! You're temp, too?"

"Right. Temp. That's how he got you, right?" The music stopped. "Shit. Not again. The Wi-Fi here sucks!" Tracy tried to reload.

"Right? I've given up. Anytime past seven, it's loaded down. I've got two providers now. Two phones. One for cell service and one for Wi-Fi. Even then, they don't work half the time." DS's eyes scanned the small space as he spoke. A couple of family pictures were scattered on the table.

"I've been scanning photos, trying to make sense of it all." Tracy noticed his interest and headed for the pile of photos.

DS reached for one. "Is that your sister? Sure look a lot alike."

Tracy grabbed the photo and then the others. "Yeah, that's what everyone says. I don't see her any more, though. I was the black sheep and she stayed with the herd."

"Hmmm, that's too bad. Wish I could see mine."

"Yeah?"

"But that's not happening." DS felt oddly comfortable with Tracy and just blurted it out. "She died when I was in fifth grade. In a car crash with my parents."

"Shit, man. Sorry to hear that. That's horrible actually." Tracy's solution to the discomfort was to roll a blunt. "Mine are out of my life too. Not an accident. Just differences." He lit the blunt, took a hit and passed it to DS.

"Blue Cheese? First time I came up the stairs I got the drift."

"Diesel. Blue Diesel." After two hits they were faded.

#

The next morning at work, Mindy was a mess. Looked adorable, but her head was scrambled. She lowered a cheek onto her desk, pretended not to see DS as he passed, but he was too much of a gentleman not to stop.

"Hey Mindy! Great meal last night. You really went all out. Loved it."

Mindy's eyelids peeled open, like the skin on raw onions, her whites red and minks now wilting. "Really? Really? You loved it?" Oh, how she loved that word.

"Yeah, it was amazing. What a cook! And that beef! Wow, that beef." If one looked deep enough, they could see the slight disgust as DS completed the sentence, but nothing that Mindy would ever take note of.

"Great then! We'll have to do it again."

"My treat next time." DS gave her a little pat on her hand. He quickly pulled back. "We'll have to watch that. Now that I'm, you know, technically your boss."

"O.K., Boss!" Mindy watched him stroll down the hallway and then lowered her eyes to her ring finger. Still, ever hopeful.

As if on cue, Frances strutted up with her arms full of glorious flowers. "Aren't they amazing? I had them delivered from Plan Decor in honor of Justin. I still think it's really weird that there's no funeral." She sniffed at the artfully assembled bouquet anchored with peonies. "Hey, did you see him yet?"

"I think I got a pass. The wine must not have really hit until he left. Thank God." She looked at her ring finger again. "We've got a date."

Frances' cell phone sounded an alert. She checked it immediately. "Oh shit, he's struck again. Same block as last time. There goes that theory."

#

The police blues were out in full force. Again, the public had little more than a black hoodie for a clue. Of course, Frances followed every tweet, had an alarm set for the keywords Tenderloin Butcher and was on top of all things SF-human-flesh. She even had a feed on the psychics who had been giving out tips on the case. A few were crackpots, but nonetheless, the policy was to regard those tips as any others that came in. Madame Devein, who had a frou-frou Parisian psychic parlor in the Marina, chimed in that the perp was a reincarnation of the Zodiac killer while another self-professed psychic swore it was a shapeshifting lizard and probably a member of Obama's security team. All the loonies came out but one, a past lives psychic from Angels Camp who had worked closely with agencies around the country and been on-the-nose in several cases, sensed a drug connection and clearly saw a little boy in poverty on the outskirts of a small Central American city.

The actual identity of this victim, whose pieces were found on Hyde St., just four doors up from DS's aPodment, was unknown. Unless the eight fingers that rained down from the corner bay window onto the guy napping on the street were in the system, they would be at a loss until the rest of the body was found. Frances followed the anonymous tweets coming from someone within the department all day. The psychic had led them directly to a huge trash receptacle by The Merchant, the premiere food center catering to the mid-Market techies. The fingers had just been a tease. The real deal was buried in a rusty bin with old short ribs, monkfish liver and other post-Fukushima fish that had seen better days.

When the victim turned out to be a wannabe small-time drug dealer raised under a tin roof in Honduras, the psychic from Angels Camp had established her cred. After crossing the boarder at sixteen, he had made his way to the Northwest to stake out some new territory and make some bucks from the flourishing heroin trade that was hitting San Francisco. All anyone had to do was count the needles littering the sidewalks outside the thriving tech companies in the early morning, before the brave street workers power-washed away the overnight piss and shit, to know that H was back in town, big time.

But still, there was nothing on the actual killer. Just that black hoodie. It was his trademark and one that everyone agreed he would maintain throughout his spree. This guy got off on tempting fate, as was evidenced by the littered body parts, and all bets were on that he wasn't about to take a step backwards. In fact, he had stepped up his game.

In a desperate attempt, the department even put out a plea for everyone in SF to pack up their black hoodies until the killer was caught, the thought being he wouldn't give up his trademark.

The response was almost surreal. Corner entrepreneurs started selling white hoodies, local merchants couldn't keep them in stock. Even the hipsters lightened up, all in an attempt to catch what the police assumed to be an arrogant killer.

#

"O.K., DS. Bad news. He's encroaching. Broke the one block rule." Frances had clearly become obsessed. By lunchtime, she had a full report. "You need to make a move. ASAP."

They sat in the organic cafeteria, The Girls waiting for Chef Louis' macadamia-encrusted tilapia over kale to emerge, while DS held out for a veggie burger. That last round of meat had put him over the top.

DS was on his third espresso and had just been powering through another David list.

Marika had kept tabs on the rental market. "Good luck. Every new tech worker stuck in the TL is looking for an out."

Mindy's brain raged ecstatic. "It's settled then. Stay with us. Come back." Mindy looked around the table for some sort of consensus amongst the white hoodies. It was surprisingly weak. Since she announced her fantasy engagement, Frances and Marika had been weary of Mindy's grasp on reality. Marika had confessed her initial DS attraction to Frances who had since reprogrammed that crush in reverse as any decent flatmate would do, so that wasn't the issue. It was just that it would clearly be like inviting a train wreck. All eyes turned to DS.

"I've got Jason Taliaferro out looking. Until then, I'll be careful. We've got security. No one gets in without a fob. I'm not worried. It's only for a couple of more weeks. He thinks he'll be able to find something in the four range that's decent."

Mindy's enthusiasm skyrocketed. Four thousand was still in the large one-bedroom range and that meant no studio, which meant more closet space, which meant he was definitely thinking couple like *choo-choo there's a potential train wreck on the horizon.* "Don't be ridiculous. You'll stay with us until he comes through. It'll be fun. Right?" Mindy couldn't wait until they moved in together or, bigger still, she couldn't have him risk his early demise by the Butcher. She once again looked for encouragement from her flatmates but there were only blank stares. "One big slumber party."

"Hey Min. Thanks for the offer, but the only way I'm powering through work these days is by regrouping alone when I get home." Mindy's smile melted. It was painful to watch. "I love being with you guys." Ahhh, there was that word. "But I need that alone time." *There. I finally said it.* But what DS didn't say was that he and Tracy were having one hell of a time binge-watching old movies.

Just as Chef Louis personally delivered the plated tilapia salad and veggie burger, Mindy excused herself with a tenuous toodle. "I'll be back." But she never returned. Instead, she went back into her office, face-planted into her favorite ergonomic neck pillow and screamed until the entrapped heat of her breath effectively steamed off one of her minks. When she came up for air and saw the damage, she booked an emergency appointment at the Lash Lab.

Mindy texted The Girls while escaping the building:

Sorry. Cramps. Heading home.

They knew it wasn't true because, as with any really close flatmates, their periods were in sync. Marika and Frances rolled their eyes, unnoticed by DS, who was digging into his veggie burger, confirming to one another that it was not that time of month.

#

By the time DS made it through the yellow tape, he had shown his driver's license and a digital copy of his lease three times. It was definitely a tight crime scene that night, heavily documented and speculated on by both the local and national media. Juan Chavez was back on camera. This time, his producer tagged DS for a comment. He was reluctant, purely because there was that remote chance that Flo would see him bust into one of her shows, but the next thing he knew he was under the spotlights with a mic shoved in his face.

"So, I understand that you live on the block. How does it feel to know that the Tenderloin Butcher has struck here twice in the last two weeks?" It was one of those vague questions meant to incite any kind of sound bite. But DS wasn't biting.

"I'm not letting it get under my skin. Just take a look around. No one is getting through this tape. I've never felt more protected. It's like having my own private security on the block." And then he broke the fourth wall and punctuated what would be the sound bite heard around the country. "So Gram, stop worrying."

No sooner did he get through his front door did the texts from The Girls and his team come vibrating in. Most of them were sentimental comments on his Grammy connection. But Mindy's observation was a bit more intense. She couldn't let it go with just a text. She downed a fatty glass of red before dialing from her bed. DS answered upbeat, not expecting the deluge. "You can't stay there. Think, really think of your Ol' Grammy Flo. How could you make her worry like that?"

"She's not worried. Believe me, if she heard anything about this latest one, she would have called by now."

"We need to talk, DS. About us."

"Us?" DS clearly had no clue. But he was going find out soon.

"You know. Us." Mindy slurped up some more red to bolster her nerves.

"Are you drinking, Mindy? You sound a little off."

"Off? No, just Blue Italy. You know how I love that. I can't believe they're out of it at Trader Jack's. Sucks, you know, when it's out of stock," she babbled on.

"Right. Blue. Italy."

"I'm just going to spit it out, DS."

"Why? You just said you loved it."

"The words, DS. The words. I think I... every time... every time I'm with you I want to give you a big hug and never let go."

DS just laughed. Not what Mindy expected. "Right. And that's why you're the best damn Vibe Manager in San Francisco. You've got those heart massage hugs down!"

"I mean... you. You DS. You're the one I don't want to let go of." He still didn't get it. It was beyond his imagination that this little toodle blonde would be interested in him that long-term way. At best, he thought he was in the friends with benefits category even though the benefits scared the fluids out of him.

"I mean I really love you, DS. Damn it, I love you."

He still didn't get it that her love was like love, love not the cutesy kind of stuff they batted around all day long for the sake of managing vibes. "And I love you, too, Min." Oh God, if only he knew the dysfunctional power of what he had seemingly divulged and the psycho that he divulged it to. Those words would stay with Mindy all night long, after DS hung up abruptly when Grammy called.

"Gram. Hi. What's up?"

"What's up? What's up? I just saw my Grandson on the national news and you ask what's up? Come home 'til they catch the crazy, Dickie. I won't have you being carved up and scattered on the street next to a pile of human poop."

"Calm down, Gram."

"Don't tell me to calm down. They say that, Dickie. They say people poop on the streets out there. Those aren't the streets of San Francisco I saw on TV. Those are the streets of some Third World country."

"Gram—" He just couldn't stop the avalanche of truth.

"You're supposed to be living in the First World. The First First World with all that techie crap, not human crap."

"Gram!!" He busted into her repertoire like never before. She halted. "Gram, now listen to me. It's complicated. San Francisco is a complicated place. It's beautiful and it's ugly. That's what makes it San Francisco. The Tenderloin Butcher will be caught. The police have really tightened up the TL."

"TL? Now what crazy are you talking?"

"The TL. The Tenderloin. I'm going to be fine, Gram. Trust me. Now, you get a good night's sleep and I'll call you in the morning. Promise. It's late there. Go to sleep."

As soon as DS hung up, he texted Randy Taliaferro half in all caps so he'd know DS meant business:

Any openings? I'll go up to $5,000. JUST GET ME THE HELL OUT OF THE TL!!

Next he emailed David, praising his generosity but asking for an advance to cover his newly-anticipated first, last month's rent and security deposit. It was a $20,000 request, a down payment in some other cities. Two houses in Detroit. He made sure that David had opened his email with the file that completed the last tasks on the list, before making the request. All the W's were in their place.

Just as he was falling asleep, his cell rang. He didn't need to check who it was. "Hey Gram. I thought I told you to get some sleep."

"It's me, DS."

DS knew the voice somewhere between the slurred lines. "I jush could dint shleep." Somewhere in those words he heard Mindy. "I mish you."

Weeks ago, this might have been a dream come true, but the more he had got to know Mindy and her habits, the more he saw trouble. And the last thing DS needed was trouble. He was living in the middle of the biggest crime mystery The City had seen in decades. That was enough in the trouble department.

"That's nice of you, but I've got a meeting with the team first thing. Talk after?"

"Now. We need to talk now."

"But we just did that"—he checked the time—"six-seven minutes ago."

"I know, but I shtill mish you."

The calls came about every fifteen minutes until the light came through the windows. DS stopped answering after the fifth one. He was clearly in a bind. If only Mindy's father wasn't a key investor.

#

By the time DS got to work, the team was busy sharing messages. He just assumed it was about his appearance on *The 10 O'Clock News*, but then he heard Mindy's voice in stereo. Apparently she had drunk dialed the entire team. It wasn't until later that morning, when David called, that he understood the extent of what Mindy had unleashed.

"Hey, David. Guess you got the email? Did all the attachments go through?"

"Email. Yeah. Email. Not a problem. Not the problem. Great work, as always. The problem is

Mindy. I want you to be honest with me, DS. Are you and Mindy in a relationship?" *Damn it. Justin. He just keeps lingering.* "No, sir. Not at all. I just sort of told Justin that—"

"Justin, who said anything about Justin? I'm talking about Mindy. I had three messages from her this morning and all I could make out was that she was in love with you." *Oh God, not back to the patriarchal incest thing, I hope.*

"Yeah, about that. I think something got a little twisted about how she thinks about us. I mean, she's great, but I'm totally focused on work. I'm sure you got that from the files, right?"

"Impeccable, DS. You addressed every concern and more. But my concern this morning is that Mindy's losing it. I won't tolerate drunk dialing, even from an investor's daughter. And by the way, her father is more than well aware of the situation. So, if you're telling me you're not in a relationship with her and she's just going nutso, then she has to go, DS. We have a termination protocol from our lawyer that you'll need to follow."

At that moment, DS nearly lost his shit.

#

When DS opened the termination protocol email, he sifted through the legalese and with each paragraph, he felt the flow going south then north then south.

By the time Marika and Frances stopped by to confirm the onslaught of VMs echoing through the office, DS had been pacing with his stress balls for nearly an hour.

"Hey. Heard Mindy had one of her meltdowns last night." Frances was being gentle.

"One of?" DS couldn't imagine that it was a regular thing.

"It happens. Seems like once every couple of months." Marika wouldn't be so kind. "She makes an ass out of herself, makes her vows, then breaks her vows." The overuse of the term "vows" wasn't innocent. She wanted DS to have a psychic imprint that Mindy wasn't the vow-taking type, just in case.

"Kk. You have to help me. Confidential. Just us. I'm in hell. David wants me to fire her." The gasp was palpable.

"No. She called David, too? Nooo." Frances was devastated. She knew the implication.

"Yes. David. Yes." DS was ashamed to even be part of the phone buzz. "Listen, I know you think part of this was me, but, honestly, I didn't do anything."

"We know. Mindy's in love with love and whoever happens to be on her radar at the time gets attacked. You just were just at the right place at the right time. Congratulations." Frances always had the practical explanation.

"She cycles. We love her, but she cycles and it gets old." Marika had just about had it.

"Mindy's great. I mean, all my life I wanted a Mindy but then—" DS didn't have a chance to reveal his loser truth or his no-girlfriend past before Marika played the message.

"Ma-reeee-kah. Pick up. I'm schtuck." As the morning fog cleared, the messages sounded even more dysfunctional.

"By the time I turned on my phone this morning and went to check on her, she had untangled herself from the sheets."

"So, how are you going to do it? When?" Frances asked.

"I'd like to be out of town." Marika turned to Frances. "Napa? We haven't been wine tasting for a couple of weeks." *Wait. Seriously? Her best friends are going to toss her from the wine train? Just like that?*

That afternoon DS learned the dirty little truth about Millennial women in the workplace. Although they had no clue what the generations before them went through to get to where they were, by banding together, The Girls were in the generation that disbanded with ease. Perhaps they were just the byproducts of a disposable society, no better that the Tenderloin Butcher. He was shocked; however, regardless, that afternoon, once Mindy dragged herself in, he knew he had to do the dirty work of disembodying a dream. Alone.

#

DS paced his office in full panic mode. He squeezed the stress balls, set the fake teeth chattering and longed for a rewind of the night before with Mindy. A better ending, any ending that would have kept her from the fateful dialing frenzy.

"Hey." Mindy poked her head in the door. She looked so pulled-together in a swingy little skirt, ankle boots and flowy blouse carefully wrapped up with a pink belt. Her hair was pristine, her smile ever pearly and her eyes... those eyes. Those blue diamonds.

"Hey. Come in. Have a seat."

"Wow. Have a seat. Sounds pretty formal. Is that what happens in a new office?" Mindy slid into one of the cushy designer chairs she had handpicked for Justin. She twisted about awkwardly, waiting for an answer. It never came. "Are we O.K.?"

"We... we're a little tired today."

"Sorry. Didn't mean to keep you so late. What time was it?" Mindy was fishing to put together the lost night.

"Which time? The first, the second?"

Mindy sunk further into the chair and freaked internally. OMG they did it. IT. More than once. And, she didn't remember a fucking thing? Her internal torture was brutal. But the clothes? Why get dressed again?

"Min? You still with me?"

Music to Mindy's ears. "Oh yes, DS. Forever. I'll be with you forever." Her smile was intoxicating, which made sense because DS had the sneaky feeling she was actually still intoxicated.

DS referred to the termination checklist on his computer. If he missed a beat or said too much, there could be problems. Her father had conferred with David and clearly agreed that tough love was the best step for his only child and that no special treatment was needed.

Just read the line. "Well, Mindy, it's been decided that it is no longer in the best interest of the company to continue your employment with us."

This was clearly a hit well below her Katy Spode belt. "What? What are you talking about?"

"You're being terminated, Mindy."

"Terminated? Seriously? Bad joke, DS."

"It's no joke Mindy. The building front desk security will escort you as soon as you clean out your desk."

Mindy stood up and gave DS one of her huge, heartwarming hugs. "Oh DS, I love you. Of course we can't work together if we're, you know, going to be together. Together that way."

Not going well. Not going well at all.

DS gently pushed Mindy away from his heart. She finally took a moment to read the sober look on his face. No words could capture the instant that Mindy transformed from sweetness to vulgarity.

"Oh my God. You're serious, aren't you?" It didn't take long for her to pull the looney trigger. "Who... wha... who? Just who do you think you are? My father owns this place. He owns you!"

"Your father made the decision Mindy."

Double-hit below the old Katy Spode. Now she was really pissed. "Who the fuck do you think you are, fucking me, then this?"

Oh dear... this is really, really not going well. He had read several items on sexual discrimination in the termination memo. Nothing in his Pent State team management classes had prepared him for this day, though.

"What are you talking about? We never, never did any such thing. Not even close, Mindy. I left right after that pecan praline heart cheesecake slice."

"The one that I had especially made and delivered from Half Moon Bay? That one? The $275 one?"

This was one spoiled little kitten and DS was seeing just how lucky he was, to escape her paws before it was too late. "Yeah. Sure. That one. And, by the way, you paid too much because there was a whole chunk of stale icing missing on my piece."

"That's called fondant in the civilized world." Mindy stomped her feet like a little girl in a tantrum. "Oh, stop playing games, DS! You don't have sex with someone twice the same night and then fire them the next morning. You just don't!!"

The accusation was driving DS out of his mind, giving sexy credit where sexy credit was not due and such. He held her at arm's length, steadied her. "Mindy, I would definitely make note of something like that. A virgin would definitely make note, don't cha think?"

Mindy's jaw nearly landed on the floor. "Virgin?" And then she almost collapsed from convincing faux laughter. "Virgin? Seriously? Virgin?" If this was true, all bets were off and DS was straight-talking. The reality short-circuited her fantasy. It was her last chance to go into complete Bitch Girl mode and she knew it. "Well, what a loser! Virgin. Of course no one would want to initiate some little nerd like you. What'd you do, spend all your nights in Shawnee," this she said particularly loud and drawly, "jerking off to some fake video game babes? And to think I felt sorry for you."

DS sent a text to the security guard who was at the ready, as he was losing the termination war. "No, Mindy. I was—"

"You are nothing but a loser Okie from Shawwww-neeeee. Hear me? Loser!" Then she did something that, under any other circumstances, would have been laughable. In a most vile motion, she formed the letter "L" with her thumb and index finger on her forehead. "Loser," she punctuated. "Little Mr. Dickie Strait..." Her next move was unforgivable. She stood in the middle of the hallway and shouted at the tippy-top of her lungs. "Hear that everyone? Little Dickie Strait here from Shawwww-neeeee is still a virgin! V-I-R-G-I-N!!!!"

DS pulled her fiercely back into his office. "Mindy, you're really—"

"I'm really what, Dickie? Stupid for getting a full on Brazilian for nothing?" She pulled her skirt up and her thong down. "See this? See this, Dickie? For nothing. Bikini bumps for nothing. No-thing!!!"

DS stared in both fascination and disbelief then quickly turned his head away. "Mindy, did you even check your phone? You drunk dialed everyone in the company last night. Including David."

"Well, he's nothing but a fucking loser, too. Loser." Mindy paused as if she was taking a deep cleansing breath, but it only re-armed her war words. "And to think I took pity on you."

The security guard, a massive man from Nigeria, stood in DS's doorway. "This way, ma'am."

Mindy spun around faster than a whirling dervish, her skirt stuck on hoist in the string of her thong. "Oh, and now you got your nigga on me? Great, DS, just great."

And that was when Mindy really started to lose it, channeling a slew of racist celebrities. No one was immune, even Marika and Frances who were now standing in the doorway. "And you bitches! You bitches did this, didn't you?" At that moment, they both knew they should have booked the Napa tasting.

Mindy's frenzy of rage started to escalate as she began to hurl anything within reach. The little stress balls flew through the air first. When she flung the wind-up plastic teeth, they nearly took a bite out of DS's cheek. Mindy went through every item on DS's shelf and then turned to the scissors on his desk. At this moment, the guard pulled out his tazer. One zap and she was down. He called for an ambulance. Mindy managed to struggle nearly to her feet. The second jolt from the tazer fully immobilized her to the point that Frances, Marika and DS rushed to her side. The Japanese blinking eyeballs in the corner of the office just took it all in.

"Oh my God. She's dead," Marika gushed.

"Dead?" Frances was morbidly inquisitive.

The guard took her vitals. "She's fine. Ambulance is on its way."

"Where's she going?" Marika mopped up her onslaught of guilty tears with the sleeve of her shirt.

"First stop is usually S.F. Main. They'll probably hold her for seventy-two hours."

Frances and Marika, now fully taking in the severity of the event, started to sob. Within a few minutes, Mindy was slapped onto a gurney like a wet noodle, restrained, just in case. DS couldn't let the moment go. He had to do, say something to regain his self-esteem. It wasn't an ego thing, more of a survival thing. If she left his office without him having a moment, he would forever be that loser. The energy would be in there forever. This now ex-Vibe Manager had expertly impaled him with the Loser Vibe and he needed to immediately take that knife out and stop the bleeding. He took a long glance at the bold black letters on the building in the distance. TRUTH.

DS approached the gurney, leaned down next to Mindy's ear and whispered, ever-so-gently, "Look who the loser is now." Mindy peeled open one of her minks but didn't have the strength to battle her demons any more. And with that, DS had reclaimed his self-esteem. It was his victory over not just Mindy, but Jessica and all the Mean Girls at school, Blotto, The Wheeler Boys and even his father all at once.

Mindy was rolled down the hall to the horrifying stares of her co-workers. It wasn't even 10:15 in the morning and DS had re-affirmed that his boss wasn't a sexual predator hot on his tail, Frances and Marika might actually have hearts and that Mindy was one real sicko.

At 10:20, DS ordered a triple espresso from Chef Louie. It had already been one helluva long morning.

#

The team was assembled for the announcement of Mindy's departure. For now, the word was that she had had an anxiety attack, although Mindy would be headed for a chichi rehab program in Malibu after her seventy-two hour hold. Her father swore the lawyers were working on the new will and everything would go to his favorite charity, some Mark Twain donkey reserve, unless she cleaned up. Mindy knew what she had to do, especially if she wanted to ever see another Katy Spode belt again. Seems that Kate was quite the powerful motivator, even though Mindy had her own bucks from a couple of winning start-ups.

It would be the most awkward assembly of DS's life. Ted, Kahlil, Perry and Hayden stood circling DS's desk in his office which was now an official emotional killing field. Their eyes, all eight of them, were cast downwards. "So, I guess you've all heard by now."

"We heard everything," Ted confessed.

"Everything," Kahlil seconded. Affirming the words was painful for DS, as though someone was pounding away at his heart.

"Every last word" Perry tugged on Hayden's sleeve.

"The V word." Hayden hammered the nail in the coffin.

O.K., then. There it was. The entire office now knew that DS was a twenty-three-year-old virgin. Now his eyes were cast downwards.

Ted, who had been concealing an intended donut behind his back, broke up the pity party. "Dude, me too." He took a big sloppy bite that defined why he had likely been stuck in Virgin Land.

Kahlil was next in line for the confession. "You're not alone, Bro."

DS raised his eyes and met Ted and Kahlil's eyes with an acceptance that he hadn't known since the pre-Pussycat Club confession at Pent State. His eyes drifted towards Perry and Hayden.

"Don't count us in. We fuck like rabbits." Perry reached his hand out. "And you will, too. Gimme your phones. Each of you."

DS squirmed. "Wha?"

"Tinder. You're all going on Tinder. The first to score gets our box seats for the Giants."

"Tinder? Is it O.K. for first timers? You think?" DS questioned.

"Right. It's time for desperate measures. If you don't get that first time out of the way soon, your dick may just drop off in the middle of the night. It's that or a hooker. An escort if you really wanna pay." Perry was already downloading the app simultaneously on their phones.

"Fuck the app. You have season tickets? For the Giants?" Ted finished off his donut between sentences.

"My old man. Box seats," Hayden glowed.

Oh great, another trust fund baby on the team.

"O.K., then. We're on!" Kahlil was genuinely thrilled by the mutual confession and the chance that his dirty little secret might soon be relieved.

DS wasn't so sure about the challenge. He still held on to that romantic vision of his first time. Just as he was getting used to the idea, Perry killed it. "If I wasn't gay, I would have done Mindy. Just sayin'." Hayden slugged him in the arm.

DS checked the time. "Guys, it's been one hell of a morning. I need to touch base with David. Let him know the deed has been done. I'll meet you in the yoga room in fifteen. Someone let the man know we need him."

And so it went. Mindy was kaput, DS was about to be enlisted into Operation Virgin via Tinder, David was relieved and Ted was about to relieve that damn gas that had been fermenting in his jumbo stomach all morning. Pity the poor girl who'd de-virginate that one.

#

Broga was indeed a big relief, not just for the team, but especially for DS who came out of the session with a renewed sense of self. He had never been comfortable with change, but a new chapter was opening and this time he was going to write it, damn it.

That afternoon, the search began for a new Vibe Manager and just two days later, Aiyanna was hired. There was little Mindy-ness about this hire. No pseudo-bubbly personality. Unlike WASPY Mindy, Aiyanna had Native American lineage and came with a stellar CV which included a supervised internship of 3,640 clinical hours in order to become a licensed Creative Arts Therapist as well as two years in a Peace NGO in the Congo. She was also really into aromatherapy which didn't thrill DS until she came into his office for their first meeting and brought out the sage stick.

"I sense there was some trauma in here recently. Shall we sage it?"

"Sage it?"

"White sage. It's one of the purest forms of cleansing a space. It will bring wisdom, clarity and spiritual awareness."

"Well, sure, I guess. I could use all of those. I mean, really, who couldn't?"

Aiyanna didn't laugh—she was on a mission. "Now, before I light the sage, you must have an intention in mind."

DS wondered if it was somehow sacrilegious to intend to win the bet and see the Giants. Or, maybe he should just focus on being the best he could be. Fuck it, he decided and grounded his intent.

"It's of the highest importance that your intention be clear before we begin." Aiyanna looked into DS's soul. "Are you clear?"

"Clear." And with that, DS zeroed every last brain cell in on getting de-virginated. Laid. ASAP. Hopefully with someone he cared for *in that way*.

Aiyanna lit the sage, gave it just long enough to get the smoke going and then began the ceremony. She gently waved the smoking, jumbo white sage smudge stick past the high traffic areas and around the computer to cleanse the mind space. She concentrated on the corners of the office, and when she came to the shelf with the chattering teeth, which now clearly had a severe case of TMJ, the flow paused. "Something painful here. Let's work through the pain together." Aiyanna did an extra sweep across the entire Mindy-chosen toy shelf. With each pass of the stick, DS felt himself closer to his intention.

He would hop on Tinder as soon as possible.

#

Frances and Marika had just returned to the office from visiting Mindy at SF Main. She was, for the most part, out of it. They had drugged her up on a strong anti-depressant cocktail. Her father had already had an employee come by the apartment and clean out her belongings. He didn't want her to have any temptation to return to that scene again. So, a room was open if DS wanted it and Marika really wanted him to want it.

"I have another call into my agent, Jason. He said he's got something coming up soon. I think I'll hold out. Besides, the Butcher seems to have gone underground. Must have been all those white hoodies." DS laughed but Marika wasn't about to let him off that easily.

"Do you know what you're being offered here, buddy? Rent control. A room in a real house with a real garden and a real garage in The Mission for under two thousand. Are you crazy?"

DS really thought about that question. *Am I crazy?* He flashed back to the last few weeks. Could any more crazy be packed into them? Sure, he was a bit of a drama magnet, but this last dose had been obscene. He really felt like if he couldn't at least be drama free at home, he'd go crazy.

"Call me nutso, but I'm going to hold out for my agent. Jason promised he'd come through. I really need my space."

Marika nearly flipped. "You're crazy. They all promise."

Frances held her back, even though she was also secretly wishing that he would take Mindy's spot. "We'll hold it until you hear back from Jason. Mindy's paid until the end of the month anyway."

So, no deal sealed, but there was still a chance that DS might move in with the leftover girls and that Marika could have her moment or two with DS. A slim chance and one that would be exponentially increased—if only the Butcher would strike again.

#

That night, DS heard back from Jason. There was indeed a unit, a really decent unit opening up in the Duboce Triangle. Small, but prestigious with a view of a magnolia tree if he craned his head out the kitchenette window.

This was the best news DS had heard all day. When Tracy came by soon thereafter and DS told him, they both felt the void. Small and as tacky as their rooms were, they had, in just a few weeks, gotten into that video game/movie binge bro-bond that would be really hard to replace.

"Hey, how about if I ask if there's another opening?"

"You're paying $4,500? That's crazy."

"It's only because I can. My boss is desperate and, I'm feeling a little that way too. If you only knew—"

That was the only opening Tracy needed. He was as good a listener to DS as DS was to The Girls. It all came out.

"Every place I've ever worked turns into a gossip-pit. Social media is just a breeding ground for the spew. I never post my ID. Anywhere. Totally anonymous. Ano," Tracy advised with passion.

"I was too until Mindy, Marika and Frances jacked my life! Next thing I knew, I was everywhere. I even have a blog! First week they ghost posted on all. But today I was gossip ground zero. I'm afraid to look."

"Yeah?"

"Yeah." They left it at that for a bit, until the bong hit hit.

"Mindy got put on a seventy-two hour hold today."

"Uh, horrible. Hate those."

"You know those?"

Tracy just shook his head "yes" with no elaboration.

"I don't think I'll ever see her again. No loss, I guess. She wasn't the girl I thought she was." The veil of grief was thin but obvious.

"What kind is that?"

"Adorable forever. Always a good vibe. A smart blonde with heart."

"Blonde your type? Didn't think that would be your fuckin' type. What about Frances?"

"Too morbid. My God, she should be out with the police tracking down the Butcher. She's mapped all his moves, profiled each victim. Put it this way, her claim to fame is that she's watched every episode of *Criminal Minds* seven times. That's Frances. A lot of episodes."

"You'd better check to see if Mindy went cyber-whack on you."

"No, she'd never." DS recognized his own complacency. "Would she?"

DS checked his phone. Before he even got to FB, he saw her texts. At least a dozen. "What is that?" He showed his cell to his neighbor.

Tracy leaned in to check out the photo from Mindy. "Looks like someone had a bad Brazilian." Apparently when Mindy woke up from her anti-psychotic drug induced nap, she was bored.

"Oh my God. That's... that's—"

"Up close and personal."

"What do I do? Shit. This is a nightmare."

"Check Facebook. She's probably pissed you didn't respond."

DS checked his FB page and nearly puked. She had been very busy. DS's timeline was full of Mindy chatter. Posts about how to get laid if you're a virgin. Very graphic posts. "Fuck."

"Hmmmm, still a virgin? Really?" Tracy regretted peering over his shoulder.

DS was shamed. "Really."

"Cool."

"Cool?"

"We're sucked into a world where deposited sperm is our social currency. If you're low, it will show. So, either you deposit some or you look like you do. Or, change your definition of love—none greater than to lay down one's life for one's friend and all that. And then it doesn't matter. To you, at least."

"Wow. Deep."

"My father was a preacher." Tracy took another huge bong hit. "Go figure. A real motherfucker."

"Mine, too. A real motherfucker."

"At least he's a dead motherfucker. Mine's still haunting me." Tracy opened up his laptop. "Let's fix this bitch right now. What's your password?"

"I don't want a war."

"No war. Just a blackout. You need to block her. Now, Bro. Check all your accounts. They're probably plastered."

Tracy was right. As they worked through all DS's social media sites, it was clear that Mindy had all but announced to his world that he was a virgin. Tracy worked furiously to block out all he could and shut down others. "You said you don't really care about this shit, right? Then just shut it down. Shut them all down.

You're not going to be able to block this babe. You can create a new one later."

"Not even twitter?"

"You can try to start that one fresh, but she'll stalk Marika and Frances and figure it out soon enough. You'll need a new username."

"No beef." DS was always good for a little self-deprecating humor.

"Seriously." Tracy thought vehemently. "Beef... butcher... virgin... values... Culture Butcher? Culture Butcher. That's it!"

"What the fuck does that even mean?"

"It's where people go chop it up. Chew. Talk about alternative cultures."

DS inhaled a big hit. "Hmmm... Culture Butcher." DS exhaled and coughed through the musty cloud. "It's workin' on me, man."

"All right. That's it then." Tracy registered the twitter name. For a moment, DS felt like he had a new lease on life. An anonymous place where anyone could post and follow him. Totally ano.

Or, he could just have been really high.

#

Things would never be the same without Mindy on board. The new Vibe Manager, Aiyanna, although seemingly perfect with the right CV, was far from adorable Mindy with her constant toodles. But on the other hand, she wasn't bat shit crazy, either.

It had been a week or so since DS had started his Culture Butcher twitter feed and his first post about the homeless in San Francisco went viral. It was linked to his photos of the human decay. Horrid photos. Tender photos. Defining photos. Aiyanna had been standing in his office doorway ahem-ing until he finally looked up. She knew the exchange should be brief.

"Oh, hey."

"I had a talk with David this morning about the launch party. I've got Chef Louis working on the menu. I'll take care of that. But thoughts on a theme?"

DS had only two things on his mind. Culture and Butcher. He just spat it out. "The culture of pets." Boom. That was it. Brilliant as always. Later, when David got the word that DS had been the mastermind behind the theme, it only affirmed his commitment to his young protégé.

"Culture? Culture, like...?" Aiyanna stood by with her massive cell which instantaneously transcribed and filed DS's words.

"Where they go. How they feel. What they like. Our NuMilieu Pets can't just be walking holograms. They need stories. Like USA Girl Dolls. Remember those?"

A sadness weakened Aiyanna's otherwise pleasant face. "I wasn't allowed to play with dolls."

"Well, we can't have that happen with our pets. We want the world to know that our pets play!" As a second thought, DS gazed up at Aiyanna. "No dolls? At all?"

"Especially the Bimbo Dolls. My mother thought they were Plastic Whores and would give me slut tendencies. Anorexia, too. You know, unobtainable body ideal and all. Big breasts, no hips."

"Right. Right. Tough to achieve that look without cutting, really."

Aiyanna needed to leave before she got even more confused. "O.K. USA Girl Doll Pets it is." Aiyanna left the office dizzy with information, or rather, the lack thereof. DS shouted a few more thoughts.

"NuMilieu Pets that play with girls, boys, adults, doctors, lawyers. Hell, flight attendants. Transgendered teens. Martians if we can find them. Our pets will play with everyone!!" DS's words followed her.

Aiyanna did an about face. "That's highly insensitive, equating trans people with Martians." Aiyanna was dead serious. Pissed.

"Oh, no. No, nothing like that. God no. I certainly didn't mean it to come out like that. No, no. Not at all." And if anyone didn't mean it, it was this kid from Shawnee who had suffered at the hands of bullies.

DS shut the door and settled into thought about the USA Girl Doll and soon a familiar flashback of his sister and what she'd left behind followed. Her USA Girl Doll, Molly. How lonely she looked in the corner of Lulu's pretty pink bedroom. How he said good-bye to her, actually kissed her forehead as though it was his sister's. And how he left to live at Grammy's, right before the estate sale which wiped out the memories that those who thought they were in the know believed had to go. They were wrong, by the way. Those relics, the dolls, his mother's spice rack, even his father's belt would live on forever, long after they were sold to the local bargain hunters and hoarders.

The flashback, as usual, set him back. It was a good hour before he could refocus on the issue at hand. How to sell NuMilieu to the world. Not just to those who have allergies and wanted a designer 3D pet that would sit quietly in the corner and occasionally on an owner's lap. A pet that might be a purple and green koala bear with an orange tuxedo that sang an original song. One that could sit down with its owner and appreciate a good martini. *Now, that is a NuMilieu Pet.*

Tech-cess

---#---

Marika and Frances piled into DS's office. They had been working on the launch for six weeks, which meant three more Butcher murders. In between the The City's serial drama, not seen since the Zodiac days, they had to get the social media storm whirling. They were tweeting like mad. Like any healthy pet, the branding of their product was morphing. DS had an inkling that the visit from the leftover girls was just going to be another protest session about the rejection of their spare room.

"O.K. It's a simple yes or no." Frances looked deeply into his eyes.

"Are you or are you not Culture Butcher?" Since his first post, DS had generated a viral storm. The feed ran itself and all the while, DS was always careful to remain ano.

"I don't know what you're talking about."

"You can't hide from us, DS. We have our ways." Suddenly, DS felt as though they might be on the verge of torture if he didn't confess. How would they do it? Nails? Water boarding? Or maybe just some basic S&M nipple clamps, whips and such? DS had seen a crop resting in Marika's room once and knew she was no equestrian.

"Culture Butcher?" He would test their convictions.

"Yes, DS. Culture Butcher. It started the day Mindy got committed. You shut down all your social media. But remember, I follow every Butcher keyword that's cross-referenced with San Francisco and I knew from the first post it was you." Frances had him.

DS was proud of his first musing: Chewing over the Tenderloin. Even more so of his second: Beds and Meds Get Them Ahead. It was a classic DSism and one that he had spouted whenever walking with The Girls and they belittled the homeless. But what had really forced that post was his own walk to work early one Tuesday morning.

It was a foggy SF morning and the sun was trying desperately to peek out early. DS was on his usual stroll to the office when he saw one small black bird, not the usual dead pigeon, flat on its back with its little curled feet sticking straight up in the air. Next to it was a small hypodermic needle which would be added to the overnight trash pile that swelled in the street. A couple of blocks ahead he could make out an Emergency Fire vehicle. As he walked closer, he started to freak that there may have been another Tenderloin Butcher crime scene in the making. An ambulance sirened up, which usually picked up the overdosed and hopeless homeless who couldn't suffer through another night. It was, sadly, a common vision. But this morning the barrage of police cars was absent. As DS approached the body that lay spread out on the street, he thought he recognized the plaid wool shirt and torn khakis. As he passed the woman, the paramedic pulled a blanket towards the ragged woman's chin, the very woman from Meet's with the vertical marijuana leaf tattoo, and then over her head. The vision sent chills up and down DS's spine. It was the third time he'd recognized the person having the blanket of death pulled over them. The other two were his mother and sister, also spread out on cement but under much different circumstances. He never saw the death pull over his father as he'd jumped from the car when those devilish eyes had shown no sign of life.

So yes, DS had become known as the only one in the office who had any sympathy for the homeless. It was a slow, sad revelation, the idea that any animal on the street who was suffering in San Francisco would have medical care, food and shelter. The San Francisco Humane Society was world famous for its kitty condos and no-kill policy. But The City treated its homeless with less compassion than it did its animals. Yes, The City treated its people worse than down and out-of-luck animals. The City had its own kill policy.

And it was, indeed, DS who had authored that first post causing a mini-riot on twitter as local tech workers debated the debauchery on the edge of their neighborhoods. It was a territorial fight and if they weren't careful, there were fears that the MS-13, the most notorious street gang in the Western Hemisphere, would come in to settle things. The gentrification had stirred it up to that point of gang intervention.

"Well, come on! Are you Culture Butcher or not?"

"O.K. Yes. Tag. I'm it."

The Girls were unified. "We knew it!"

Marika expanded, "That first post… My God! You lit it up!!"

"I'll never look at them the same. I would literally step over the bodies like they were trash. Never again." Frances was emphatic.

"So, that's settled. Now what?" DS knew something was gearing up.

"We talked to Mindy and she really wants to talk to you. She can't believe you closed down all your accounts."

"Marika almost let on about your new twitter feed." Frances all but got punched by Marika.

"But I didn't! And the point is that I didn't!!"

"And don't. Ever. I can't have her little private bumps posting there. Even if they get taken down. It's a… it's a distraction."

"Well, that's good to hear." Frances was blunt.

"What's that supposed to mean?"

"Good that a little genitalia is actually a distraction for you," Frances clarified. "We thought maybe you were asexual. A lot of that going around."

"Especially in Japan," Marika added expertly. "And how is that whole de-virginating scheme going? Ted told us about the bet. He's obsessed with grabbing those box seats. Really Tinder-ing it up, I hear."

DS started to fume. "Well, good to know the gossip zone is alive and well." He pretended to busy himself with work. "I have the app. I just haven't really used it yet."

At this point, Frances knew this was Marika's chance to lunge in. She pretended to take a call. Just as she exited, Marika braved, "About that whole thing.

Listen, you wouldn't be my first. I mean, friends with benefits is right up my alley. On Mamas. We Gucci?"

It took a moment for DS to get her drift. Her Bay Area slang rarely drifted in. Her eyes were moistly zeroing in on his, much like Mindy's had after her first glass of red. "I'll not be shamed into sex, Marika. With you or anybody. Maybe it's my potentially hearty upbringing, but I'm waiting."

"Oh please, don't tell me for marriage? Or that you and Grammy had a commitment ceremony." What she thought was an innocent giggle was a roar in DS's ears.

That comment just killed the one-percent chance that he could get drunk enough and do it with Marika just to get the damn thing over with and sit in those box seats. "No, not marriage, Marika. I just need to like the person I do it with the first time." He morphed the sarcasm. "On Mamas. But thanks for the offer."

A well-plotted hit below Marika's studded belt.

#

DS googled the app just to make sure he got it right. Tinder made some vast promises and he wanted to make sure he was privy to all of them. But first, he'd have to create a new Facebook page for Tinder to link up with. Actually, this was perfect. DS could stay anonymous by posting some new, select selfies. He took off his glasses, swept back his hair, dipped his chin. No one would recognize him. He changed shirts and put on a few that Grammy had overnighted him over a month ago when she heard he'd lost his suitcase. They'd been stuck at the bottom of his drawer, waiting to donate to Out of the Closet. He was certain no one would be offended that the photos looked so far off from his usual.

He quickly loaded up his profile with soft, non-specific accolades: a tech worker, new to The City, liked to bike, skateboard, drink beer, and on occasion, sip Old World wine—just in case there was a wine snob sniffing him out. After he loaded up the info, he opened the app and saw the magic begin. He still wasn't exactly sure how to use it—this was just his beta moment. And what a moment it was. He saw things that surely he thought should be illegal. Things that made Mindy's little bumps look like teenage acne. There were some big, big things being imaged on Tinder. DS felt himself blush and just kept swiping right. The pictures and messages came at a furious pace; it was hard to get through the parade of men and women in various forms of undress and with their short messages, that ran the gamut of lofty high English to trash talkin', slurrish ramblings. *Yikes.* He knew he'd messed up the settings somehow and was just about to go back to tweak them when a familiar photo came up. It was Tracy, not at all ano. DS was shocked and quickly swiped right which he later re-learned was an accept and that he should have been left-swiping all along, and certainly he would have wanted to left-swipe Tracy because, well, just because he wasn't looking for a man. He was looking for his dream girl and he knew she was out there somewhere.

Then the message came in:

Hey, interested in coffee? I'm pretty close.

Oh God. Now what? Did he know it was me? And how did I not know he was gay? Or was he? Or was he just on

Tinder autopilot like me. Awkward. DS left it at a firm no response, but couldn't help but try to sneak back in to see how this guy billed himself. *FTM. O.K. Whatever. Fit Man. Sure. We all think that.*

DS went back to the directions and found out that his right swipes were opening the door to anyone. Sort of like Chatroulette on steroids. Time to start over. Within minutes, DS was having a lovely chat with a darling blonde whom Grammy surely would have approved of. Darcy. She was sitting in the café in The Merchant, having a demitasse of Black Bottle. It only took him ten minutes to charge out the door and swing open the thick glass doors of The City's upscale market. Surely a safe place for a first meeting. Sort of like the New World Way of meeting someone over a sensuous squeeze in the veggie aisle in the 70's. It wasn't perfect, but people always swore it did happen.

DS, of course, had his glasses on, which threw Darcy off. He made a beeline for her.

"Hey, you're Darcy, right?"

"Yeah." Darcy—one hottie blonde with perfectly manicured nails—was not particularly enthused. "Please don't tell me—"

DS stuck out his hand, an ejaculation of confidence, just like he had been coaxed to as a kid, "Pleasure to meet you."

Darcy's hand limped up to his for a most unceremonious handshake. "Did you seriously think that selfie looked like you? I mean. You look totally different."

"Oh, these. Right, I just lost a contact today and didn't have a refill." He left-swiped off his glasses. Darcy was not impressed.

Needless to say, it was little more than a quick hello before Darcy got the planned girlfriend text. "Wouldn't you know it? That's my flatmate. She needs me. Great to meet you, Samuel. Good luck on Tinder." And with that, Darcy left with a cruel little giggle that brought DS back to his insecure elementary school days, glad that he had used a Tinder pseudonym. Later, he would pretend it just sort of happened to a different poor soul. Whatever. Thank God they served beer in The Merchant. DS kicked back three before heading back up the hill to the TL.

When he got home, he ran into Tracy in the hallway and any thought of his Tinder profile had dissolved into the suds. DS was just glad to have someone to chill with. They binge-watched *Game of Thrones* until 1:30 and then DS called it in. "Gotta to get up early. But this weekend—"

"Sure. This weekend." Tracy's eyes followed DS to the door, diverted from the American fantasy.

DS scooted back into the room. "Hey, this weekend we have our launch party. You should come. It's going to be crazy. Lemme know."

"K."

#

The office was hopping the rest of the week as the preparations for the launch party got set in motion. Chef Louis hired extra servers and assistants. He wanted to go with San Francisco traditions but with an added flair.

Frances and Marika were in power play with Aiyanna over Vibe Management. Who would execute what without wanting to execute each other? Mindy had hired premiere event planners and flowers from Plan Decor. She had booked The Neiman Mansion, a pastiche of a turn-of-the-century Frenchchâteaux with magnificent Bay and Golden Gate views. Mindy been fired with the plans inside her rummy little head. Since there hadn't been any time to download them before her departure and she couldn't take calls at her Malibu Rehab, everyone had to rely on deposit receipts to piece together the venue and vendors.

DS's team worked insane hours to make sure their pets were ready for play. It was a dream challenge that, if turned into a nightmare, could mean the end of their start-up. Everyone's career depended on the launch. From DS down to poor Aiyanna, who had some big, soggy designer shoes to fill, all scurried to put the start-up's best foot forward. The invite list, menu, the flowers, the DJ, the swag bag, the designer cocktails, the valet, the after-party spot, even the twitter hashtag became a source of contentious negotiations as workers realized that this was their moment to introduce their pets to the world. It was their time to let people know that they could still have all the fun of owning a pet, even random admiration from like-minded (read: QR code-savvy) strangers on the street. NuMilieu Pets would be the status symbol of the Millennium. Designer pets, one of a kind, with programmed personalities tailored to their owner's whims.

Frances and Marika led the PR outreach. They assembled a team of social media interns who tweeted, Facebooked the launch day and night. They even sparked interest for those who couldn't actually attend to participate through a live stream on NuMilieu.tv. In just two weeks, the event had gone viral as people from around the world guessed exactly what the pets could do. The owner voice recognition was generating the most buzz. But it was the look they waited for.

Until the launch, everything was a trade secret as with most high tech company policies. The difference was that NuMilieu was a fresh company that had attracted the curiosity of techies around the world with the promise of their pets' unique interactivity, over some already established hologram animals. It was always a temptation for DS to take a personal pet home for the night. In his fantasy, he had already designed the perfect one. A pink elephant named Tipsy who would burp on command as they traipsed up the streets of the TL.

David was on top of all the activities via Skype from his office back in Ohio. Since the Mindy ordeal, he'd checked in three times a day, morning, noon and night, just to make sure things were on target with the launch party.

"Marika and Frances just brought in the numbers. Over 61,000 likes on FB and the YouTube video has the potential to go viral," DS assured David.

"Don't discount the skepticism. It's like the moon walk. Until real people interact with our pets, it's just animation." DS thought deeply about David's words. "I want full coverage of the launch, including traditional. Every local station. Your job is to reel them in. Set up a network feed that's irresistible."

"That's our goal and we're getting there. All the Bay Area stations are committed. Still working on Sacramento. May have a lead for L.A."

"Keep up the good work." David let out an uncomfortable laugh. "Or else."

"Will do. Bye, Sir. Talk soon."

Kahlil, Perry and Hayden sat nursing their morning coffees as DS finished his call with David. Ted bounced late into DS's office with an intense glow. DS figured he must have just finished a dozen donuts. His round belly produced a nice baritone. "Take me out to the ballgame—"

"Sit down Mr. Jollykins. We've got work to do. I want a performance review of every pet that's premiering at the launch party by three this afternoon."

"And yes, speaking of performance—" Ted was ready to explode.

Hayden butted in, "No fucking way."

"Way."

"Photos?" Perry wanted proof and Ted was quick to provide it. He had indeed hooked up. The picture on his cell of him blissfully naked next to a heavily-tattooed Rubenesque woman was a bit much for DS so early in the morning. After the initial recognition, he turned his head. "O.K. O.K. You win."

"But wait, she's really into selfies. I've got more." Next thing, Ted was sliding through dozens of photos of the two of them in various stages of repose.

Kahlil was both impressed and jealous. He took them all in, even the last where they kissed over a chocolate chipotle raised glaze at Dynamic Donuts.

"You'll meet her. She's coming to launch."

"O.K. Enough! So you think you might have held those back if we were going to meet her in the flesh?" DS was really coming off like the virgin he was.

"No luck on Tinder?" Perry asked.

"One date. It lasted about three minutes."

"Hey, that's all it takes sometimes," Hayden chimed in.

"Coffee. The coffee date only lasted three minutes and then she got a call from her flatmate."

They all knew that routine, but Kahlil drilled it in. "Ahhh classic. The fated flatmate rescue device."

"Huh?"

"It's an app for dating disasters. It listens for a coded word then calls with a distressed roommate or mother in need."

"Great. Well, congratulations on the de-virgination. Now, we've got work to do."

"Spoilsport," said Ted as he buried his cell in his pants' pocket between layers of toppling fat.

#

Mindy had been in Malibu for nearly a week and was checking the calendar to see if she could make it back in time for the launch.

Her father walked into the plush meeting room with a vibe that he thought for sure his little girl would appreciate. "I'm so proud of you, Min. One week. Must feel great, huh?"

"I hate this place. You can't keep me here." When it became obvious that her thirty days collided with the launch date, she wanted to bolt.

"You're right, I can't. But I can cut you off, which is exactly what I'll do if you leave."

"Go ahead. I've got savings. You can't touch that."

"It's your call, but you'll have nowhere to go. Your room at Marika and Frances' has been cleared out."

"What the fuck?"

"The fuck, Mindy, is that I'm not letting you go the down the same path as your mother. You need help and you're in the best place for that now."

"But I planned the launch. I picked the venue. It's all me."

"That's the problem, Mindy. It's always been all you and I take responsibility for that. Stick it out. Then you can start over. There will be other start-ups where you can begin with an intact reputation. Right now, it's all up at NuMilieu."

"But Daddy."

"No 'but Daddy.' You're twenty-four and it's not too late to grow up right."

#

The night of the launch party, Hollywood-esque spotlights highlighted never-before-imagined birds in the sky above the Neiman Mansion. Pink Pterodactyls grouped together to sing "Somewhere Over the Rainbow" under a projected arc of colors. Giant neon hologram lizards in tuxedos lined the black and white carpet and greeted each guest by name as they arrived. Once inside, the attendees, many launch staples who had been to several events at the mansion, were awestruck by the caliber of the event. Toney neighbors gathered in the street drawn to the fantasy displays.

A polka dot sheep, walking upright with a large satchel, came up to one group and bleated, "And how is your evening so far?"

The neighbors, most dressed in upscale street clothes, just laughed and bleated back. "Fine."

They certainly didn't expect what came next. "Well, we can't simply be fine tonight. We want you to feel spectacular!" The sheep reached into her satchel and grabbed a handful of magic. She tossed it up into the sky and a hallucination of stars, hearts, kisses and peace signs rained down on the neighbors. They craned their heads upwards, relishing the bombardment of fantasy, transformed by the experience.

And it was all caught on KZO news by Juan Chavez for what would be a national feed. But this was nothing compared to what he found up the granite steps, between Lexi and Leonard, the Neiman's marble lions, that were now in 3D and who ironically meowed and purred as guests walked past them to the enormous ornate oak and plate glass double doors.

Aiyanna wore one of the dozens of concealed earbuds that workers had tucked in their drums to receive precise instructions. Workers had had to pass a test to confirm that they had memorized the orders. The mansion was coded by floor, then by room. The instructions ran the gamut from more champagne to more toilet paper to party crasher warning. It was Ted's signature launch party system and it had a flawless reputation.

DS was trailed by his own personal pet, a magnificent albino buck that tossed out hearts as it pranced beside him. DS had coded instructions for the dispersion of all the pets. He would whisper into his collar the floor and room where each pet was needed and what their mission was, whether it be to enjoy a cocktail, sprinkle some magic, blow a kiss, make a toast or do the tango, and then the magic would simply happen.

Marika and Frances, gorgeous head to toe, were in charge of charm. Marika wore an ethereal red maxi dress while Frances opted for an elegant ecru original. They flittered their way about the elegant rooms; the gorgeous dining rooms, the ballroom, the library and the solarium with its Tiffany stained glass that overlooked the Bay. Around every corner was a breath of history and that history was rewritten with the NuMilieu Pet ready to surprise each guest.

DS checked out each room before the angel investors piled through the grand front doors. When he hit the food display in the corner of the ballroom he nearly flipped. He coarsely whispered into his lapel for Chef Louis who was overwhelmed trying to keep an ice sculpture from melting next to the Tiffany glass before the sunset. DS gave one last breathy command. Chef Louis appeared within seconds, fully disheveled.

"What the fuck?" DS grunted under his breath.

"What, what the fuck?" Chef Louis wiped his hairy brow.

"Shrimp? Whose idea is this fucking mound of shrimp?" DS waved his arm grandly over an enormous pile of shrimp that was the centerpiece of a huge table in the ballroom.

"Mr. Strait. I've worked at four start-ups and we always have shrimp at the launch. Lots of shrimp. Jumbo shrimp."

"Exactly! And where are they now?" Chef Louis was dumbstruck. "Where are those start-ups now?"

"Under. Sir. They went under."

"Exact-fucking-ly! Get rid of them! They're oxymorons!" He motioned grandly to the chef who stood motionless, only to wipe the fresh beads from his brow.

"But Mr. Strait—"

"Do you have a problem with that? Get them out of here. Now!" DS got a buzz in his ear from Frances that the angels were arriving. "Now. This minute! Down the disposal. Quick. If I see one fucking shrimp in this place, you're finished!"

"But, sir—"

DS reached for the chef's kerchief for emphasis but he backed up out of arm's grasp. "Yes. Sir. I will dispose of them." And with that he snapped his fingers at two elegantly dressed staff members, who carried the four-foot-high mound of shrimp delicately through the side halls into the kitchen, where it was stuffed down the disposal, handful by handful, and ground into history.

From that moment on, the chef thought DS was a pure madman, but in the end, the mission was accomplished and the largest mound of shrimp that any launch party in the history of San Francisco launch parties had ever seen was now neatly ground up and disposed of, to the horror of the catering staff at the Neiman Mansion.

David, Frances' and Marika's parents and Mindy's father were the first guests to enter the ballroom. They were each accompanied by gigantic NuMilieu cats especially designed for their personality. Marika's mother's pet walked carefully, balancing a cup of tea. Ed's carried a stem filled with red wine. Frances' and Mindy's father's NuMilieu kitties each swirled a snifter of brandy. Once they had delivered the guests, the animals put their drinks down on the table. The guests marveled as the glasses magically disappeared.

"And this is what we pay DS for. This. This is perfection. Pure—" before he could complete the sentence, David started sniffing wildly. "Shrimp? Do I smell shrimp? Please tell me, DS?" His glared, frantically scouting the room. "If I taught you one thing, it was my mound of shrimp theory. Please," he nosed through the entire room, "please don't let me find a mound of shrimp."

DS laughed off his concerns. "It's their treat. An olfactory feed for the pets. I'll change the scent immediately if it bothers you. We wanted potential owners to get the real pet feel experience. Perhaps it's overkill."

"Well, turn it down or change it to beef."

DS whispered the directions into his lapel. "By the way. Genius, David." He pointed to his earbud. "Pure genius. Love the connectivity."

The pets gravitated to the row of hologrammed crystal bowls lining a corner of the grand ballroom and began to chow down, while DS gravitated to Mindy's father.

"Good to see you, sir. I'm sorry to hear about Mindy."

"Well, she's in good hands. Her mother had the same damn allergy to alcohol. It's what brought her down. She'll nip this in the bud. She has to."

"I hope so, sir. She had a great vibe."

The evening was a fantastical success. Once the party started rolling, DS made it a goal to personally greet each guest. It was a lofty, likely unattainable goal, as the responses had filled the Neiman Mansion's maximum of one thousand. One thousand! Just the thought of that success alone was staggering. The launch had become the buzz of The City and anyone who was or who thought they were anyone wanted to be there. It wasn't just for the new SF tech money, but for the old money ballet and symphony crowd as well. They were relevant and the angel investors knew it.

One of the biggest hits was the elaborate mini-zoo which housed the traditional Mother's brand pink and white sprinkled animal cookies. No one could resist grabbing a handful of childhood memories as they walked past. Buried within the mound were mini pink-and-white-themed NuMilieu Pets that would motion-activate when a guest approached. A specially designed box full of cookies were in the swag bags along with a first edition of a QR code book for pet toys.

"Hey, you made it!"

"Fuck, man. This is over-the-top! You did this?" Tracy looked handsome and so different from the slouchy guy who lurked around the apartment. All trimmed up and tailored in a cool black jacket and collarless dress shirt.

"Hey, I'm just part of the best team ever." DS saw Marika and Frances floating their way across the ballroom floor, trying not to slosh their Zootinis that the mixologist had created for the event.

"Wow! Tracy!! You look fabulous!!!" Marika was all over him now that DS was off limits.

"Thanks for the invite. This makes our start-up's launch look like peanuts."

"Well, you're in the real zoo now!" Frances dragged all three out to the dance floor where the band, Dogpatch, played on stage. Classic breeds redefined in neon colors played sax, drums and guitar with gusto accompanied by the Pit Bull Singers which brought the mansion down. The dance floor was full. By the end of the first song, Marika and Frances, still balancing their Zootinis, were grinding against DS and Tracy. The pressure went on for two more songs when DS feigned earbud interruptus and excused himself. Tracy followed.

The balcony overlooked the Bay. The distinct damp, salty air was invigorating. DS and Tracy propped against the balustrade, mesmerized by the view. Tracy reached into his pocket for an elegantly rolled joint and lit up. DS obliged looking over his should all the while.

"You did an amazing job."

"Like I said, it wasn't just me." DS appreciated each breath.

"Take off the modesty hat. It's just me. Tracy." DS looked into his friend's eyes, again noting they were the same starry blue as Mindy's.

"It's like a dream, right?" DS wanted to pinch himself. "I'm afraid to close my eyes. Afraid it will go away."

"Go ahead, close them. Nothing will go away."

DS closed his eyes as Tracy leaned in slightly. He wasn't sure if it was the Zootini tasting the mixologist had put him through earlier that evening, the sudden fresh air or (most likely) the weed, but he felt faint, weak kneed. He propped open his eyes and saw the blue diamonds. He pushed himself away and nearly screamed.

"Mindy!?!"

"See what you were missing, DS?" She took a sip of her Zootini then rested it on a small wrought iron table and took DS's hands in hers. "But that's O.K. We're together now. Forever."

DS, Tracy and Mindy stood in an awkward circle, DS's lips smeared with hastily-applied red Etienne lipstick. "How? I thought—"

"It wasn't easy. I hitched all afternoon. Lots of shady rides. Finally got a guy who took me straight from Livermore and dropped me off under the zoo in the sky. We did it, DS!" His eyes had been stuck on her deep blues. DS refocused and saw the shape the ex-Vibe Manager was in. Tattered clothes, smudged face, a cut across her cheek. The application of lipstick was her only attempt at arriving in style. "Our launch is a success! Did you see the press outside? They're everywhere. Everyone wants to know about the zoo in the sky!!"

"How did you get in?" DS turned and discreetly whispered into his lapel as he awaited her answer.

"I just showed my I.D. and told them Daddy's little girl was left off the list by accident. Let's dance, DS. I've been dying to dance."

DS looked over to Tracy who was tottering between shock and amusement. He prayed for some relief. It came a moment later when John Montgomery arrived.

"Mindy! My God. My Mindy." Her father was livid at first, but when he saw the severity of his daughter's condition, all he could do was hold her. "Come with me, dear. Let's have a chat."

"Go. We can dance after." DS gave Mindy a gentle pat on the shoulder.

"Promise?"

"Promise." DS knew it would never be fulfilled that evening.

And so the launch party continued with the sour taste of Mindy on DS's red lips.

In the Blink of an Eye

———#———

If the launch party was a fantasy come true, then the after-party was a notch above the illusion. Marika had scored by renting out a comic gallery in the Mission which her friend from the Institute of Art was showing in. But she really wanted to win points with DS. Not employee points. She wanted to give "it" one last obnoxious shot. The "it" that Mindy had never got. The competition between them had never been non-existent, and Marika wanted to win this one big-time while Mindy was out of the picture. Marika thought "it" was a shoe-in after Mindy's brief appearance. She thought the field was clear, but DS seemed more interested in his pet team more than anything else.

"Here's to my bros! We did it guys!! The all-nighters you pulled... it's all paying off!!"

Hayden, Perry, Kahlil and David circled around DS. He had brought not only his vision, but the technology needed to create the zoo. "Cheers to DS. None of this would have been possible without that eccentric brain." Kahlil was exuberant. They joined in a human chain with DS in the middle and reveled in the applause from the hundred or so post-partiers who were positively swerved at this point.

When the chain unlinked, Ted grabbed his Rubenesque Tinder friend, Rebecca, who Frances could have sworn, after five too many Zootinis, was actually Penelope from *Criminal Minds*.

"Penelope!" When Frances sloshed the bulky girl's way, DS headed her off.

"Frances. Water. Coffee. Something. Anything but this." He took the half empty champagne flute from her hand.

"But DS, we're friends, right? Come on... with benefits?"

The begging was obnoxious. Pathetic. Tracy observed it all with a smirk on his face.

#

The glory of the fantasy launch party barely had a chance to kick in when the reality of San Francisco hit full force. The Tenderloin Butcher struck yet again, this time raining eyeballs onto an unsuspecting pedestrian walking down Larkin St. The accounts were all over the news.

"It's just one block over from your aPodment and less than a block from his last murder. This guy has definitely switched it up." Frances pointed at Marika's cell phone as if for evidence. "There are no boundaries now."

"That's it. You're with us until this guy is caught." Marika would have it no other way.

"Now, let's not overreact here." DS looked up to the giant eyeball which had stayed in Justin's old office throughout DS's move-in. He could have sworn the eye rolled in disbelief. He made a mental note to have it removed.

"Listen. I should be approved soon. We all agree he's stretched out the kills, right? The pattern's gone. But let's not panic. I'll be out of the TL soon enough. One week tops."

Marika fired up her news feeds. "He's down to one week intervals. That's all you've got."

"Soon enough is not soon enough. I have an itchy feeling about this." Now Frances had jumped on the persuasion bandwagon.

"Keep your itches to yourself. He's not that predictable any more. Meanwhile, any news on Mindy?"

"Her dad tucked her back into a new glam rehab in Novato. They reset the thirty days."

"Well, let's hope she stays put. And social media monitoring? What's the response?"

"We're beyond social media. The national news picked it up and the Sky Zoo went viral!"

"As expected. Great news."

#

DS's cell rang. "Hey, Gram! I was just—"

"Oh, don't waste your breath with that 'I was just going to call you' jazz! You got more going on out there than a quakenado!"

"That's a pretty fair assessment."

"First I see that company you been pluggin' away at has hit the big time. I saw the Sky Zoo, Dickie! On TNN!! I nearly wet myself!!!" Frances and Marika were highly amused by her enthusiasm. "But then, they busted into that to say now it's raining eyeballs out there. Dickie, if you tell me you're still in that God-awful neighborhood, that Tenderhip, I'll scream. Just scream."

"Loin, Gram, Tenderloin. And calm down. I've got a commitment from the agent. I'm first in line. They're just processing the paperwork now."

"A commitment? A commitment ain't no damn safe roof over your head. A commitment. Sheesh... Ain't no damn marriage. Now, I have an idea. How 'bout you hightail it home for a little visit 'til that agent person done get you a new roof? A safe roof. I can't get any of these inventions you been orderin' up to work. I got boxes here, skinny, weird lookin' televisions there and wires everywhere. Everywhere, Dickie. I'm trippin' all over 'em. And they all lead to nowhere. Take a little trip home and help your Grammy set this crap up, would ya, Dickie?"

"Gram, we're right in the middle of our big splash."

Frances kicked him under the table. Both of The Girls nodded concurrently, "yes" as in "get the fuck back to your Grammy Flo."

"O.K. Gram. Let me see what I can do. Soon. I promise. Soon."

"Oh, and Dickie. Did you get yourself that cat, yet? I've been waitin' for a video. Just dyin' to see a video. By some miracle, I got that lap Mac whatever working just fine and I've been checkin' that email account you set up, and know what? No cat."

"Right. The cat. The cat's on hold 'til the new place."

"Well, just one more reason to take care of that. Hope this agent person isn't one of those fast-talkin' BSers. Nothin' worse than a fast-talkin' BSer."

"He's not."

"Well then. Let me know when you got your ticket an' I'll pick you up. Oh, and bring that girlfriend if you want. I can make room."

"We'll see, Gram. We'll see." DS rolled his eyes.

Flo hung up, thrilled that her little Schnicklefritz would be on his way soon. Frances' and Marika's mouths hung open. "Girlfriend?" Marika fished.

"It's just a thing. It helps her sleep thinking I've got someone special."

At that moment, The Girls thought that Little Dickie Strait could not have been more adorable.

"Hey, I'd be more than happy to go if you need a cover-up." Marika would elbow her way in any way she could.

"That's a generous offer, but I'm solo on this one."

Marika sang a weak version of "Call Me" as she followed Frances throughout the sunlit hallway.

#

"It's yours. One hundred percent. You can move in next week. They want to do some work in the bathroom. The prior tenant took long showers and the paint's peeling like crazy."

"Thanks, Jason. Sounds like a green light!" So, with the move-in date in one week, that gave DS time to pack up, head to Shawnee for a long weekend and get back to work. Fresh.

The trek home that night through the TL once again inspired a detour around yellow crime scene tape since DS wanted to see, like so many other murder tourists, exactly where the deed had taken place. This time it was a bit too close for comfort, and the thought of eyeballs rolling across the asphalt was particularly egregious. He stopped at the local market run by a couple of Pakistani guys who had more dirt on the Butcher than the police department. But that's not saying much.

"The eyeballs didn't roll, like they say. By time they hit street, near flat." The devil was in the details. "The guy, they say he had black hoodie, but street people, they say dark gray. Guy with dark gray look 'spicious." Azeem gave DS three damp vegetable boxes for packing as long as he bought some tape. "Be careful. Keep your eyes open." The cashier laughed at his own irony.

"O.K. Thanks. I'll keep my eyes. Open."

DS packed up his sparse possessions, recalling the housewarming that Mindy had arranged just two months earlier and how drastically things had changed since then. He looked across the light well, looking for Tracy to do his familiar heads up welcoming him home which was a code for come by later. But the shades were drawn which was rare. It wasn't so weird that DS worried and, in fact, gave DS the evening to get all his packing done. He shot Tracy a text but by the end of his packing, there was still no response. He put Mindy's rubber ducky, the one that had taken up residence on the shower floor, atop the last box and declared to himself that he was, finally, finished.

The quiet was both unsettling and restorative. DS plopped down on the twin bed that he'd be so glad to depart from and, intending to shut his eyes for just a few minutes, conked out. It was only 8:35 and it had been years since he turned in so early. When he woke up, the sunrise was streaming slightly through the light well, beating onto his face and warming the puddle of drool that had escaped his mouth sometime early that morning. It was that kind of deep, paralyzing sleep that only comes with sheer exhaustion.

After he showered and glanced across the way, DS thought the shades from Tracy's place were slightly higher, different from the night before. Odd, he thought, that Tracy would open then close the shades at night. Regardless, he figured Tracy had just got in late and had drawn them up slightly to see if he was still awake. With that in mind, he left for work in comfort.

#

DS had Aiyanna get his plane tix, so everything was in order for a Thursday departure.

"Right, I'll be leaving tomorrow night, coming back early Monday morning." David wasn't thrilled with the call and hearing for the first time that his star start-up partner was taking off in the middle of the denouement from the launch party. "I just realized I had some loose ends to tie up. My grandmother has some issues. She needs me back home for a few days." He rearranged his office toys on the shelf as he spoke on his cell.

"Well, make sure Frances and Marika and the rest of the Pet Team know where you are at all times. We've got a lot of requests coming in for interviews. I think you're the best for that job, DS. I really do."

"Not a problem. Our calendars are synced."

"Very good. Enjoy your time back home. Oh, did your rental agent get the references? The check?"

"He did. And thanks. I can't tell you what it means to be able to get out of the Tenderloin."

"Well, I can only imagine with all those body parts and all." They disconnected on a good note.

Not too many minutes later, Aiyanna came in with the details of DS's flight home. Frances and Marika followed. "So you're on US Flightways—"

DS spun around like a madman. "Didn't I tell you specifically no US Flightways? I had a horrific experience coming here."

Aiyanna looked shell shocked. "It was the only flight available. I'm so sorry. I can probably change it, but it won't be non-stop."

"Anything but that airline. I told you that."

"Fine. I'll change it to Alaska Air, but it will take you two stops and over twelve hours."

"Anything but US Flightways," DS grunted to himself.

Aiyanna backed out of the room, leaving a bad vibe just as Frances and Marika were entering.

"Just don't go stuffing your duffel!" Frances tried to lighten it up.

"No duffel. No nothing. On and off. Laptop. That's it. I learned my lesson."

"Did David tell you about the requests? Every talk show wants an interview. And TNN is following up. It's crazy!"

"Any time after Monday works. I just need this weekend to get a few things together. I did all my packing for the new place last night, so that's out of the way."

"Promise you'll tweet? Your whole little adventure. Little Grammy-Grams. We set up a special twitter account!" Marika was so proud of their plan.

"Yeah, we want it all. Recipes, too." Frances begged.

"Right? How the hell does anyone fry a pie?" Marika wondered.

"Yes, yes, yes. I promise. I'll start the minute the trip officially begins. 6 a.m. sharp. I'll be in my Uber. Happy?"

"Happy," The Girls grinned.

Grammy Flo was already a legend in her own time around the office because of The Girls re-enacting, with endearment, her conversations with "Little Dickie." Thank God the Schnicklefritz hadn't slipped out. He wouldn't be able to live that one down.

"Fine. Fine. I'll tweet. I promise. Every crazy little thing she does. And, trust me, there will be lots." DS beamed as he thought of Flo, his once-in-a-life-character-to-end-all-characters.

"We thought it would be fun to go live with it. You know, sort of a PR piece on you, the real brains behind NuMilieu, and how you still remember your roots."

"Don't you think we're getting ahead of ourselves? The company hasn't made a red cent. And may not for months. Years, even."

Frances and Marika looked at each other, knowing that they were about to blow the lid off DS's reality check.

"I think you'd better sit down for this." Frances and Marika shoved him into a chair before releasing the news.

#

Apparently behind the scenes, the office was like rush hour at Penn Station. Controlled chaos with a touch of panic. The texts, emails and phone calls came in at a rapid pace. The world was curious and celebrities, wealthy oil barons and Wall Street brats alike, all wanted the new status symbol. It was snob squared. And NuMilieu had the patent on the whole deal.

Frances read the list of requests. "We've got a guy in Abu Dhabi who wants to throw a party just like our launch. He saw it on BBC News."

"What?"

"Yeah! And that's just the beginning."

"Wait, go back to... what? He wants the same pets? Wha?"

DS paced, wound up the chattering teeth. The weird rhythm helped him think. "No. That's diluting the brand. We're selling personalized pets. Lemme think." He wound the teeth up yet again. "O.K., tell him we'll give them half those pets for free and design a dozen new ones if he agrees to let us film the event with exclusive rights to distribute the images."

"O.K., but their party is in six weeks. You came into the company with your own designs ready to go. How long will we need?"

"I'll need a team of 3D artists stat. David said HR has been in touch with the local digital schools. I want four-dozen butts in chairs by the time I come in on Tuesday morning. We'll start training then. My code has streamlined the process. That's what we're marketing. Unique, tailored 3D pets. As unique as anyone's pet. Collectibles."

"Teensy Babies," Marika blurted out.

"Teensy Babies?"

"Oh, come on. Don't tell me you never heard of Teensy Babies. I had every one ever made. With tags. My parents wouldn't let me cut the tags. Assholes." Marika was obviously still pissed at her parents over this.

"I never got into those. Grammy sewed me her own version though. Little Miss Tiddles and her kittens. Named them all, wrote a little note about their history. She loves cats, but swore she'd never own another after her last one passed."

"Ahhhhh..." Frances moaned. "Sort of like USA Girl dolls, but kitties."

"Ugh... USA Girl Dolls. Again? What's next? Furlies?"

Everyone in the room groaned, recalling the evil toy.

"Never mind. It's not important. What else?"

"O.K. then. We've got another from Queen Leila. She wants a pink poodle for her little Princess and she wants it to sing her national anthem. It's for the Princess' birthday in one week." Frances was reading from a long list of notes.

"Done. But a pink poodle? Couldn't she come up with something more original?"

"Her staff thought that was original."

"Pink poodle it is then," DS declared.

"And what about the White House? Can they have their red, white and blue eagle's nest? In time for the announcement of a new trade agreement in three weeks?" Frances had that order circled in red.

And so it went. The orders came in fast and furious. By the end of the list, DS was overwhelmed.

"Maybe David was right. Not a good time to go home."

"This is my third start-up. Let me tell you. It's now or never because once the sales go up, it's hard to get off the roller coaster."

"So, why didn't you stay? At the others?"

Frances and Marika chimed in together. "Options. Once you exercise your options, what's the point? Then it's party time."

"You've had options? And you're all still renting?"

"Just waiting for that bubble to burst. What blows up must deflate," Marika summarized.

DS felt like he was back at day one. Intimidated by The Girls who were just partying their way to riches.

So, DS finally got the full picture. Here were these two girls whom he thought were simply soaking their parents, but in reality, they had it together. "What about Mindy? Was this her first?"

"Yup. She was really hoping the stock options would pave her way to independence," Frances divulged.

"Well, that bubble may have burst." DS was sickened by his own words.

#

"So bros, looks like we're on our way! I heard some numbers this morning and these stock options are going to be lookin' good sooner rather than later." Ted, Kahlil, Perry and Hayden cheered DS as he made the announcement in the conference room over signature cafe drinks before he dropped the bomb about the workload.

"What about new hires?" Kahlil was genuinely concerned.

"I'll be looking into that when I get back next week. Suffice it to say that the investors are really excited and the next round of funding should be a breeze and then we should be going into the black. In the meantime, I think it's safe to expect that we'll be expanding the team which should give most of you some well-deserved normalcy. And sleep. After we get through these first few orders."

"Great, I'll let Blue Bull know." Perry quipped.

"Exactly. And someone contact Mountain Rain, too." They all knew the references of nearly IV pumping caffeine energy drinks throughout the day and night to meet the target deadlines. "Anyway, here's to my bros. Seriously, we are quite a team!"

"And here's to you, DS, for bringing on the creative juice to fuel the NuMilieu Project." Perry and Hayden were beyond sincere, they were near tears.

"Geez, let's not get sentimental." Truth was, they were all ecstatic that the hard work was about to pay off. They were all about to reach above and beyond any geek's dream of success, if DS's projections were anywhere near close to reality.

Kahlil left for a few minutes and returned with a magnum of champagne. The team split it and then later topped it off with oysters at The Merchant, although DS passed graciously on the wobbly bites, opting for a plate of tacos he imported from their upscale taco bar next to the butcher shop.

"Livin' the life. We are about to be livin' the life!" Kahlil slurped down the last of a dozen oysters and snapped his fingers shamelessly for more.

Livin' the life. Livin' the life. Livin' the life. DS chanted the phrase in his mind as he stumbled through the TL later that night, past the barefoot homeless couple and echoing bum fights, barely able to find his temporary-and-soon-to-be-forgotten home.

#

The news conference was set up on the steps in front of City Hall. The Mayor and top brass from the department created a very official-looking line. All local stations were there and a few cable ones as well with their sky-high antennas shooting into the morning fog.

The Mayor, a buffoonish character who was great at giving out tech company tax breaks but did little for the homeless population, knew that his ass was really on the line with the Tenderloin Butcher. There was panic on the streets, and ironically, the homeless were moving further up Market St. which infuriated the tech workers who had staked out that real estate as their own homeless-free zone. There was even a conspiracy theory that the Butcher was a hitman hired by the mid-Market Exploitation Association to clean up the Tenderloin and intentionally get the encampments to move on. Then again, there were also conspiracies that Gene Tech, the City's biggest drug manufacturer, in conjunction with Google, was working on genetically modified bees that would seek out the stench of the homeless and attack. Conspiracies aside, there was one undeniable truth—there was a vicious killer on the loose and the police were nowhere closer to the killer than when he'd first struck, three months and six murders earlier. Demands to catch the killer and really see some action from the police were haunting the Mayor and his re-election counted on catching the killer.

"As we all know, the Tenderloin Butcher has broken his pattern. Now the department will be out in full force, monitoring the comings and goings of all individuals in the Tenderloin. Some may call this a police state, but I can assure you this increased presence is only to protect our fine citizens."

Marika, Frances and DS watched as the conference streamed live. The camera panned the people who had gathered in front of the dome. It settled on a close-up of a hipster clearly mouthing the word "windbag." It was a common nickname for the mayor who had made many long-winded speeches about making The City a safer place—and well, now this.

. #

That night there was indeed an increased presence. DS got through the blue line even after showing his ID which still had his Shawnee address. He was, stupidly, wearing a black hoodie that evening.

"How long have you been in The City?"

"Almost two months, sir." Grammy had taught DS to always be respectful of the uniform. Any uniform. Even flight attendants.

"Can you document that?"

"Document?"

"Airline tickets. Anything?"

The officer was just doing his work but others being questioned were obviously offended. DS searched on his cell phone and brought up his reservation confirmation. The officer took a look, really scrutinizing the image on the cell. DS thought that would be it and he'd be on his way, but little did he know that the airport security had linked DS to the airlines' terrorist watch list, thanks to Old Iron Balls from Flight 147. "Is there a problem, officer?"

"How long are you planning on staying in The City?"

"Forever."

"But you're leaving town tomorrow. That's not exactly forever."

Well, then. This is getting weird.

"Listen." DS looked at the officer's badge. Officer Maples. "Listen, Officer Maples. It's true that I'm leaving tomorrow to go see my grandmother in Shawnee. Help her out with a few things around the house."

"Sounds good in theory, but given the circumstances, I've got a few more questions." Officer Maples was transforming before DS's eyes. His fairly soft spoken, pleasant demeanor shifted. DS felt like a mouse under the watchful eyes and sharp claws of a curious kitty.

"Listen, I've got work to do tonight. As you saw, I'm leaving tomorrow."

"Right. Grammy Flo." Officer Maples whispered into his lapel mic then got back to DS. "Let me put it to you this way, Mr. Strait. You can either answer a few simple questions here, now, or come into the station."

Getting real weird.

"Whatever you say, Officer." At that moment, three other officers surrounded DS. "Ask away."

The officers did just that, as DS tried desperately to convince them that he was, indeed, working in San Francisco and had, in fact, been the brains behind the Sky Zoo and that he had emphatically not been in San Francisco prior to that dreadful Flight 147 that had landed him on an international terror watch list.

It wasn't an easy feat, but one of the officers, Officer McInerney, a rather short, waxy-looking man, had, himself, been a victim of Flight Attendant Abuse and shook the whole thing off with the confirmation that DS had been the mastermind behind the NuMilieu event that had captured The City's heart just days earlier.

"Well Mr. Strait, it appears that you've been very busy. My little girl saw the Sky Zoo on the news and she was in heaven. Any chance of getting one of them pets for her birthday party? It's not for three months."

DS gladly handed over a business card with a wholehearted promise if it would just get him out of this mess and on his way up the hill.

#

DS was hoping that Tracy would be around and they could catch up before he took off for the weekend. When he got back to the aPodment, he looked out across the light well and this time thought it was really getting strange that Tracy's shades were drawn yet again. Seemed to DS that he would have at least come by to say something about the launch party sometime in the last few days. He went by Tracy's door and knocked vigorously. No answer. He tried his cell. Nothing. And no text back. He'd check again later to see if any lights went on inside once it got dark. Maybe the guy just needed a crash day or two. Or three.

For that half hour, he had absolutely nothing to do. Everything but what he was taking to Shawnee, which was next to nothing, was packed for the move to the new apartment. He paced for a bit, finished off the lone bottle of craft beer in his mini-fridge and ate the last of some goldfish crackers which he dipped in peanut butter from a jar that was quite thick, dry and grainy around the edges.

The room across the light well was pitch dark. DS dug through a box aptly labelled "randomness," that was the accumulation of care packages of knickknacks that Grammy had sent over the weeks. He pulled out a little laser light, and simply out of boredom, beamed it across the empty space into Tracy's place. In the blink of an eye he thought he saw fingers creep along the side of the shade, pulling it aside slightly, as if to make way to peer out. But, like a blink, it was over. He'd find out soon enough if it was Tracy or an illusion.

Oh Snap!

———#———

Sure enough, just minutes later there was a knock at the door. DS opened it wide for his neighbor, but no sooner had it swung open did a dark gray-hooded figure push into the room and shut the door behind him. He wielded a switchblade.

"Oh shit. Who—?" It took only a second for DS to assimilate that the stranger also came equipped with duct tape and rope. *This is not going to be pretty.*

"Sit the fuck down. Now! And not a word or else I'll slice your lips right off." He had a thick Latino accent.

Fuck. Fuck. Fuck. Fuck. The Tenderloin Butcher. Live. Fuck. Fuck.

"Right. Not a—"

"—word!" The bulky stranger brought the knife up to DS's trembling mouth. *The word is the future. The word is the future. The word is the future.*

With lightning speed, the stranger tied DS up to a chair and duct-taped his mouth, which was something of a weird comfort to DS, knowing that he did still have lips to apply the silver strip to. "I'll be back when I'm done with your little pussy friend." *Done. Did he mean done-done? Kaput done?*

His own inevitable demise was quickly sinking in. The stranger took one of DS's cell phones which sat atop the stack of boxes.

Four minutes had taken him from life to death. It was 8:37 Wednesday night and if this guy was the Tenderloin Butcher, as DS more than expected, he would be on the menu very soon.

It was stifling, listening to the hiss of the radiant heat and watching the minutes pass on that fucking microwave clock with not even the thickness of a dime between the sweaty skin on his hands and the rope that dug into his protruding veins. Yes, DS was fit to be tied. He felt the outline of his phone in his pocket and rocked his pelvis back and forth praying at first for a butt dial but knowing that PT&T didn't have the bars for that dream. His best bet was dislodging the phone from his pocket, hoping it would default to his Internet, and trying to tweet with his thumb that had, as of 11:43 p.m. according to the microwave, the slightest bit of movement. It was, literally, a stretch.

DS assumed the stranger would check back in, but even by 5:16 on Thursday morning, just about the time he was supposed to Uber to SFO for his 7:30 a.m. flight, he had had no check-in from the stranger. A part of this was reassuring because he thought maybe the Butcher had gone on to other things or got sidetracked, until he reminded himself that getting sidetracked might very well mean his friend was being dismembered across the light well. The realization and discomfort spread throughout his body, landing in his bladder that wanted to suddenly, desperately, expel that last beer he'd finished nearly nine and a half hours earlier.

The speculation and restriction was, in itself, torture. He could only imagine what was to come. And then, as if by some miracle, a final movement dislodged his cell phone from his pocket. Instinctively he dove to the phone, forgetting that he was tethered to a chair, landing his thumb next to it. Nearly a half hour later, all the while wishing that he had the foresight not to create such an intricate and loooooong passcode, he had turned the fucking thing on. About two minutes after that, after nearly a dozen ineffective thumb stabs, he managed to get signed on to his new twitter account that The Girls had set up for his trip. HELP was his only tweet. He simply didn't have the mobility for 140 characters. So HELP it was. He retweeted it again. And again. And again. And again. Every second, rhythmically, he retweeted hoping that someone, anyone, would get it that something was drastically wrong in DS's life.

And someone did. Just not who he expected.

#

Mindy hated her new Novato rehab even more than the Malibu center, mostly because her routine now started at sunrise. But this one allowed visitors and thank God for Frances and Marika, who came through in times of need. Besides DS, who'd had no intention of visiting any time soon, they had been the only names she'd put on her visitor list. After an hour of humiliating begging during their visit, they had smuggled in a cell if she promised to only use it for data. They gave Mindy another little crumb if she swore not to abuse it. They told her to check the

NuMilieu website for their latest social media blast about DS's trip back to his roots. Anyone could follow him on twitter so this way The Girls didn't feel like they'd actually divulged anything, and gave her DS's twitter news. They simply led Mindy to a guilty little pleasure that would give her some kind of joy in what she called her "rehab prison"—a sprawling luxury compound complete with pool, spa, yoga room and an impossible list of rules including a wardrobe limited to casual active wear and no make-up policy. Bare skin to bare it all.

So, poor thing was left with cyberstalking as anything else would certainly get back to the staff. Not that it really mattered as everyone had blocked her anyway. Mindy usually started first thing in the morning, same as the chirpy little birds she found so annoying after years of city living. As usual, she started the stalk with DS. It was a routine she'd developed since the first day they set up his social media accounts. When he shut each and every one down because of her manic posts, she had been despondent. That withdrawal was, she thought, worse than any caused by drying out from Old World Red or the freaky little diet pills traded like baseball cards outside her locker in high school.

Little did she know until her daily cyber stalk began that her DS was obviously in some sort of trouble. When she read the hundreds of HELPS on his twitter feed, she slipped on some furry lined boots over her sweats, grabbed a white hoodie, her empty Katy Spode clutch, a piece of paper and a marker from her art therapy supply kit and hit the road. Literally. She figured it would take under an hour to get back to

San Francisco if she could just snag a straight shot ride. Much better than the long hitch from her first rehab from Southern California.

As luck would have it, Mindy found that ride in a pearly sedan with heated seats and tinted windows heading right into the heart of The City. The sign had worked: MOTHER DYING. NEED RIDE TO SAN FRANCISCO.

#

The ride from Novato over the Golden Gate was uneventful at first. The man who had picked Mindy up, Simon, a spiffily dressed, metro-ish guy, maybe fifty, talked incessantly about his own mother. They covered it all, from toddler to college and everything in between.

"Oh, and could she ever play the piano. My own private concerts. Gershwin, all the Broadway greats. And sing, just like Babs! I mean, really, how lucky is that?" Mindy's gaydar was passing the metro mark and had now moved onto I-can-be-safe-with-this-guy-because-he's-gay which, of course, is a good thing if you're a hot twenty-something, even sans make-up, and have just crawled into a stranger's car.

"She sounds amazing."

"Yes amazing! The pies. Let me tell you that woman knew how to bake a pie like no one else. No one. Apple, peach, berry. Lattice top."

"You must have grown up in the country." Mindy just wanted to keep the conversation going as she continued to respond to the new "HELPS" on DS's twitter feed:

I'll be there soon, My Love.

Little did Mindy know that DS was in no particular position to actually read her tweets.

"Actually no. Down on the Peninsula, but we had fruit trees. Succulent fruit trees."

"Me, too. The Peninsula." Mindy looked up just as the car in front of them slammed on the brakes and flipped over the barrier in the middle of the Golden Gate. It was an efficient end to any chitchat about who came from where.

Simon swerved and missed the Mercedes by an inch. He narrated his observation through the rearview mirror. "Oh dear. That's not pretty. Someone's getting an ambulance ride."

For the first time, there was silence throughout the leather interior of the sedan. It wasn't awkward or forced, just necessary, as they both slowly realized no one could have survived what they just witnessed. There were several minutes before either could fully adjust.

"Your mother. What hospital is she in? Pacific West? St. Andrew's?" He expected some response. "SF Main? Wherever. I can take you. I've got an hour before my meeting." He smiled at her gently as she tucked her cell into the otherwise empty hot pink Katy Spode clutch.

"She's not in a hospital."

"But I thought you said she was dying?"

"I did. In the Tenderloin."

"Oh, poor dear. Well then, maybe it's for the best." His sarcasm had slipped, and had Mindy still had a mother alive who was dying in the TL, she might have been genuinely pissed, but whatever. She got her ride.

"I don't want to put you out. You can drop me off on Van Ness and Turk? I'll just hop out."

"Don't be nutty. I'll take you right there."

"O.K. then. How about Hyde and Turk?"

"Ewww... Butcherland. Sure thing, but I'll pull over and see to it that you make it in safe." And in a few minutes, he did pull over, in a safe spot away from the cops and blocks from Hyde and Turk.

"Thanks. You're a really sweet guy for taking me all the way." Mindy didn't notice that she was only on the edge of the TL in a quiet alley, until she went to hop out. And then, her door was locked. She looked over to Simon who was unzipping his well-tailored trousers.

"You can thank me here or in the back seat."

"Are you kidding me?" Apparently Mindy's gaydar was off that morning as this pig had just gone from snow job to blow job in seconds. But Mindy was a quick study in these kinds of situations, especially ones that she didn't instigate. In fact, she would have none of it if she didn't instigate it. "Back seat."

Mindy crawled into the back seat with her Katy Spode clutch and Simon followed, nearly jamming himself between his heated seat and the roof. He finally propped himself atop her, tugged at her sweats and then thong, ready to enter. "Hey wait. Come on. Protection at least. I've got some." With that, Mindy opened her Katy Spode, took out her cell phone and then, with all the might she could summon, shut the clutch bending the metal slightly but securing the clasps around what could only now be called a broken penis.

"Shiiiiiiit Biaaaaatch!" Simon screamed in excruciating pain as Mindy hopped back into the driver's seat and fiddled with buttons until the door unlocked.

"Thanks for the ride, Pencil Dick. Have a great day." She burst through the heavy car door. "Oh snap!" were her final words.

#

All this and it was only 6:50 in the morning. Mindy got her bearings and headed for DS's aPodment in the hope that someone would exit for work soon and let her in. Officers stopped Mindy a filthy block away, but didn't really grill her too severely as odds were the Butcher was a man and they thought her story about losing her purse to a "stick-up" was credible, although an old school word choice. Mindy, though, knew it was the perfect choice of words.

"You be careful now, miss. The Butcher is still on the loose."

Mindy speed walked to Hyde and Turk until she found DS's place. She paced in her comfy boots and sweats outside the aPodment long enough to hear the siren stop blocks away in the direction of Simon's car. She pictured the look on the medics' faces as they saw Simon's penis clutched in her Katy Spode. Just as the sight gelled in her mind, out popped a temp tenant who readily let her in when she said she forgot her keys. It was just about 7 a.m. as the stranger slammed shut the ornate iron gate that protected the front door to the refigured aPodment building. A horn honked. Mindy turned around and saw a black Uber pull up and park at the curb. Out piled Frances and Marika, in sweats and a full panic.

"Mindy! You made it!!" Marika was shocked but it just seemed fitting that the three of them were there together to investigate.

"Open the gate. I couldn't believe it when you texted." Frances was panicked. "The twitter feed's scary. Something's definitely up."

"According to the company account, he never ordered a car this morning." Marika had checked it all out. Frances followed Marika through the gates and the three stood in the lobby. There was an eerie sense of calm.

"Maybe we should have just told the cops," Frances second-guessed.

"And see DS dead for sure? You know they'd kill anything that moves if they thought it was for the greater good." Marika pulled both of The Girls together. "Now listen to me very carefully. According to my calculations, there's a fifty-seven percent chance this area is a target."

"What are you talking about?"

"You've been out of the loop, Min. This guy does have a pattern. Fuck what the cops say. And by the way, balls to the wall that you're even here, Girl!"

"Oh, you have no idea." Mindy couldn't believe it herself.

The Girls tiptoed up the steps to the second then third floor. They stood outside DS's door and listened. The muffled sounds of insane wriggling—the scraping of furniture across the thick plank floors freaked Mindy. "Oh no! DS. My Baby!!"

Frances slugged Mindy in the shoulder and whispered through clenched teeth. "Stop that shit now. Right now. It's time to grow up. Here and now. This is reality. And reality could get really fucked up real soon." Frances and Marika pulled pepper spray and tazers from their designer bags.

They jiggled the doorknob. More muffled sounds came from within. "Here, I've got it." Mindy pulled a hairpin from her updo and with a sleight of hand, picked the lock.

Even Marika was impressed. "No way."

"Way," Frances echoed. Mindy just stood wide-eyed, afraid to make a peep.

They opened the door, pointing the pepper spray in through the crack first. At that point, DS couldn't hold it any longer and pissed himself big time. By the time The Girls fully entered the room, he was drenched. It didn't matter to anyone. They ripped off his duct tape. "Undo me and then get the fuck out of here before he comes back!"

"Oh, DS—" Mindy went to give him a heart hug.

"What happened?" Marika wanted the details but DS didn't have time.

"And what the hell? Mindy? What are you doing here?" He pushed her back, careful not to get her wet.

"If it wasn't for Mindy, we never would have seen the tweets this early. She texted on her way," Frances defended.

"And you'd still be tied up." Marika backed her girl up.

"Then I owe you, Mindy." DS grabbed some fresh pants, zipped into the bathroom.

"Was it a robbery? Not much loot here." Marika begged for details.

"He didn't take anything really, except for my old cell."

"Well, thank God for that. When I saw all those HELPs, all I could think was it was the butcher." Mindy dumped out all her relief in one big sigh.

"Geesh. We thought the same thing." Frances nodded spasmodically with Marika.

DS whispered through the door. "There's no cell service. All three of you get out of here. Go downstairs and get the police. Tell them the Butcher is in 317." The Girls were, for once, speechless. But that didn't last.

"The—" Marika started.

"—Butcher?" Frances completed.

"Butcher?" Mindy chattered as if through toy teeth.

"Did you fucking hear me? Now!"

Mindy reached into the bathroom and grabbed onto DS's arm. "No, I'm never leaving you."

"Please, Mindy." DS burst back into the room in fresh clothes, Mindy still holding on. There was no backing off. DS just had to go for the big lie. It was in everyone's interest. "I love you. Mindy. I love you. O.K. Now go. Please."

"You do? Love me? Oh, DS. Really? Now I really can't leave you. Ever." Mindy beamed pathetically as she latched more securely onto DS's arm.

DS looked at Frances and Marika. Despondent wasn't even close to what he felt. "I'm sorry Mindy, but I don't have a choice." He took the duct tape left by the Butcher, taped her mouth and wrapped her to the chair. Her muffled pleas only fortified DS. "Who's next, huh? Or are you going to go get the fucking police?"

The other girls were frozen. DS paced like a madman, pulling his hair, dribbling great amounts of spittle as the words rustled through clenched teeth. "Get the fuck out. Now!" They remained frozen. He had no choice but to shuffle through his box of randomness. When he got to the item he was looking for, he pulled it out with a force none of them had ever imagined he possessed. DS waved his father's buck knife at them both. "Now!!" He turned to Mindy who was on her way to paralysis. "And you. Don't even try. Don't move. For anything!"

With that, Frances and Mindy scurried like naughty little mice down the stairs but not until DS retrieved their tazers and pepper spray. Frances motioned to the hairpin on the floor by the door before disappearing.

DS tucked the weapons into his dry pants and slid along the side of the wall and around the corner to 317. Mindy's muffled rebellion followed him all the way down the hall. DS craned his ear against the door and heard nothing but jiggling, snoring and deep-throated grumbles. Assuming Tracy was still alive to produce a muffle of any sort, he might be in decent shape.

DS fought silently with the lock and finally thrust open the door, which knocked over a chair the Butcher had tried to lodge against it. The chair busted with a fierce warning. *Fuckin' cheap ass Swedish furniture!* The snores halted immediately and the

Butcher pulled his hoodie up from over his bloodshot eyes. It was a split second, but not enough for DS to figure out how the hell to work either the pepper spray or the tazer without turning it on himself. And in that same split second, he managed to make eye contact with Tracy, who was tied up and pleading with his bruised and bloodied orbs.

DS was his own version of one of the Keystone Cops he had giggled at so profusely next to Gram on endless Saturdays. But this morning he was the pseudo-cop buffooning about, tossing tazers and spray through the thick, stressful air. This was not only no laughing matter. It was one where, in his past life, he'd just break down in tears, collapse to his knees, bow his head. But not this morning.

"You wanna fuck with me? Good luck with that!" The meaty Latino raged towards DS, scooping up the tazer from the floor. His eyes were wild, dilated with excitement and his movements as quick as any creature DS had ever seen.

Worst of mine. Worst of mine. Worst of mine.

The scrawny little nerd-turned-hipster finally pulled the buck knife from his pants, slicing the skin on his own belly, and summoned up every Ninja Turtles' move he'd ever practiced to clutch The Butcher in a headlock with the buck knife at his neck. This wasn't a time for heroics. He knew he'd just got lucky. This guy only needed a second to summon up his strength, then Tracy and DS would be goners. *And where the fuck are the police, anyway?*

Too late. DS took a deep breath filling his lungs with The Butcher's musty odor, then one last look into his eyes. He needed to see that instant before death.

The evil that needed to be slayed. And there came the summoning of the devil, his father's words piped into his brain like they had so many times in the past, only this time, they were revered. "Just cut, damn it." He took the knife and shoved the blade closer, causing a bit of blood to trickle from the Butcher's neck. And then he pressed in deep and swiped his arm rapidly through the soft skin-hide, past the membrane that was watery and thin, cutting both carotid arteries. DS turned away as the red meat was exposed and immediately covered with the forceful gush of blood.

Worst of mine. Worst of mine. Worst of mine.

After some seconds, he looked to see if the deed was, indeed, done. The body had gone limp and slid to the floor. DS bent down and searched the dead man's eyes, the dilated black pupils, the reddish-brown tache noire strip that formed across his eyeballs and then, feeling an odd sense of peace, knowing another evil had passed, he stood up and raised his eyes up to an imaginary heaven. Then he vomited.

Now he could collapse. DS fully dropped to his knees, and as if coming to from a rage blackout, he became aware of the muffled, tortured screams again. Tracy was drenched in sweat and urine, his eyes still wild with fear. With a final burst of adrenaline, DS pulled off the duct tape and untied his neighbor. The strip was full of a nest of brown hairs. They slid against one another's bodies to the floor, each reaching out, feeling the patches of missing beard from each other's faces. Their eyes, themselves nearly mere tache noire strips, were now alive and full of tears. Tracy pulled DS towards him, chest against chest, cheek against cheek, until the officers, guns drawn, burst through the door followed by Marika, Frances, and eventually, Mindy. In that precise order.

"Police! Don't move."

Both DS and Tracy raised their innocent, spent eyes. Officer Maples, still on double duty, recognized DS. "Mr. Strait?"

"I got your Butcher, boys." With that, DS fainted. Blood trickled through his plaid flannel shirt onto the pile of cottage cheese-like vomit beside him.

Tracy leaned over. "Shit, DS! You're bleeding!!" Tracy's eyes were filled with tears. "He's bleeding," he pleaded and then swooped in over the flaccid body, wrapped his arms around DS, tightened his grip and whispered into his ear. Perhaps a firm, "DS, don't leave." Or maybe, "Come on buddy, you're O.K." Whatever it was, it was the verbal injection that DS needed. His eyes flickered open to great applause from all around the room.

"Yay DS!" Marika threw her arms around both DS and Tracy. Then Frances joined the love huddle.

Officer Maples put on some latex gloves and pulled open DS's shirt where a bit of blood had already begun to coagulate from a superficial wound on his alabaster stomach. "I don't think it's anything serious, but call an ambulance. We need to get this cut checked out."

An officer off to the side called it in. "Requesting ambulance. Non-life threatening. And a coroner."

As if on cue, Mindy appeared at the door of the aPodment in what could only be called her own miraculous feat. Still tied to the chair and stifled by the duct tape, she had shimmied her way down the hall with a *bounce, bounce, rickety bounce* and then burst through the wall of officers who were dumbfounded when she appeared.

"Holy shit!" One of the officers screamed what everyone in the room was thinking. Particularly Marika and Frances who were so caught up in the action that they'd forgotten about their former roomie.

"Fuck Mindy! I'm soooooo sorry!!" Frances beat the path to her ahead of the police and ripped the duct tape from her mouth.

"Thanks assholes!" Before Mindy could launch into her tirade, she saw DS in Tracy's arms with Officer Maples dabbing at the blood on his belly. "DS!!!!!! My baby!!!!!!!" She began to wriggle over to them, still tied to the chair, but the officers unwound her and once given that freedom, she was unstoppable.

Marika whispered to Frances, "Let the show begin." And it did, with little disappointment. An Oscar-worthy performance. Full of drama, tension and tears. All it needed was a dramatic score and the little gold statue would be hers.

"Oh my God, DS! I thought you were dead!! You have no idea what it was like being tied up there thinking the worst." Once freed, she literally strong-armed Tracy aside. "Oh my baby. Don't ever leave me again. Promise?"

In that moment, DS seriously thought of just feigning faintness until the ambulance arrived, but he avoided that temptation and opted for a little well-deserved praise, hoping it wouldn't inflate a fantasy.

"Mindy. I could have been butchered if you weren't on twitter. Thanks, babe." Oh dear, pure music to her ears. Mindy grinned lobe to lobe.

A gruff policeman elbowed into the room. Officer McTeague gently pulled Mindy back from DS. "Miss, we have some questions for you."

"No, I can't leave him. Don't make me."

"We just want to know about your interaction with The Butcher."

"Well, that's easy. None. I didn't have any."

"Then who tied you up?"

"Well, DS, of course."

There was an inevitable chain of eye contact amongst officers around the room.

"It's complicated." The words spilt from DS's mouth could never have been truer.

Marika took the officers aside to begin to try to explain just how complicated Mindy Montgomery was. The audience gathered around her like moths hanging on every thread of detail.

Meanwhile, Tracy had moved back in to comfort DS under the distant jealous surveillance of Mindy's minks.

McTeague barked at Maples, "Check on that ambulance."

Officer Maples chimed in, "There's a five car pile-up on 101. And some weirdo got his dick caught in a purse two blocks over."

McTeague was furious. "Let the perv suffer. Get that ambulance here. Now!"

Mindy nodded ferociously. "Yeah. Let it rot off!" The dozen or so officers now crowding the aPodment all turned to Mindy, noting her exceptional conviction.

Officer McTeague added, "We've got us a hero to take care of."

\#

Word that the Tenderloin Butcher was dead spread on twitter and all the Old World news feeds. Soon the area was swarming with local news trucks, including TNN, a sea of reporters, crime scene tourists, and the usual colorful TL locals.

Juan Chavez stood under the spiraling antennae next to the KZO news truck, waiting for the signal.

"On the air," a producer signaled.

"This is Juan Chavez from KZO News reporting on what appears to be the end of the terrorizing murders that have paralyzed The City for twelve weeks now. What we have just learned is that the Tenderloin Butcher appears to have been killed. Details are still coming in, but from what we know so far, he was killed by one of his potential victims, Richard Strait, whom some of you may recall as the mastermind behind the recent San Francisco Sky Zoo. We will keep you posted as we try to piece together these extraordinary events. As far as we know, The Butcher did not claim another victim."

Juan Chavez was distracted by a homeless guy wandering behind the camera. Chavez did a double take. "Hey, you're da man. 'Memba me? Da man! Wat d'ja got now? Eyeballs, fingers raining' from da sky?" He leaned in closer to Chavez. "Any more dem flying' saucers?" Chavez' producer was tipped off by the saucer reference and the crackhead's red Nikes. He tried to swoosh him away before he totally derailed the broadcast. "Come on now. 'Member me? I ain't never got me a red cent from The City to get that damn blood outta my shirt. 'Magine that. Not a red cent."

The crackhead pushed in next to Chavez. "Hey, I'm makin' a movie, ya know?"

Chavez backed away, repelled by the man's scent. Before he knew it, the man had grabbed his mic and began putting on his own show. The broadcast was rescued by the synchronistic action coming out from behind the iron gates. Frances and Marika led the way. Mindy filed behind, looking over her shoulder. The crowd of reporters nearly bum-rushed them.

"Here! Here!! What can you tell us about what's going on inside?" The cameras panned to the reporters who shoved microphones at them from every direction, like an aggressive game of pick-up sticks. Frances and Marika had every intention of barreling through the invaders. But Mindy would have nothing of it. She poised herself like a debutante and dug in. Another Oscar-worthy performance.

"My lover is a hero today. DS, Mr. Richard Strait, single-handedly slayed The Tenderloin Butcher and rescued the intended victim from a fate worse than death—live dismemberment. The City owes a debt of gratitude to him."

The mics pushed and prodded. Mindy commanded their presence like a Queen. "Miss! Miss!! What is your name?" Several reporters asked.

"Mindy Montgomery. Like the street. That's spelled M-O-N-T-G-O-M-E-R-Y. Mindy Montgomery."

"Mindy! Mindy!!" The reporters shouted out her name like she was a rock star. "Tell us about your hero. What can you tell us about Richard?"

"DS is the most wonderful man I've ever met. From the moment I saw him, I knew my little hipster from Shawnee was for me." She offered the crowd the cutest little giggle.

"Shawnee?"

Another reporter shouted from aside. "Tell us about that."

"My DS came to San Francisco from Shawnee, Oklahoma. Worlds away from our vibrant life here and in that time, as you can see, he has taken The City by storm. First the Sky Zoo and now, well, now he has single-handedly put an end to one of the most horrid crime sprees any city has ever endured. He's slayed the Butcher."

\#

Grammy had to take a seat in one of the slippery Alaska Air lounge seats. Like everyone waiting in the arrival area, she was watching the news that had broken into all local programming. She took a deep breath and then cringed as a figure in the distance walked out of the building in a blood stained shirt surrounded by officers. Her gasp was noted by a like-aged woman, who elbowed her husband, who then made eye contact with a young mother rocking a stroller up and down with an annoying squeak. Grammy focused with an unlit Morley in hand as the camera panned to follow the medics towards a waiting ambulance. The press rushed to them, leaving Mindy alone with Frances and Marika on the steps of the Hyde Street building. Shouts of "Richard! Richard! DS!!" echoed through the streets. They literally mobbed him. He stepped inside the ambulance but emerged just minutes later with a bandage across his belly. It was a medium shot, just enough to confirm her fear.

When Grammy saw this, she yanked out her cell phone and rang and rang and rang. She cursed at the screen as others in the arrival area looked on. "Come on, Dickie. Pick it up you little shit."

One of the officers answered the phone, which had been tossed in the kitchen in Tracy's apartment. "Hello?"

"Well, just who the hell is this?"

"Officer Schouler. Who's this?"

"I'm Dickie's Grammy."

"I'm sorry, you must have the wrong number."

"Richard Strait, you nincompoop! I'm Richard Strait's grandmother and I'm staring at him right now on the TV screen at the airport where he's 'posed to be gettin' off the plane and I'm watchin' him with a bloody shirt. On TV!"

Schouler held the phone away from his ear for others to hear. Grammy cupped the phone and informed the curious loungers, "That's my Dickie. My little Schnicklefritz."

"Better give that to DS. Trust me, he'd want to talk to her right away." Tracy was still being interviewed by the police but was emphatic that Grammy took precedence.

Officer Schouler tried to calm Flo over the phone as he jammed down the stairs and shouted for DS. "Mr. Strait, a phone call. Sounds important. Your grandmother."

The awes from the reporters were audible as DS spun around and reached out for the phone with tears in his eyes. The cameras immediately zoomed in on the tender, emotion-worthy shot. He grabbed the phone from the officer's hand. "Gram?" He looked right into the camera and the tears came raining down. "Grammy?"

DS broke the fourth wall and stared straight at Grammy Flo in that lounge over seventeen hundred miles away, along with the dozens of strangers who were awestruck as well. She was ready to lose it, but quickly jolted herself together.

"Are you O.K? I'm worried sick!! There you are bleedin' in that TenderHip."

"Loin, Gram. Tenderloin."

"In your loin, too? From here it looks like you're bleedin' from your tummy, Dickie."

"It's literally just a scratch, Gram. I'm fine. Really. Totally fine. Nothing a little bandage won't fix."

"Well, that's good, but, but... Dickie?"

"What Gram? I sorta need to get going." The mob of reporters was thickening around DS. Somehow one of their miracle mics picked up Grammy's words and broadcast them around the world. Live.

"First off, why haven't I heard about this love of your life before? And second, is it true, Dickie? Did you slay that Butcher?"

"Slay?"

"Yes, slay. That's the exact word that your girlfriend—that adorable Mindy Montgomery—said."

"It's complicated, Gram. I'll explain everything when I get home."

"Speakin' of which, I've been at the airport waitin' on you. I'm here right now with a buncha people staring at me like I'm some kind of lunatic talking to you here on the phone and lookin' at you up on the TV."

"I'm so sorry, Gram. I just got, I got tied up."

"Well, you could have called an' saved your Ol' Gram a trip."

"I'm so sorry. I love you."

Within moments, the exchange had gone viral. And it certainly wasn't wasted on Mindy who came rushing towards him. Frances and Marika managed to hold her back.

"He's got to go, Min." DS hopped immediately into the ambulance before the cameras got any closer.

As the ambulance snaked its way through the crowd and vehicles, Mindy went into Vibe Manager mode. "Now if any of you have any questions or I can help you with anything, you can reach me on Facebook or twitter. I'm here to help. Don't be shy. And remember to breathe."

Enough was enough. Marika dragged Mindy from the scene as the police blocked the iron doors of the building off with yellow crime scene tape. The Girls crawled into the backseat of an awaiting black Uber SUV, collapsing on each other like a pile of hungry kittens. "Toast, anyone?"

"Depends on what kind of toast? The Staff or Runi?" Mindy asked genuinely. "I vote for The Staff. DS deserves a sober lover. Don't you think?"

Frances and Marika answered in sync. "It's complicated."

Officer McTeague approached the Uber. "Hey Girls, you'll need to come down to Bryant St. for questioning. Just while everything's fresh, if you don't mind. Some time tomorrow."

DS and Tracy were taken there directly after the briefest hospital visit.

#

The Hall of Justice was bustling this brisk day, not just with the usual drug dealers, prostitutes and thugs but also DMV-worthy lines of citizens who would undoubtedly write Yelp reviews about the police assholes. But, for this moment, DS was glad to be in their care after a quick checkout at the emergency room. The gauze secured across his abdomen was mostly cosmetic to cover a four-inch scratch that could have been life-threatening had it gone deeper, as the Butcher surely would have gone.

He looked over at Tracy who had also been tended to at the scene and cleared. His bruises were just beginning to ripen and the darkness made his blue eyes sparkle in the barren room where they gave their statements.

Officer McTeague stood in the background as the victims' statements were documented. Tracy was up first. He was in the room for over an hour.

"I thought the guy was a tenant. He followed me in and I didn't really think anything of it. There are so many people coming and going. I just assumed the officers had checked him out on the street." Tracy's account was specific.

"Can you tell us any more about the perpetrator?"

"He just kept telling me my heart was defective."

So there it was. That was the tidbit that Marika in all of her searches and police blog-stalking had never got ahold of. Every victim was missing their heart. The

Butcher would boil the hearts and presumably ate them before discarding body tidbits out the window and escaping.

"Can you talk more about that? Why he thought it was defective?"

Later it would be learned that there was a deeper perversion to the Butcher, but in that moment, the questioning was halted, as Tracy was given time to recompose.

DS's questioning, in an adjacent room, was similar, although the details that could be used to profile the Butcher weren't as specific as Tracy's who had spent hours on end with the monster.

When it was all over and the two were released, the sudden freedom, the smell of life in The City, the mustiness carried by the fog, the pungent smell of human waste, the slight essence of bakeshop scents mixing with ripe cheese that traveled miraculously from blocks away, the faintest mix of eucalyptus, grilled onions, garlic and weed. It was a fulfilling blend that DS and Tracy inhaled deeply as they waited outside on Bryant St. for their Uber driver.

"Now what?" Tracy looked up at the fog literally rolling across the sky.

"Home."

"To yellow tape?" Tracy giggled awkwardly at the absurdity.

"McTeague said my aPodment is clear. You can stay there."

"What a fucking day," they echoed in tandem.

#

That night and each following, the hauntings occurred. DS relived the sound, the smell and the sight of the final slice. The deep cut that halted at the neck bone. The media claims of heroism were hard to swallow, as DS knew he had taken a life. Just as his father had taught him to do.

#

DS had every intention of heading straight back to Shawnee, but the requests from media outlets were a P.R. dream according to David who was beyond elated at the heroism DS showed. "How much would it hurt to fly to L.A. or New York and do Pimmel or Stephen Sherbert? They both want you. Hell, everyone wants you, DS! Shawnee can wait for a day or two."

"I just really want to get home."

"And you will. Just one interview."

"I've already done dozens. Every time I try to escape a building, they're there poking questions at me."

"Then do just one before you head to Shawnee. For me, DS. For the company. Your grandmother will understand."

"I suppose it couldn't hurt."

"That's my boy. I always knew you had an incredible spirit, but I never knew you had such a savage instinct. I'm proud of you boy. Damn proud of you." The phone call had prompted DS to close his office door and reflect on his father. How he had wished those words could have come from him. Once. Just once.

The lights on stage were so much brighter, so much hotter than DS ever imagined. He was star-struck by Sherbert. His grandmother thought him only second best to Letterman and was "just sick" that he had retired before her Dickie had his moment of glory on *The Not So Late Show* with her Dave.

"You'd have to be living under a rock not to have heard about this guy. First that crazy menagerie in the already crazy city, San Francisco, and then, like that wasn't enough, the guy goes and butchers The Butcher. So, here, tonight, is a true hero, Richard Strait!!" Stephen Sherbert was clearly impressed.

DS paraded out on stage to wild cheers and catcalls from the audience. He looked like a hipster extraordinaire—half hip and half (finally) Armani. Sherbert graciously stood while the applause went on for an unbearable amount of time. "Maybe I shoulda tried the hero route instead of this comedian stuff!" Sherbert quipped. Eventually the audience calmed and DS finally sat down.

"So, I understand that you don't like to be called Richard."

"Right. DS. I go by DS."

"One of those techie things. Everything's an acronym, right?"

"I guess you could say that. SS." The crowd loved DS all over again.

And so did Grammy as she watched him from her Morley-infused living room. She chain-smoked her way through the interview, nervous as a Catholic schoolgirl walking by the boys' playground on a windy day. "That's my Dickie."

"Tell us about that morning."

"Well, Stephen, that morning started the night before. The aPodment is a temporary living space in the Tenderloin, mostly a stepping-stone for tech workers. The last thing I expected was to get a knock on the door, and instead of it being my buddy from across the way, it was The Butcher. He had tied up my friend Tracy and we believe he would have been the first to go."

"There are rumors that there may have been some cannibalism involved." Sherbert was morbidly curious and licked his lips, Hannibal-style.

"If you're asking if there was a pot boiling on the stove, ready to go. Then no. Even so, my neighbor will probably get rid of his hot plate and pasta pot. It's O.K. SF has great delivery." The audience let out a guilty little laugh.

"Right. I hear they deliver anything there!" Sherbert mimed smoking a blunt into the camera.

"Absolutely. And we have an app for that." The crowd cheered. "But let me put it to you this way, a little piece of me thinks I may have been the main course." The audience roared awkwardly.

"Well, hey, I'm glad you and your buddy are O.K. and the streets of San Francisco are a bit safer today. Although, from what we've seen of the Tenderloin, safe is a negligible word." The audience laughed knowingly.

"Well, you know Stephen, San Francisco has been a magnet for the homeless. People live, breathe and die on these streets every day. Here we're talking about the murders of a few people over a few weeks, yet maybe we should ask ourselves how we can help those folks who we step around on our way to work every day.

The ones sleeping on manholes for warmth or under a tarp made of newspapers. These people were born just like all of us, naked. Most of us had someone to feed us, wrap us in warmth and love. To guide us. I had my Grammy Flo." A huge applause went up. Sherbert was stuck on serious. "But some people weren't so lucky. They were born with psychological challenges or they got involved in hard drugs, maybe out of boredom or to self-medicate. And some of them suffer with their wartime memories as they try to survive the streets."

"So, what do you think the answer is?" Sherbert really wanted to know.

"Well, for one, the tech industry in San Francisco has the ability, and I think, the responsibility to give back. They can start by not sheltering money offshore and begin to pay their taxes. But if they truly had a heart, they would commit to solving this problem, just as I will be asking our company to do. We all need to commit to the homeless challenge until the problem is under control. They need shelter. Shelter without going through hoops and a checklist. Let them have a small roof over their heads unconditionally and begin to get them well again before you ask them to make promises. These people are ill, but I believe they can heal. They need our help. We treat our pets better. If we see a sick dog or kitten on the street, we call the animal shelter or, better yet, bring them there. The San Francisco SPCA has kitty condos, but who do we call when we see a sick human on the street? No one."

As the music started to play, indicating that DS had gone way over time, Stephen Sherbert stood up and joined in a standing ovation for DS.

"Man, I could talk to you all night. Keep up the good work. You are our hero!"

#

DS called Gram on his way to JFK just to ease her mind that there weren't any other hitches in his travel plans this time. At least he hoped. "And, by the way, Gram. I'm bringing a guest."

Well, that's all Flo needed to set her head spinnin'. "A guest? Why, who Dickie?"

"It's a surprise. You'll just have to wait and see."

Of course, it could only be that cute Mindy Montgomery. Grammy heard the wedding bells loud and clear.

The line for security was impossibly long and DS was already late. Again. Déjà vu. And then he got pulled.

"Sir, would you please accompany us? We need to search you. You'll be more comfortable in the private screening area." The TSA screener was a tall, hunky guy, about DS's age but with twice the meat on him.

"Search? For what??"

"Nothing in particular. We just choose random passengers at times. And, bingo, your number came up." Hunky Guy thrived on sarcasm.

"Well, my flight number is coming up and if I'm not on that plane, well, you just have no idea how dreadful it will be. You see, my grandmother has been waiting."

The officer jerked his arm. He meant business.

"I said this way." The screener spoke into his lapel which, DS knew, was not a good sign.

"Yes, sir. But I really do have to get on that plane."

He looked off into the distance and saw his travel partner freaking out. DS shouted emphatically. "Just get on the plane. I'll be there soon." He was surrounded by what looked like a small army of Airport Police Officers who pulled him by his arms and dragged him into an office furnished with a heavy metal desk, with one very sharp corner that DS imagined may have felt a head or two.

One officer, wearing baby blue latex gloves, examined his driver's license. "So, you're Richard Straight?"

DS beamed. Bet he saw me on Sherbert. "Yeah. I'm the guy that whacked the Butcher." DS motioned as though he was slitting his own neck. One of the officers drew his gun. DS put his hands up. "Oh God. Please... please! Hands up! Don't shoot!!"

Another agent signaled to the gun-toting one. "Down, Officer." That other officer, much shorter but equally as meaty, slowly lowered his gun. "Now, Mr. Strait, can you tell me where you're off to this fine afternoon?"

"Well, if I make my flight," DS checked his cell, "and that's a big if, I'm off to Shawnee Oklahoma to help my grandmother with some things around the house. Grammy Flo."

The officers all made suspicious eye contact. "Your Grammy Flo?"

"Exactly. You see, I was just on the *The No So Late Show* last night. I mentioned her."

"Hmmmm, were you now?" The doubt was palpable. "And I guess you were on Timmy Pimmel, too?"

Oh my God. Here we go again. What is this with the airport gangs? "Perhaps you've heard of the Tenderloin Butcher?"

"Well, of course. Who hasn't?" The larger officer began an invasive pat down that climaxed with a giant, lingering grope of DS's groin. He, the officer, that is, seemed to enjoy the linger.

"Strait. I'm Strait."

"Well, that's great, but no one asked you about that, did they?" Did this idiot really not know just who he was talking to?

"No. In fact, they didn't. But, I'm the guy who killed him. I killed the Tenderloin Butcher."

"Sure. Sure you did."

"Hey, what about the Sky Zoo?" DS tried to rally enthusiasm. "You guys see that? Anyone got kids? Need a 3D pet for a birthday party? I'm the man!" DS did all but a song and dance.

"Suuurrrree you are." The officer who had drawn the gun was clearly mocking DS.

"Honest. Honest truth." Truth. Where was that getting me now? Nowhere with these guys who are about as sharp as marbles.

DS checked his phone again. The text was in all caps. He was in big trouble now:

TURNING OFF PHONE BC WE'RE TAKING OFF!!

"Fuck. See what you've done now? I've missed my plane." DS threw his phone. "What now? I'm stranded in hell and my travel partner is about to be up in the heavenly skies."

The officers went into alert mode and moved in on DS. One twisted his arm behind his back.

A random officer poked his head inside the room. "Story checks out. Chief says release him. Doesn't matter that he's on the list. The guy's a hero."

The officers backed down slowly. Well now. That's more like it!

"So. What was it like? When you carved into his skin?" asked the shorter meathead.

"Oh, just lovely." He wasn't about to let this little creep get under his skin.

"Sorry for the inconvenience, Mr. Strait, but we have to follow protocol. Once someone is on that list, it haunts. We'll make sure you get on the next available flight."

An officer was checking schedules and in contact with a reservationist. "We can get you on a one-stop that will get you into Tulsa before your travel partner. That was a two-stop, right?"

"Right," DS sighed. "Well, then. That's a relief."

The officer confirmed the flight. "US Flightways—"

No fucking way.

"Excuse me? You were mumbling something."

"Oh lucky. Way lucky." DS forced the words.

Some Like it Hot

—#—

No fucking way.

DS reached into the upper cabinet to try to stuff his satchel in and was immediately bombarded by Old Iron Balls.

How is this possible?

"Well, if it isn't our friend on board for a return visit?" The bags under her eyes elongated like roasted almonds as she smiled.

DS returned the smile. A pure, pleasant smile. "Yes, in fact. Back to Shawnee to see my grandmother." *Maybe that'll work. It usually gets the women.*

The attendant leaned into DS and whispered with breath so hot he thought his ear would melt. "Listen, you little motherfucker, you give me one problem, even for a millisecond, I'll have you hogtied so fast your head will spin. Think Linda Blair in *The Exorcist*."

Actually, DS thought that was a fabulous visual because in his mind this babe needed an exorcism. "Yes, Ma'am."

As DS turned to sit down, someone shouted from three rows behind. "Hey, it's him!" The passenger, a pudgy businessman, pointed his pale, thick index finger directly at DS. He cringed.

Just then, Old Iron Balls craned her neck and then made an about face. She called out. "Captain! Get the Captain here now!!"

No fucking way!

"That's the hero! That's the guy that killed The Butcher." Before he knew it, the entire plane was giving DS a round of applause.

A Mindy-ish girl behind him tapped his shoulder. "I saw you on Sherbert. So awesome. I can't believe it's you!"

"Thanks. Thank you." DS bowed and sat down, quiet as a mouse. He looked up to see Ms. Balls winding down the applause from the rest of the cabin.

She leaned back into DS's ear. "I don't give a fuck who you killed. Be good or you'll be next."

DS waited until she was well down the aisle to call Grammy and tell her about the flight change. He got her machine. He whispered, "Hey Gram, I had to change flights. Same-ish time though. I'll call you when I hit the ground."

For the entire flight DS sat frozen in his seat. At cruising altitude, he took a good look at Ms. Balls, thinking he would see that sort of angelic light about her, the one that most attendants have at cruising altitude if they use the right reflective make-up, but she had none. Just a mean sallowness that followed her through the cabin.

DS drifted off in the sky. The heaviness of the last few days forced his eyes shut as if to give his brain time to breathe. A montage of events starting with Mindy's adorable smile and climaxing with the tremendous buck knife swipe across the Butcher's neck lulled him asleep that afternoon. And for nights afterwards, the same dysfunctional montage would haunt him. But for now, he was just grateful to breathe, even if it was recycled air.

The violence of the turbulence shook him awake. Like Grammy, he had the inner fear of flying, but after narrowly escaping death, the motion was simply a minor inconvenience. And after all, no one ever died from turbulence, or so he had heard. His body shifted every which way, up, down, left, right and variations in between. Sounds went off warning to secure all belts and OIB strapped herself in for the ride. "Ladies and Gentlemen, we're about to enter some strong turbulence. Please make sure all items are secure under your seats and keep your seat belts tightly fastened." The pilot was unnervingly calm and had that generic Pennsylvanian accent that an uncanny number of pilots echoed.

DS was seated in between two lonely women. One quite large who certainly looked like she could fend for herself in an emergency and to his right, a frail woman who, until now, had her nose buried deep in a steamy romance novel. She shoved the fresh novel into the pocket in front of her and braced her wrinkly body against her seat. She shut her eyes, a wince really, that reacted with every movement of the plane. Without notice, her hand crept over to DS's side. He looked at the wormy veins and thin, transparent skin that reached out. When he covered that hand with his, he felt her coolness and wanted to transfer all the warmth from his body to hers. It was twenty or so tortuous minutes before the flight stabilized. It wasn't until the pilot announced that they could move about the cabin that DS's little seatmate opened her eyes. When they shifted to meet his, DS saw her glow, an aura about her. Angelic.

"Thank you." Her voice was ethereal as she slid her now warm hand from his. In that moment, DS realized that it was not the woman who needed support, but that this stranger had given DS the gift of touch to power through his own fear.

When he off-boarded, he thought for sure Old Iron Balls muttered a "fuck you" to him under her breath.

And under his breath DS responded so quietly that she wasn't quite sure he even spoke. "Back at ya."

#

DS was in no way prepared for the chaotic scene that would greet him at Tulsa International Airport. The media was fully assembled and flashes blinded him as he wandered the waiting area looking for Flo. And then he saw her, elbowing her way through the reporters, dodging and pushing cameras.

"Dickie! Dickie!! Here!!!" The cameras followed her movements just in time to catch the money shot of their reunion.

"Gram!!" DS lurched towards her. She was dressed in her Sunday best, a little one-piece outfit with a matching print belt. A Morley was lodged behind her ear, not at all covered by the coif she had had done up in the beauty shop that morning.

The two locked bodies as the passengers passed, all smiling, some patting them on the back. DS's seatmate gave him a wink as she meandered by.

"Well, where is she?" Grammy's head twirled in search of her houseguest.

"Who?"

"Well, you know that cute little—" Grammy saw her. The Mindy lookalike. "Oh, there she is!" Gram took off in a billy goat charge for the unsuspecting passenger. DS had no choice but to chase after her.

"Gram Wait! Gram!!" The cameras followed it all as DS snagged her before she toppled the girl. "That's not her... him... her."

"Him... her... what? Make up your mind. Which is it?"

With precise timing, Tracy appeared. "Hey, DS!" The cameras panned left as Tracy rolled his bag over to the confusion. "I made it! Finally!! And you made it." Tracy put down his bags.

"Oh my God. And you must be the infamous Grammy Flo." Tracy gave her a huge heartwarming hug.

She motioned a "Wha?" behind DS's back. "Yes. I'm Flo, but who the hell are you?" She looked over to DS.

"This is Tracy. My neighbor, the guy the Butcher almost—"

"Butchered," Flo chimed in, impressed.

"Right. That's me."

"Didn't recognize you. Well then. Good to meet you. Now that we've got that straight, let's head home. I've got a nice chocolate cake waiting on the table."

Before they walked to the ol' Nash Mechanic, trailed by media stringers, Tracy dashed into the men's restroom. Gram pulled DS close in for a confidential. "What happened to that adorable Cindy?"

"You mean Mindy?"

"Whatever. It's just a word. But I thought for sure she was the one."

"We'll see Gram. It's complicated."

"What in the world is all this complicated? Nobody's perfect, DS."

"You're right on that one. Nobody's perfect, Gram."

#

Twenty minutes later, they were on I-44 in the good ol' Nash.

"Coolest car ever!" Tracy sat in the backseat as the old gem chugged along.

"This was my Daddy's last car. I swore on his deathbed I'd treat it like my baby 'til the end." And Flo had lovingly cared for it all these years, putting on only minimum miles, although infiltrating it with the smoke from hundreds of cartons of Morleys.

"I've never been in such a cool car." Tracy peered out the window watching the flat fields go by.

"You an' me gonna get along just fine." Gram pressed in the lighter and pulled the Morley from behind her ear.

"Hey, what about the nicotine patches? You got the patches, right? They came, right?"

"Of course they came, but it's just not the same, Dickie. It's all in the process. I tried. I did try, though."

Gram looked up in the rearview mirror. Tracy was successfully dodging the whirls of smoke in the backseat so she just left it at that.

"Well, I just want you to stay healthy."

"I'm healthy as a horse, Dickie. Healthy as a horse." With that, she let out a congestive whinny of a cough.

"Gram... patches. We're getting you on the patches. Final."

Her eyes raised once again to the small mirror. "Can you believe this? Tryin' to tell this ol' Okie what to do?"

"Ah look... sheep!" It had been years since Tracy had seen any kind of farm animal and he pointed out each one from Tulsa to Shawnee. And that was the end of the patch conversation.

#

"Tracy, you like your pie regular or you like it fried? I got some dough ready to go." Tracy had just risen from the makeshift guest room made up in the sewing room that had been stuffed with deliveries from DS over the past couple of weeks.

"Fried, I guess. Never tried it, but I went to a fair once and they fried everything and it was all good. Especially the candy bars!"

"Well, I can't say much about frying' no chocolate, but my fried pies are well known in Shawnee."

"Then bring 'em on!" Tracy knew how to butter this babe up.

By the time DS got up, the hour hand on the kitchen clock was past noon. No one dared wake him—he needed the rest. But what he didn't tell either of them was that he had never really slept. His brain was still full of that montage, all the scenes from Mindy globbing on to him through the throat slit. The scenes played over and over and over and over.

"Mornin'."

"Afternoon." Grammy was quick to correct. "You feelin' rested, Mr. Sleepyhead?"

"Surprisingly, no. Still exhausted."

"Well, it'll be some time before it all settles in, I imagine. Pies comin' out in twenty minutes. How 'bout some juice. Coffee?"

"Coffee, please." Gram poured her tar-like concoction from a French press that DS had sent. "How much coffee did you put in?"

"Well, you didn't send directions, so I figured half coffee, half water."

Tracy and DS looked at each other. By now, Tracy's eyes were electrified from his two morning cups. "Hmmmm... maybe a bit of overkill."

"It'll put hair on your chest. Stop complainin' an' toss in some milk." The phone rang. "It's been going off all mornin' Dickie. They want to give you some kind of award downtown. You talk to them."

DS answered, and sure enough, Shawnee saw this as a way to get on the media map. "Five o'clock? Yeah, we can be there. Down at the Depot? Alright. See you at five."

"You'd think Brad Pitt done come back into town the way the phone's been ringin' off the hook. Off the hook, I tell ya, Dickie. Off the hook ever since you done slayed that Butcher."

Tracy's eyes still had evidence of his capture, the dark purple bruising turning an aqua green, thanks to a constant application of Arnica. But DS's wounds were deeper, and like his childhood, he evaded them well. "So, Gram. The boxes. Let's get to the boxes."

By the time 4:30 rolled around, DS and Tracy had tricked out Grammy's place with technology. A flat screen TV with surround sound. Her new laptop now ready for Skyping, and her own personal 3D pet, a Japanese snow monkey named Hiro.

"Hiro? What kinda name is Hiro?"

"Generous, abundant, tolerant, prosperous. All the things you are and deserve."

"Sounds like you been bit by the New Age bug out there in Cali. Does it bite, Dickie? That's what I need to know. Does it bite? I don't need no biting monkey. 'Specially no Buddhist biting monkey."

Tracy found her fear adorable. "It's a 3D image, Mrs. Strait. Totally safe."

"For the last time, you call me Grammy Flo. Is that clear young man?" Tracy loved those words.

"It's safe, Grammy Flo."

#

It looked like the whole of Shawnee had turned out at the Santa Fe Depot late that day. Crowds gathered by the limestone building, an oddity resembling a Scottish lighthouse, which now served as a historical museum.

Gram, DS and Tracy putted up in the Nash only to find themselves swarmed by local and national news trucks, their spider-webbish antennas reaching high into the clear Oklahoma sky.

"DS! DS! Richard? Mr. Straight? How is it to be back home again?"

The Mayor of Shawnee, a bloated little man, a hunter at heart and civic leader who lived his own code of Moral Re-Armament, personally ushered the group from the parking lot to a stage set up in front of the Depot's thick tower and multi-arched portico. The cameras followed relentlessly.

DS recalled one fond time his dad took him to Shawnee's Santa Fe Depot Museum, which was not far from their house. He was just a little guy then, when it was still somewhat O.K. to shed a tear or two. They explored the railroad memorabilia and artifacts of the settlement of Shawnee. It was in this building that he got his first lesson in hunting. "Persistence is a hunting technique, son. Hunters track their prey until they're exhausted. Why, in some parts they'd run, walk, all mounted on horses or with dogs. They'd just keep tracking, beat them down sooner or later. Persistence is everything, Dickie. Everything." His father's words now had more meaning than ever. As he approached the mic on the stage, DS was beat down. He was both the hunter and the hunted. He looked out over the crowd and took in the withered, familiar faces. Of course, The Wheeler Boys were there looking on in awe, as were the local business people who hoped that this media circus would put Shawnee on the tourist map.

The Mayor spoke with a perky enthusiasm usually reserved for used car commercials. "Our fine citizen, Richard Straight, like this building behind us, is a

National treasure. His creativity has launched a new industry in the tech world, but it's his heroism we're here to cheer today." He proudly handed a key to The City to DS.

The crowd stood in deafening applause as bunches of balloons were released into the sky. DS was escorted to the mic by two stodgy city council members. After a few long minutes the Okies quieted down. DS tapped the mic as he had always seen it done in the movies. "I want to thank the Mayor for such a warm greeting. This town is my foundation. It held me together when my family was killed and now you're here to take their place in making me feel like a hero. And most of all, my greatest thanks are to my grandmother, Flodina Strait, who has been my lifeline forever."

Another wild round of applause from the townsfolk broke out. The Boys elbowed each other and mugged stupidly for the cameras that panned the crowd. When the applause finally subsided, DS continued. "The road to a hero is often paved with pain and challenges so, in my mind, I created a fantasy world to escape in. Today that world has evolved into NuMilieu." Another round of applause erupted. "And although I am most appreciative of this welcome, it's not always been so. I look out at what the deadness of this town has done to individuals that should have flourished. Instead, their skin is full of scabs and their souls are blistered." There was an audible breath of concern from the gatherers. "As I look out on this crowd, I see faces, now withered from meth and heroin, that did some things to me, unspeakable things, in the past. I see some of the bullies here today and you know who you are. The memories come back, one flash at a time. In fact, one night, not blocks from here, I was brutally attacked by half of the football team just for the fun of it."

Grammy followed his words with tears in her eyes. Had she only known. "My Lord." Tracy nudged in instinctively to support her.

"For these people, if my good fortune prevails, I plan on opening a wellness clinic where people in this town can build their self-esteem so that drugs will be not be the default of choice. And cruelty will not be tolerated."

The camera feed was live locally and editors were ready for the sound bites. No one expected such a salacious feast, though.

"And for those who called me everything from faggot to queer to fairy all throughout my school years just because I didn't play sports or bully the next weakest kid"—DS had to take a breath—"for all of those, and you know who you are, I can stand here today and say I don't care what you think. I have considered the source and it's pretty sad. But for me, now and forever, it's in one ear and out both. Although I forgive, I will not forget."

And then, without warning, he reached over to Tracy and pulled him towards him and gave him a thick, rich kiss on the lips. Whether Tracy was more shocked, or Grammy, who mouthed her confusion, or the crowd, it really didn't matter to DS. After the kiss melted away, DS faced the cameras which, by now, were close-up. "Let's see if I'm still a hero tomorrow or if the bullies will have their way."

In the very back of the crowd, Jessica Herz was sobbing as she smoothed a finger over the scar on her leg which had once had a rudimentary bandage hiding it but was now, as though by miracle, healing.

And on stage, Grammy, perhaps by accident or on purpose, snapped in half the Morley that had been lodged behind her ear.

#

After the commotion of being honored by the whole of Shawnee, DS, Grammy and Tracy, sitting on the couch in that order, spent the evening watching a rerun of the event. Afterwards, they shared caramel popcorn and a movie marathon.

In the Mission, Marika, Frances and Mindy sat on their velvet sofa. They lit a fat blunt, turned on the news and nearly flipped when they saw the kiss. As the camera closed in on Grammy, they agreed her lips clearly read: "Oh well, no one's perfect." Flo would have no idea just how insightful her seemingly frivolous comment was.

Mindy took a lazy sip of her Old World Red as she tweeted:

The Tenderloin Butcher's killer lives on in my heart. Forever.

She poured another glass of wine and watched it go viral, unaware of just how prophetic her words were. Before long, Mindy had slipped into a dream of the perfect world.

And somewhere on the sidewalks of San Francisco, a homeless man spread his cold, tenderized body over a cast iron manhole, wishing sleep, desperately wanting to slip away from his nightmare and into a dream of the perfect world, but knowing that it would be just that. Just a dream.

Author's Note

All humankind falls on a continuum between female and male. This story explores a harsh patriarchal world that doesn't recognize or respect that mosaic. Yet...

www.bononeill.com